The Monstrous Member

by

Patterson Gregory

Published by James Patterson and Julie-Ann Gregory in 2019

Cover image by Gavin Thomas

Chapter One

"That's just not fucking good enough!"

Ana Novak MP hissed these words with venomous ferocity. Her assistant Marianne Stuart stood silently, her cheeks stinging.

There was a short pause before Ana resumed her attack. She looked away briefly and shook her head.

"I have tried to give you a chance. I really have. You've *fucked up* at every turn and now…and now, you want to FUCK UP MY CAREER!"

Marianne opened her mouth to remonstrate before deciding it was pointless. There was another pause. Her attention settled momentarily on the view of Big Ben behind the office window.

Ana sighed. She looked down at her desk and then back up at Marianne. Her voice softened. "I have to ask Marianne, what were you thinking? What *were you* thinking? *Who* starts a fight on the House of Commons FUCKING TERRACE?"

"I didn't start the fight" said Marianne trying to keep her voice even. "I barely even defended myself."

"I don't give a shit. All I care about is that the press have dragged my name into it. And it is your fault. It really is your fault."

"All I can say is…." Marianne began.

Ana violently banged the desk cutting her off. The gesture was of such force that Marianne wondered, afterwards, if it had hurt. She sat back in her chair, closed her eyes and massaged her temples.

"I really have no choice now. I'm going to have to take advice and make this formal." Her eyes flicked open. "You know what that means, don't you?"

Marianne nodded sullenly.

"I suggest you go back to work today" said Ana. "We'll talk more about this."

Dismissed, Marianne closed the door to Ana's office behind her. She had toyed with the idea of slamming it in a gesture of defiance. Still, she was probably in enough trouble.

She began walking down the corridor back to her office. Her cheeks were still stinging. She could feel her eyes welling up with tears. Crying on the parliamentary estate was not a good look. She'd been at Westminster long enough to know that.

Needing to compose herself, she dived into the nearest ladies'. She blew her nose and dabbed her eyes in front of the mirror. A couple of deep breaths seemed to restore her to some sort of equilibrium. She stared at her reflection.

Her situation was truly miserable. She was facing unemployment having been embroiled in political ignominy. It was the disgrace more than anything that bothered her. In some ways, her predicament was extraordinary. A couple of years earlier, politics hadn't been part of her life. Politics was on the news and in the papers.

How has this happened to me? she asked herself. *How have I ended up trapped in this life, in this mess?*

She knew the answer really. It had all started more than a year ago. In February 2015, she and Euan returned to a frosty West London after eighteen months away. They had worked their way across the Far East: Thailand, Vietnam, Cambodia and Indonesia. Eventually, they ended up in Australia before coming home via Los Angeles.

The trip had been Euan's idea. "Let's get the old mid-life crisis out the way early" he said. She'd laughed about this when they celebrated her thirtieth birthday on Bondi Beach.

Marianne had worked in publishing. She gave up her job as a copy editor to go travelling. This hadn't been a difficult decision. Her job had never felt like a career as such. It was something she'd fallen into after leaving university. Euan made his living playing the violin, and trying to teach others to do the same. He was pretty much able to take or leave work as he chose.

Initially, Marianne felt elated to be back in London. Their families and friends had celebrated their homecoming. It was like they'd returned triumphant from a crusade rather than an extended holiday. To her surprise, she didn't yearn for sandy beaches, palm trees and balmy evenings. It was fun to share their adventures over Sunday pub lunches. Still, Marianne had no desire to be back in paradise. She was delighted to be home in their tiny, ramshackle flat. London seemed to teem with life and possibility. Tube journeys, once irksome, now felt sort of invigorating. Marianne discovered new joy in people watching.

In the evenings, Euan cooked Thai or Balinese dishes for dinner. They would eat in front of the TV news on their bedroom sofa. The 2015 General Election was in full swing. Marianne found herself becoming slightly hooked.

"He's such a weaselly little twat" she said of David Cameron when he was interviewed.

Euan grunted indifferently. "Prefer the other guy do you?"

Marianne thought for a moment. "Yes. Yes, I do as it happens. At least he seems to want to do something positive with the power."

"They always do until they get elected."

"Yes, Victor Meldrew."

For the next couple of weeks, Marianne was left alone in the flat for long periods. Her early sense of contentment began to evaporate. Euan would leave and return carrying his violin case and satchel. She began to get bored. Their money situation wasn't desperate but she would need to find work. She registered with a couple of temp agencies but heard nothing. To pass the time, she read the *Guardian Online* religiously.

"You're becoming obsessed" Euan told her when she became irate about a story on *Newsnight*. She felt Ed Miliband was getting a raw deal.

"Fucking right I am. I am sick of hearing about bacon sandwiches. This is supposed to be about the future of our country."

Euan put down his fork. "*Well*, why don't you do something about it?"

"What do you mean?"

"You're at a loose end at the moment. Why don't you volunteer on the Labour campaign, or something?"

"How would I do that?"

He shrugged. "Go online?"

The next day, Marianne filled out her details on the Labour Party website. A week passed without her hearing anything. She had begun to think more about finding work.

An unknown number called her 'phone. She answered hoping it was one of the temp agencies.

"Is that Marianne?" asked a brisk female voice.

"Yes."

"Marianne, It's Karen from Greenwood Labour Party. I gather you've volunteered for our campaign."

"Erm…yes."

"Marvellous. What's your availability?"

"Well, anytime really. I am…"

"Fantastic" interjected Karen. "We're running a session tomorrow afternoon. Just pop into the office at two. I'll send you an e-mail with all the details. See you then."

The line went dead. Marianne wondered why she hadn't piped up to ask what exactly was involved.

Despite her misgivings, she kept the appointment. She arrived at the Greenwood Labour Party offices the following afternoon. The entrance was a shop front opposite the tube station on Greenwood High Road. In the window was a campaign poster for Ana Novak, the Labour candidate for Greenwood Central.

Having done a spot of online research beforehand, Marianne knew a little about Ana Novak. In fact, she vaguely remembered seeing her on TV. Novak had been the social affairs correspondent for a London news programme. At the time, she'd made little impression on Marianne. She was blonde, slender and well groomed but not especially memorable. Her sweet smile and beseeching brown eyes seemed suitable for her medium.

Marianne gleaned that she was the child of Polish immigrants. They'd worked in blue collar jobs. Their daughter, Ana had read history at Cambridge before training as a journalist. That was where she had joined the Labour Party. Her career established, she became an advocate for the local Polish community. The London Borough of Greenwood had one of the biggest. That was how she'd earned her political brownie points. Her media profile helped.

At the door, Marianne pressed the buzzer. A disembodied voice ushered her in. She was directed upstairs to the first floor. Once there, she found herself inside a dusty smelling, cavernous office. A number of smaller partitioned rooms led off from it. The whole place was strewn with boxes of envelopes and leaflets. The walls were adorned with paraphernalia such as election posters from 1945.

There were about a dozen volunteers milling around. They seemed to be awaiting instruction. Marianne concluded that most of them were either students or retired teachers. She hung around in front of the door for a moment. A couple of older women nodded and smiled encouragingly at her.

"Beep, beep" said a brisk voice behind her.

She turned to see a tall, dark haired woman, about forty, in the doorway. The woman was carrying a cardboard box. She wore an oversized rucksack, a woolly hat and tortoiseshell glasses. Marianne stood aside to let her past.

The woman dropped the box on a table with a thud. "Got another fucking parking ticket" she said to no one in particular. The attention of the room seemed to be focussed on her. Clearly, she was the one in charge.

Addressing them, she said "Are you all ready to go out? The candidate will be joining you later."

Marianne realised the woman was Karen Giannapoulos, the paid organiser of the Greenwood Labour Party. It was her who'd called the day before. Something about her appearance and manner reminded Marianne of Lucy from the *Peanuts* cartoons.

She stepped forward to introduce herself. "Hi, I'm Marianne…"

"Yes. Marianne". Karen took her hand and shook it firmly. "Thank you so much for coming. Have you done this before?"

"No, I meant to ask…"

"No problem. There's nothing to it. I will send you out with a crew and they'll show you the ropes. It's on-the-job training here, I'm afraid."

With brutal efficiency, Marianne found herself dispatched, with six others, onto the streets of West London. She was somewhat perturbed to find that she was expected to knock on the doors of total strangers. She had to ask them how they were going to vote. The others called this canvassing or "voter ID".

She followed another woman, who was clearly an old hand, for the first couple of doors. She had expected to be berated by disgruntled voters for the intrusion.

Instead, she found that most were just politely indifferent. Her nervousness subsided. She soon found the confidence to knock on doors on her own. Being in a team made it easier. Marianne had this agreeable sense of being part of a gang.

They returned to the office a couple of hours later. It was there that Marianne met Ana Novak for the first time.

The office was even busier than it had been earlier. The crowd were a bit more diverse. Some had clearly knocked off work from their office jobs. Karen was issuing instructions to a group who were about to be sent out. There was a general hum of chatter. This subsided a bit when the candidate herself arrived.

That afternoon, there had been very light horizontal rain. Ana entered wearing a grey trench coat with its belt tied at the waist. Her blonde hair was tousled by the drizzle. Somehow, the effect was of casual, effortless elegance.

I would just look like a drowned rat Marianne thought ruefully.

She was struck by Ana's slenderness. Marianne herself, after eighteen months of backpacking, was leaner than she ever had been. Still, Ana's petite frame, and somewhat misleading impression of tallness, made her feel rather squat by comparison. Ana wore scarlet lipstick which suited her despite her pale skin and delicate cheekbones.

The candidate immediately began working the room, shaking hands and chatting. She had an agreeable laugh. She used it a lot. People seemed very pleased to have her attention for a few moments. Before long, it was Marianne's turn. Someone introduced them.

"*Cool* shoes" were Ana's first words to Marianne.

She looked down at her gold converse trainers.

Marianne was rather flattered by this. She instinctively trusted Ana on matters of fashion.

"Thanks. I got them in Thailand" she said.

"I *love* Thailand" said Ana. "I spent a couple of months backpacking in Asia. About a hundred years ago."

"We've just come back from travelling in Asia" Marianne told her. "My boyfriend and I. We've been away eighteen months."

"Wow. I wish I'd done an epic trip like that. I'm even more impressed that you're straight out on the doorstep."

"I just *had to*" Marianne said with a vehemence that surprised her. "This government is just trampling all over my values and dismantling public services. The worst thing is all this divisive immigration rhetoric. It's like we're going back in time."

"Absolutely" said Ana. "I have been dealing with the consequences of this sort of thing for years. I can tell you this much. The Tories will always pander to people's worst prejudices. The important thing is never, ever legitimise them. Never descend to their level."

"God, I wish more politicians would say that."

"I'm going to keep on saying it. Whether I win this election or not"

"How are things looking?" asked Marianne uncertainly. "Do you think you're going to win?"

Ana sighed. "The canvassing returns are looking good. They're consistent with the national polls. But you never can tell. The Tories aren't giving up this seat without a fight."

"Well, if there's anything I can do…"

"Yes. Just keep doing what you're doing. Keep coming along. We will also find time to compare notes on Thailand."

"I'd like that."

Ana patted Marianne on the shoulder.

"She's not like other politicians" Marianne told Euan later that evening. They were in bed, snuggled up under the duvet. "She actually seems interested in you. And she's drop dead gorgeous.

"Should I be getting jealous?" Euan murmured sleepily.

Marianne hit him with her pillow.

Throughout March, Marianne went out canvassing most days. She gave up trying to find a job. She would arrive at the Greenwood Labour office in the morning and leave in the evening. Some days, she would find herself knocking on doors with Ana. This always felt like some sort of treat or reward.

Between canvassing sessions, Marianne would enjoy a cigarette break with Karen who insisted she was giving up after the election. They smoked in the yard outside. Marianne herself identified as a social smoker. She and Euan had given up before they went travelling. After a couple of weeks, Karen asked her to lead some of the canvassing sessions.

One evening, Marianne had been part of a crew that canvassed a block of flats. A resident had let them in. Marianne knocked on one door. The angry, red-faced man who answered it screamed at her. His language was peppered with obscenities. For a moment, she'd thought he might hit her. Still, she remained calm and held her ground. This impressed Ana who was out with them. She put her arm around Marianne and gave her shoulders a sisterly squeeze.

"I met scarier creatures in the Outback" Marianne said. Ana squealed with laughter.

On the last Sunday of March, Karen called to speak to her.

"We're in the last six weeks of the campaign" she said.

"Yes" said Marianne, wondering where this was leading.

"We're recruiting a volunteer coordinator. It's a paid role, just until Polling Day mind."

"*Okay...*"

"Well, would you be interested?" Karen asked. "Ana's keen for you to do it."

Marianne was in the office at 7am the next day. Her new job involved chasing up offers of help and welcoming new volunteers. There seemed to be a surge of humanity though the office that day. Marianne felt energised by it, even getting frequent adrenaline rushes, until she left office after 9pm. Then, she was exhausted.

"How was your first day?" Euan called out when she got home. He was in the kitchen cooking spaghetti bolognaise. By now, he had tired of recreating dishes from the Far East.

"Fabulous. Mad. Tiring" replied Marianne. She hung up her coat on a peg in the oblong hallway.

She went into the kitchen. There was just enough room for her and Euan's gangly, rambling form. She dipped a spoon into the sauce to taste it.

"Needs more salt" she told him.

Euan took the spoon off her. "Your palette isn't refined enough to know. Now piss off and have a bath. I'll bring you in a glass of wine."

Marianne's role was based in the main office. She began to perceive the scale of Ana's campaign. It was far greater than she'd realised. She was just running a tiny little operation within it. It was like an empire with many different satellites. There was just so much else going on: fundraising dinners, photo-calls and hustings. She went to regular meetings with Karen and other volunteers. However, she knew that there were other meetings attended by more important people.

The partitioned offices off the main one were always in use. Marianne wasn't entirely sure what for. One was used by a slightly-built, intense woman called Joni. Of indeterminate middle age, she had a slightly hippyish appearance. She was doing something with postal voters. Marianne thought she seemed pleasant and friendly enough but had little interaction with her. Another was periodically occupied by a local councillor called Pete Samuelson, a large, thickset man in his early forties. He said little to her and seemed gruff. Karen had told her, during one of their cigarette breaks, that he was the Leader of Greenwood Council.

"What does he do?" Marianne asked.

"He's the big boss on the Council" Karen explained. "Sort of like a mayor would be in another country. We control the Council. He's the Labour Group leader. So he runs everything."

"This has all been such an education to me" said Marianne.

The General Election was held on Thursday 7th May 2015. Marianne's day began at 4am. She let herself into the office and dispatched a team of early, enthusiastic volunteers to deliver leaflets. People had been telling her for days they thought Ana was going to win. The candidate herself gave nothing away. The national polls suggested the election would be close. Marianne had no instinctive feeling about it herself.

At about 9am, there was a lull in the office. Believing herself to be alone, Marianne poured herself a mug of filter coffee in the office kitchen. Ana strolled in.

"Hard at it?" she said to Marianne grinning.

Marianne felt slightly embarrassed. "Oh, I was just..."

"Just kidding. You're entitled to a coffee break. Would you mind getting me one? Just black. No sugar. I've just got to go to the loo."

She disappeared and returned a few minutes later. Marianne handed her a chipped mug.

"How are you feeling?" she asked the candidate.

"I'm a bag of nerves" replied Ana. She seemed preternaturally calm and collected.

They sipped their mugs of coffee in silence for a few moments.

"Tell me" Ana said. "What are you going to do when this is all over?"

Marianne blinked. "To tell you the truth, I haven't thought about it. I've just been living and breathing this for the last couple of months..."

"I know the feeling" said Ana.

"I guess I might go back into publishing" said Marianne. "It's all I know really. I might have do some temping to tide me over."

"After today, I might be doing the same. You know I gave up my job at London News don't you?"

"No."

"Yep. I haven't been paid for nearly two years."

"How have you…"

"Politics involves sacrifices, Marianne." Ana took another sip of coffee. "Anyhow, look. You've been a great support to me this campaign. I hope you'll think about other jobs in politics."

This was unexpected and slightly overwhelming for Marianne. "Thank you. Thank you so much. You have been such an inspiration to me and…'

She tailed off. She felt clumsy and inarticulate. Ana smiled at her fondly.

After lunch, several hundred volunteers seemed to trudge in and out of the office. It wasn't humanly possible to keep track of them all. Karen had joked about electronically tagging them. The pace was frenetic. It was beyond anything she had experienced before. Marianne found that as the day wore on, the volunteers needed more and more cajoling to go out. She was frequently asked "How's it looking?". She didn't have any intelligence to gratify them with.

Karen appeared about 3pm. She had been supervising operations across the constituency. On arrival, her face was a picture of barely suppressed fury.

"What's up?" Marianne asked.

"I've got to take the candidate to the *fucking hairdressers*" she snarled. "There's nothing fucking wrong with her fucking hair. She'd be better off knocking on some fucking doors. I *really* have better things to do today".

Marianne privately thought that the candidate's attention to her appearance wasn't wholly unjustified. She was the subject of increasing media attention. Apart from anything else, she needed her armour to go into battle like many women. Still, she decided against arguing the point with Karen.

The election count was taking place at Greenwood Town Hall. The result was expected to be announced in the early hours. Marianne went home to change about 11pm. Euan was still out having a beer with friends.

She thought carefully about her outfit. What would Ana wear? Something simple and understated. With that in mind, she pulled a navy blue Reiss suit out of the wardrobe. She'd bought it for a job interview five years earlier. She had never cared for it much.

Hundreds of party activists had congregated at the Town Hall when she arrived after midnight. They weren't just differentiated by the colours of their rosettes. Marianne thought they resembled tribes. She could tell the Tories from the Greens with half a glance.

There was an atmosphere of expectation. The tribes stood around chatting to each other, trying to glean intelligence from the enemy. A couple of hours earlier, she and others had gathered around a laptop in the office. They'd learnt the BBC exit poll predicted a Tory majority. There had been gasps of disbelief. Nobody had seen it coming.

The implications for Ana were unclear. The word on the street was that she was ahead. Still, the national polls had been way off.

Marianne saw Karen and Pete Samuelson in the foyer. She went over to join them.

"As people have been asking me all day, *how's it looking?"* she asked.

Pete sort of grunted. Karen replied.

"It's looking good. We think Ana's got it by about fifteen hundred votes."

Pete said: "It's just the national picture that's the disaster".

The count went on, as predicted, until the early hours. Information from inside the count was obtained. Ana's predicted majority gradually increased to two thousand. This was later upgraded to nearer three.

There was no sign of the candidate herself until about 2am. She arrived wearing a fitted red shift dress. The local media descended on her. She smiled graciously. Marianne realised that she wouldn't be seen dead in a boxy navy blue suit. More to the point, she knew she had won.

At 4am, the candidates gathered on stage for the announcement. The returning officer cleared his throat. Ana looked cool and poised. The Tory MP she'd vanquished was clearly determined to be magnanimous in defeat.

Each result was greeted with cheers by the candidates' supporters.

"Mark Llewellyn, the Conservative Party candidate", intoned the returning officer, "sixteen thousand, three hundred and twenty-four votes".

Team Llewellyn roared supportively. The returning officer continued.

"Ana Novak, the Labour Party candidate." He paused for a few seconds, clearly enjoying the expectant silence. "Twenty thousand, seven hundred and forty-two votes".

The effect on Ana's supporters was positively explosive. Marianne herself actually screeched. Their cheers might have broken decibel records. Ana's reserved, poised smile expanded into something more overtly triumphant.

The returning officer made his final announcement: "I hereby declare that Ana Novak has been duly elected as the Member of Parliament for the Greenwood Central constituency".

That was that.

Ana's victory speech lamented the majority Tory government. She said she was delighted Greenwood Central had bucked the national trend. She vowed to fight for local people and their public services. However, Marianne realised later that there had been an omission. She hadn't thanked her volunteers.

As she left the stage, Ana was surrounded by suited men Marianne didn't recognise. They pulled her though the waiting throng of supporters. Ana nodded and smiled distractedly.

Marianne decided she wanted to congratulate the new MP herself. She touched Ana on the shoulder, as she was escorted past, and said "Well done." Ana didn't respond. She just continued looking ahead with her glazed smile.

"It wasn't exactly like she blanked me" Marianne said to Euan the next day. "It was like she didn't see me."

"Weird" said Euan.

"I guess it must have been a bit overwhelming for her."

"I suppose."

"It's a bit odd she didn't thank anybody in her speech though."

"That's politicians for you" said Euan. "They're all looking out for number one."

"Oh, I don't think that's totally fair" Marianne protested. "I think many politicians are very principled. It's high pressure stuff. "

Still, Marianne couldn't quite throw off her sense of unease. She had this disagreeable feeling that she'd been somehow used and discarded. She tried hard to talk herself out of it, to rationalise. Of course she had just been one of many who'd helped on Ana's campaign. She wasn't owed any special favours. No one else was either. In the end, it was all about the greater good. People's delicate feelings shouldn't come into it.

She had gone back to the office the next day to help clear up. Her paid job was at an end. Karen had been pleased to see her and thanked her effusively.

"I hope you'll stay involved" she'd said. "We have a new MP to support now."

"Absolutely" said Marianne. "As long as you give up smoking."

In truth, she had decided against staying active in the Party. She wanted to rediscover some feeling of contentment, spend more time with Euan and keep more regular hours. She knew that politics wasn't conducive to that.

A week later, she started a temp job. It was in a university admissions office off Kensington High Street. The work was dull but easy. It was an undemanding way of earning some money. She'd also applied for a permanent job at another publishers. They had a vacancy for a new copy editor.

One lunchtime, she decided to nip out to buy a new dress. Euan had been invited to a cocktail party by a client. She was to go as his plus one. Her wardrobe at home was full of clothes but she had nothing to wear. She decided to try her luck in the charity shops on Kensington High Street. They were highly recommended.

She searched the rail in Oxfam where she found a patterned Vivienne Westwood dress. At that moment, her phone buzzed inside her handbag. She reluctantly decided to answer.

"Hello" she said.

"Marianne, it's Ana. How are you? I haven't seen you since election night".

Marianne was stunned. "Erm, I'm fine. In fact, I'm very well. And you? How's Westminster?"

She supposed Ana had rung to thank her, finally.

"That's what I wanted to talk you about" said Ana. "I need a parliamentary assistant. My office is in chaos. And I haven't got any staff."

"Okay".

"And I can't think of anyone else who I'd rather offer the job to."

Silence.

"Marianne, are you still there?"

"Yes" said Marianne. "When would you like me to start?"

Chapter Two

The toast popped up. Marianne pressed down the plunger of her coffee maker. Early morning sunlight streamed in through the window.

It was the first day of her new job. Marianne had woken very early, and now she and Euan ate breakfast standing up, in their tiny kitchen.

Marianne took a sip of her coffee. Euan scraped some marmalade onto his toast and took a bite.

The transistor radio next to the cooker was on. Bruce Springsteen's 'Dancing in the Dark' was playing. Marianne sang along.

"*I get up in the evening. And I ain't got nothing to say. I come home in the morning. I go to bed feeling the same way.*"

Euan joined in.

"I ain't nothing but tired. Man I'm just tired and bored with myself."

Spiritedly, if not especially tunefully, they sang in unison.

"You can't start a fire. You can't start a fire without a spark. This gun's for hire. Even if we're just dancing in the dark".

Marianne was excited. This was not something she usually felt before starting a new job. Apprehension, yes, but not this shivery thrill of anticipation. A whole new world of possibilities had opened for her.

She left earlier than she needed to. Euan kissed her on the mouth, as she went out the door, smearing toast crumbs on her lipstick. She walked briskly to the tube station in the morning sunshine and took the eastbound Central Line.

Ben Harrison, Ana's researcher, had sent her an e-mail a few days earlier. This explained how she was to get into the Palace of Westminster. Marianne had only been there once on a school trip, many years earlier. Her abiding memory was of queuing up outside with tourists in the rain.

She changed onto the Jubilee Line at Oxford Circus and got off at Westminster. As instructed by Ben, she made her way to an office building off Whitehall. She was perfunctorily ushered in, photographed and given her security pass.

Returning to Westminster tube station, she entered Parliament though a 'secret tunnel' Ben had told her about. Her heels clacked on the floor of the long corridor. There were security men, at the end, stood next to an airport-style metal detector.

Marianne presented her new pass. To her mild surprise, she was just waved through. There was no need to walk through the metal detector. She wasn't subjected to any further scrutiny. She felt a strange sensation rising through her body. Only months earlier, she had been an aimless backpacker lounging around on beaches. Now, she was being ushered into the corridors of power as if she actually belonged there. She already knew which she liked best.

The ornate splendour of the place bore down on her as she made her way to Central Lobby. She was to meet Ben there. Arriving a few minutes early, she took a seat on a bench. Until Ben appeared, she was at leisure to observe.

Instinctively, she was able to distinguish between insiders and visitors. The insiders appeared from one corridor, leading off the hexagon of Central Lobby, and strutted down another. They tended to be very young, in their early twenties, sharply dressed and possessed of terrifying self-confidence. The visitors walked at a difference pace. They were often waiting, eager and slightly anxious.

An announcement was made by loudspeaker: “Marianne Stuart for Ana Novak MP.”

Marianne sprung up, her train of thought interrupted. She made her way to the reception desk. Ben Harrison was stood in front of it waiting for her. Slightly built and boyish, he certainly looked like one of the insiders.

He introduced himself, shaking her hand firmly. Closer up, she could tell he was older, perhaps in his thirties. His eyes gave away a certain world weariness. “Nice to meet you at last” he said. “I thought we’d start by showing you where you’re going to be working. Then I’ll take you up to see Ana.”

He led her out of the lobby through a maze of corridors. Marianne wondered if he would be showing her out at the end of the day. Directions had never been her strong point.

They came to a set of elevators. Signs indicated that some were for the exclusive use of MPs. Marianne was slightly taken aback. She sensed that Ben had registered her reaction. Still, he didn’t say anything. They took a non-designated lift to a lower floor.

Ben pushed open the door to the office they were to share. Marianne’s immediate impression was that it was windowless and dusty. It was also very cramped. Chairs, desks and filing cabinets seemed to merge into each other. The far wall was adorned by shelves bulging with files. An unplugged electric fan was balanced precariously on the top shelf.

“You can have either of the desks to the side” Ben told her. “Middle one’s mine.”

Marianne picked the one on the left and dropped her coat and bag on the chair behind it. “Who’s the other desk for?” she asked.

“It’s for the caseworker we’re in the process of recruiting. Ana also has an office manager based in the constituency. Trudie. You may remember her from the election.”

Marianne vaguely recalled a seemingly sensible, grey-haired woman. She thought she had met her on the campaign at some point.

“Right” Ben said. “Let’s take you up to see Ana”.

Ana’s office was a couple of floors above. Ben knocked on the door and entered before waiting for an answer. Marianne gingerly followed.

“Here’s Marianne” Ben announced.

The room was bright and uncluttered. Ana rose from her chair beaming, her arms outstretched as if she were going to give Marianne a hug. Ben exited discreetly.

“Marianne, welcome” said Ana gesturing at the chair in front of her desk. “It’s so nice to see you! Feels like ages since the campaign.”

“It really does” said Marianne as she sat down. “I’m very excited to be here”.

“Well, I’m so glad you were available. It’s all still a bit chaotic here. We need someone with your sort of resilience and can-do attitude.”

“Oh, well…”

"Anyhow, I'll reiterate the purpose of your job" said Ana. "You are here as my parliamentary assistant. You're *not* my caseworker. *However*, we need you to lend a hand with casework until we hire one."

"No problem" said Marianne. "I guess Ben and Trudie have been managing it between them."

There was a brief silence. Ana sighed.

"I'm afraid Trudie has been...*struggling* a bit." She spoke quietly. "You know, I really wanted to do something nice for her. She lost her husband last year. But she just can't seem to cope."

"Oh" said Marianne.

Ana leaned slightly closer. Her tone became more confidential, more intimate. "To tell you the truth, I don't actually know what it is *she does.* She moans about her workload. But I've seen no evidence of any productivity. Meanwhile, poor old Ben gets lumbered."

Marianne didn't know what to say. She wondered why Trudie hadn't made more of the opportunity. Surely, she should have been powered by enthusiasm. She'd been part of a successful campaign and got a job out of it.

"Sorry to offload to you on your first day" said Ana. "I know we'll be ship-shape very soon now that you're on board."

Marianne felt a surge of warmth from the confidence expressed in her. "I'll certainly do my level best" she said, trying to keep her voice even. She wanted to sound suitably coolheaded.

Ana looked at her watch. “Bollocks. I’ve got that bloody photo shoot with *Marie Claire*. I have to get a move on”.

“That sounds very *glamorous!”* Marianne said.

“Oh” said Ana waving her hand dismissively. “It’s just going to be a lot of hanging about and being asked stupid questions. They’re doing a feature on me and some of the other new women MPs. I’m not really into all this makeover malarkey.”

Nice work if you can get it though Marianne thought to herself.

Ana rose from her chair. This was clearly her signal the conversation was to finish.

“Seriously” she said to Marianne before she left. “Thank you for taking this on. I really appreciate it.”

In the following days, Marianne was inducted into her new job by Ben. He helped her set up her computer and her parliamentary e-mail address. She spent most of her first week responding to queries about the new welfare bill. Ana was opposed but it was unclear whether she would vote against. The Labour Party had begun a leadership election.

“Ana likes to sign everything that goes out in her name.” Ben told her.

“Really?” Marianne was very surprised by this. She’d assumed the sheer volume of correspondence made this impractical.

She found herself warming to Ben. He had seemed brusque at first. However, their relationship quickly developed a companionable rhythm. He volunteered little information about himself. Still, he was very willing to share his experience and insights. He involved her in a piece of casework she found fascinating. A constituent of Ana's, one Mr Al-Nawazi was facing homelessness. The apparent cause was a miscommunication between the Home Office and Greenwood Council.

Marianne said "It's sort of Kafkaesque and Monty Pythonesque at the same time."

"There's a lot of it about" said Ben. "We have to try to cut through all the crazy bureaucracy and get some sort of outcome.

On the tube home one evening, she had picked up a copy of *the Evening Standard.* Flicking through without much interest, she came across a profile of Ana. Other new MPs were also profiled. There was a quote from Ana about the importance of community to her politics. She described herself as a 'changemaker'. The paper predicted greatness for her.

On the Friday of her first week, Marianne had drafted a couple of letters about Mr Al-Nawazi. She gave them to Ana to sign.

"Might be a good idea to remind her about them next week" Ben advised.

Marianne was meeting Euan for dinner at eight. It had been his idea. He wanted them to celebrate her new job. Beforehand, she and Ben went for a drink in the House of Lords bar. They'd finished work slightly early. Ana was out of the office in the constituency

It was a warm early summer evening. The doors onto the terrace were open. Marianne and Ben ensconced themselves on plush red chairs.

"Congratulations on surviving your first week" said Ben. He took a sip of his Sauvignon Blanc.

"I have loved every minute" replied Marianne. "It just feels amazing to be here, to be part of all this."

“I was a bit worried we’d thrown you in at the deep end” Ben said. “Things are a bit chaotic at the moment.”

“No!” Marianne protested. “I think we’re doing a bloody brilliant job. Just think about all the e-mails and the letters…we’re understaffed. *And* the constituency office manager is completely incompetent…”

“Sorry” interjected Ben. What do you mean Trudie is completely incompetent?”

He looked at her with an unreadable curiosity.

Marianne had this sense of having made a faux pas. Her mind scrambled desperately to rescue the situation. “Oh, I’ve just heard that she’s…just…not that…competent.”

“Trudie is perfectly competent” said Ben quietly “and she is very hardworking and decent too.”

“It’s just that Ana said…she’s struggling a bit at the moment.”

Ben put his glass down on the table. “Yes, she’s struggling a bit with Ana at the moment” he told her.

“But why?” Marianne’s sense of mortification was growing.

“She’s inherited what I call the *baton of blame”* said Ben. “Happens to us all. She can’t do anything right by Ana at the moment, and she won’t for a while.”

Marianne struggled to comprehend this. Ana had hardly struck her as given to arbitrariness.

Ben continued. “I’ve worked for a few politicians in my time. They can be somewhat…mercurial, especially if they’re very ambitious. And Ana *is* very ambitious. I don't want to disillusion you but you need to know what working here can be like".

Marianne nodded but remained silent. She found the conversation unsettling. Perhaps Ben had just misread the situation with Trudie. Perhaps he was just so cynical and jaded that he'd misread Ana too. Her own experience was so different, apart from that weirdness on election night.

She decided not to let it spoil her evening. Euan had reserved a table at a fish restaurant on Kensington Church Street. In the late '80s, it had been an ultra-fashionable eatery. The glass front and minimalist décor were of its time. She'd wanted to go there since her publishing days. One of her bosses had regaled her with tales of long lunches and celebrity sightings. It now had a sort of faded chic.

They drank a bottle of Champagne with their meal. Marianne had battered haddock. Euan opted for the ribeye steak. By the time they had coffee, Marianne felt agreeably light-headed on Champagne bubbles.

Their conversation had turned to Mr Al-Nawazi. Marianne's account of his predicament had become increasingly incensed as she told it. She was exercised by the petty officiousness more than anything.

Euan watched her as she spoke. He looked sort of amused, affectionate. "I've never realised you are such a social justice warrior" he said.

"I'm sorry?"

"No, I think it's great. This new job has given you…something, a sense of purpose. I've never seen you like this before. I've never been sure what it is you wanted to do before. You've always been sort of aimless."

"Aimless?"

"I don't *mean* aimless!" Euan said. He clearly thought he'd been a bit tactless. He sometimes was after too much alcohol.

Marianne took a sip from the dregs of her Champagne glass. She picked up her coffee cup and swirled its contents. For a moment, she sat in contemplation. "That's just it" she said eventually. "I think *I have* been a bit aimless."

"I can't talk" said Euan. "I'm just a glorified busker!"

"It's not that I'm some sort of social justice crusader" Marianne said. "I don't even think I'm even very political. It's just that I've always wanted to make my life count for *something*. If I'm going to be on this earth for however many years, I want to do something, make *some sort* of contribution."

"And you do."

"I just want people to have a fair dea." Marianne said. "I'm not out to ferment revolution. Take Mr Al-Nawazi. He's in this nightmare situation. All because of a couple of useless office workers who won't talk to each other. He's a Syrian refugee. It wouldn't happen to us. It wouldn't happen to people like us. Purely because of circumstance. We have relatively easy lives. Not because we're cleverer or more deserving. *It's just circumstance.* If I can iron out just one anomaly, square just one circle, I feel like I've justified our existence."

"This sounds like the famous middle-class guilt I've heard about" teased Euan.

"It's not that' said Marianne. "I feel absolutely no guilt. I just want a bit of basic common sense to be applied. To everybody. Across the board."

Euan took her hand. “You have loads of common sense. More than enough for both of us. That’s why I…didn’t marry you.”

Marianne laughed. “No sensible woman would marry *you*. You can take that from me.”

The following Thursday, Ana swept into the office without knocking. Marianne was at her desk. She was reading yet more e-mails about the welfare bill. Ben had gone to the House of Commons Library.

“Marianne, I need to ask a small favour” said Ana.

“Sure...”

“I have to go to a drinks do tonight” she told her. “It’s the Greenwood Polish Business Guild. Could do with some moral support. These things can be a bit turgid.”

“Erm yes. I can do that.” Marianne couldn’t think of a reason not to.

“Fantastic. I know it’s a school night. Just come round to my house for seven. We’ll get a taxi. It will be nice to have another woman with me”

“Fine. Sounds like fun” said Marianne.

She remembered that she needed something from Ana.

“I finished that letter about Mr Al-Nawazi” she said. “Just wondering if you’ve had a chance to glance at it.”

“On my list” replied Ana. She breezed out.

Marianne was flattered by Ana’s invitation. Still, she suspected that it wasn’t *really* an invitation. She wondered how Ana would have responded if she’d had plans that evening. She mentioned it to Ben when he came back.

"Hmm. Bit short notice" was all he said.

That evening, Marianne went to Ana's house as arranged. She lived in a new-build townhouse on the other side of Greenwood. Marianne took a tube and a bus to get there.

She pressed the buzzer. Ana opened the front door in a white bathrobe.

"Come in!"

Marianne looked around the open plan ground floor. Ana's taste in décor was not what she had been expecting. She had imagined achingly hip minimalism. Instead, she was confronted by magnolia walls and bulky, bland furniture. It suggested Ana wasn't hugely interested in her own home.

"Very nice place you have" she said.

"I love it" replied Ana. She led Marianne into the kitchen. "Here. Get this down you."

She handed her a glass.

"What is it?" Marianne asked.

"Vodka and tonic. It will make this evening more bearable. Trust me. Drink up."

Feeling obliged, Marianne downed the drink as Ana watched her. She immediately felt flushed and slightly tipsy.

Ana stepped back and looked her up and down. "We need to do something about your clothes" she said.

Marianne was wearing a plain blouse and skirt under a beige trench coat. She had come straight from work. "Isn't this suitable?"

"It's an evening do. You can't go in your work clothes" Ana insisted. "Come upstairs. I have just the thing for you."

Ana's bedroom was as impersonal as the rest of the house. She opened the door to a fitted wardrobe. She pulled out a flowery dress on a wire hanger. Presumably, it belonged to her. Marianne found it difficult to imagine her wearing something quite so matronly.

Ana handed it over. "Go on" she instructed.

Marianne hesitated. She thought Ana would leave the room while she changed.

"Are you sure?" was all she could muster as any sort of protest.

"Don't be silly!"

Marianne felt weighed down by the vodka she'd drunk. Her inhibitions were loosened. Still, she thought the situation a little odd, even in her involuntarily inebriated state. She stripped down to her underwear. Ana watched.

"You have great legs" she said. "And a good bust."

Really? Marianne thought to herself incredulously. *I'm a bit bloody short to be told I have good legs.*

She pulled on the dress. Ana zipped her up at the back. It felt uncomfortably tight and too baggy at the same time.

"You look gorgeous" Ana told her.

There was a mirror on the inside of the wardrobe door. Marianne looked at her reflection. She thought she looked middle-aged, frumpy and awkward. Still, she reflected, her judgement might be impaired by the vodka. Surely she could rely on Ana's good taste.

"Now for myself" said Ana. She was still her bathrobe. "Help yourself to another drink in the kitchen."

This was clearly her cue to leave. She waited downstairs for about twenty minutes. She didn't have another drink.

Ana emerged wearing a black fitted blazer, skinny jeans and suede ankle boots. The effect was sharp.

They took a taxi to the hotel where the reception was being held. The function room was crowded when they arrived. Marianne felt hot, sweaty and disoriented. The guests seem to be largely, though not exclusively, swarthy middle-aged men. She and Ana were surrounded from the moment they arrived. Their entrance had clearly been anticipated.

Glasses of champagne were dispensed by teenage waiting staff. Ana declined as did Marianne. The room was oak-panelled with French doors that had been left open because of the warm evening.

Ana greeted, in turn everyone in the huddle surrounding them. She spoke in Polish. She acted as though she knew them well or had, at least, met them before. Whether that was the case, Marianne couldn't tell.

A podium and microphone had been assembled on one side of the room. Ana was to deliver a speech to the gathering. This was clearly the main event. After an hour of mingling and exchanging niceties, she took to the stage.

To Marianne's relief, she spoke in English. This meant that she could follow. The speech itself seemed to be an expanded version of *the Evening Standard* piece. The content was fairly bland and dripping in platitudes. Ana paid tribute to the local Polish community. She said she owed her career to them. They'd taught her everything she knew about politics. Now, it was time to apply these lessons to the national stage. Once again, she used the term 'changemaker' to describe herself.

The speech was greeted with rapturous applause. This seemed to last for about half a minute. Other speakers followed. They were mainly Polish-speaking dignitaries. Ana stood next to Marianne, nodding attentively at times.

Eventually, the speeches finished. They were once again surrounded by another throng of guests. Marianne stood close to Ana, unacknowledged but somehow vital. She felt as though she were some sort of bodyguard or minder. Her role hadn't been discussed beforehand. It all seemed to work instinctively. The guests had their moment with Ana once she gave some sort of subliminal, hidden nod.

It was nearly midnight by the time Ana broached the subject of leaving. She had almost run out of people to talk to.

"We'll get a taxi" she said. "On me. I insist. If you want to come into work a bit later tomorrow, that's fine."

The taxi delivered Ana to her house first. She touched Marianne's elbow as she got out.

"Thanks for tonight. You've been brilliant."

It was after 1am when Marianne arrived home. Euan was in bed. He'd had the night off and had been home all evening. Marianne went into the kitchen and drank a large glass of water. It cooled her down. She stood at the sink for a moment.

It had been her intention to go into the bedroom, undress and get into bed without disturbing Euan. She wasn't quite ready to discuss the strangeness of the evening. However, his bedside lamp snapped on as soon as she opened the door

He sat up in bed, looked at her and let out a high-pitched laugh

"What the fuck!" he exclaimed

Marianne realised that she was still wearing the frumpy, flowery dress. Her own clothes were still at Ana's.

"Don't ask" she said.

"How was your evening?"

Marianne wasn't desperate to answer this question, which she'd anticipated. "Erm, it was sort of *interesting*" she replied.

"Can't wait to hear about it" said Euan. With that, he went back so sleep. He had an amazing ability to just do that at will. It had made international travel very easy for him.

Marianne took her 'phone out of her bag and put it on her bedside table. She pulled off the dress and climbed into bed. Leaning across Euan's comatose form, she switched off his bedside lamp. He'd left it on.

Sleep came surprisingly easy. She had expected to replay the events of the evening in her mind. However, she was overruled by her body. She hoped she wouldn't sleep through her 7am alarm.

Her slumber was abruptly interrupted at 4am by her 'phone buzzing. She sat up. Euan stirred.

She looked at the screen. It was a new e-mail notification. It was from Ana to her personal address. The word 'Urgent' appeared in the subject line.

It read: '*Marianne, I need an urgent update about Mr Al-Nawazi first thing in the morning. The letter should have gone out on Monday. We need to get on top of this asap!*'

"Christ on a bike" Marianne said aloud. She tried to process this in her state of bare wakefulness. Wasn't it her who had been chasing Ana about the letter?

"What's up?" murmured Euan sleepily.

"Just had an e-mail from Ana. About Mr Al-Nawazi."

"A work e-mail? At this time! Doesn't she sleep like normal people?"

"Clearly not" said Marianne.

She tried to get back to sleep but couldn't.

Chapter Three

"You *are* an angel" Ana said to Marianne.

It was a couple of weeks later. They were in Ana's office. Marianne handed Ana her dry-cleaning. She'd collected it on Greenwood High Road and dragged it across town on the tube. One of the items, a dress, was particularly heavy. Marianne noticed its label, 'Prada'.

The case of Mr Al-Nawazi had been resolved the previous week. Ana had written to the Home Secretary. Marianne and Ben had drafted the letter for her. As a result, it was clear that he could stay in the country. Greenwood Council had capitulated. They would house him for the foreseeable future.

Ana had laughed off her 4am e-mail to Marianne. "I was just in a panic about that poor man" she said. "It's easy for people to get lost in the system. Especially when Greenwood Council are involved."

She paused to give Marianne a knowing look

"Don't tell any of the local councillors I said that."

Marianne herself had been overjoyed by the outcome. She'd phoned Euan in the middle of the day to tell him. It was proof that her work made a material difference. Inwardly, she wondered if she too could describe herself as a "changemaker".

Back in the present, they were going through Ana's diary. Changes had had to be made. Meetings had had to be moved.

"Did I mention I had a drink with Yvette last night?" said Ana.

She hadn't. Marianne was curious. Yvette Cooper had just announced her candidacy for the Labour leadership. She and Ben had been speculating about who Ana would support.

"Erm no..." said Marianne

"Well, she's asked me to join her campaign team" Ana told her

"Oh..."

"I know what you're thinking" said Ana. "She has too much baggage. She's too associated with New Labour. And her husband might put people off."

Marianne hadn't thought any of this. She'd decided she was quite neutral about the leadership election.

Ana continued: "Labour has never had a woman leader. It's definitely time. The thing about Yvette is that she looks like a Prime Minister. You can imagine her taking the proverbial 3am call."

All of this sounded entirely credible to Marianne. She was unsure how the leadership election would play out. The grassroots didn't seem wildly enthused by any of the candidates. She knew this because she'd become active in her local Labour Party again.

Her Sunday mornings were now spent canvassing. Initially, she had gone in response to an e-mail. Euan groaned when she mentioned it. Still, it had been good to reconnect with people she knew from the campaign. They would meet at 11am, knock on doors and retire to the pub afterwards. Their conversation was mainly local Party gossip and speculation about the leadership.

The regulars consisted of local councillors and activists. The latter often held voluntary positions in the local party. Marianne made her own friends among them. They included Bridget, a lady of a certain Edinburgh genteel and vintage. They'd met during the election. Despite her outwardly reserved manner, Marianne had found her warm and welcoming.

Bridget was a retired journalist. She had been education correspondent for *the Guardian*. Her career had taken her all over the world. She had, at different points, lived in France, Hong Kong and the United States. The Labour Party seemed to be her retirement project. She was very dedicated to it.

Marianne found the pub conversations instructive. She began to get a feel for internal Labour politics. There was a general consensus about the leadership election; either Yvette Cooper or Andy Burnham would win. Some thought there might be a strong challenge from the left. Jeremy Corbyn, a veteran backbench rebel, was making a wild card bid. This had created a surprising buzz.

"I really can't see it" said Bridget. "He won't get the nominations. His sort of politics died out in the 1980s. I remember because I was there."

Sometimes, Joni Lessing would pitch up. Marianne had met her on the campaign. She hadn't really got to know her. At the time, she had seemed inoffensive. However, her presence was a cause of unspoken tension. She hadn't been active in the Party that long. That didn't stop her telling others about how to canvass. Her unwanted advice was, for the most part, politely ignored.

Interestingly, Joni was one of the few championing Corbyn. She would deliver lengthy soliloquys on the subject. That was to anyone who made eye contact. Before long, Marianne knew her arguments off by heart. They went like this: The

Labour Party had become too rigid and stuck in an intellectual rut. Corbyn's candidacy would excite debate about policy.

Marianne had also gone to a local Party meeting. She had found it a convivial and friendly. There were perhaps about twelve people there. They'd had a fairly lateral discussion about the welfare bill. There were differences of opinion but these didn't seem to be the cause of rancour. Everybody had gone to the pub together afterwards.

"Ana's supporting Yvette" Marianne told Ben when she returned to their office.

"That's because she thinks she's going to win" he said.

"I hope I'm never as cynical as you" said Marianne.

"Give it time."

Ana had summoned Trudie, her constituency office manager. Marianne saw her when she and Ana had finished going through the diary. She was waiting outside the door. Marianne knew relations had deteriorated further. Trudie looked tense and rather miserable. She nodded in response to Marianne's greeting. Ana wordlessly, unsmilingly gestured at her to go in. The door slammed shut.

The following week, Ana said to Marianne "I need to ask a small favour".

Oh God! Not another drinks do thought Marianne. Euan had started making jokes about being a political widower.

"Absolutely" she said.

"I need you to help Karen with a photo shoot" said Ana. "We're doing new leaflets with the councillors. Not quite *Marie Claire*, I'm afraid."

Marianne was a little surprised to be asked. Still, she agreed. She was perfectly happy to do it. Later, she learnt from Ben that it was something that would normally be Trudie's job. However, Trudie wasn't available that morning. She was meeting with Ana and her trade union rep. The purpose of this meeting was unspecified.

Karen picked her up from Greenwood Central tube station. She was late. Marianne waited for about ten minutes in drizzly rain. She realised that nobody had explained how exactly she was to help. Surely they weren't relying on her to take the photos.

Her train of thought was severed by the screeching of brakes. Karen had arrived. She abruptly halted her aged BMW convertible on the street. The roof was down despite the weather. She was wrapped in a large woolly scarf. A fag hung from her mouth. Missy Elliot's 'Get Ur Freak On' blared from the car stereo.

Marianne got in. The back seats were heaving with boxes of leaflets. There was a jolt as Karen drove off. She didn't say hello to Marianne. Instead, she sang along to Missy Elliot.

"*Get ur freak on. Get ur freak on*."

"How are you!" Marianne shouted above the roar of the engine. She had barely seen Karen since the election.

"Oh alright. Could do without this fucking bollocks though. How's life in the big house?"

"I'm loving it" said Marianne. "Best job I've ever had."

"Yeah? Is madam treating you alright?" Karen asked.

"Ana? Yes, she's been great so far."

Marianne was always a little taken aback by the way Karen spoke about Ana.

They drove to an industrial estate on the outskirts of Greenwood. During the election, Karen had often complained about parking tickets. The big mystery for Marianne was how she'd managed to avoid speeding fines.

The photo shoot was at the offices of a multimedia company. It was owned by a local Labour sympathiser. As she parked, Karen explained Ana was paying for the new leaflets. They would bear her image and contact details, as well as those of the councillors. The leaflets would be used for canvassing.

Marianne helped Karen carry boxes and carrier bags in. The councillors were to be photographed against a green screen. A professional photographer, a young French woman, had been hired for the occasion.

The councillors were milling around in a reception area when Marianne and Karen arrived. There was an adjacent kitchenette. Some had helped themselves to drinks. Pete Samuelson, the Council Leader, was there. Marianne thought he looked surly and bored.

To Marianne's surprise, she spotted Joni Lessing. She knew that Joni wasn't a councillor. There wasn't any obvious reason why she'd be there. Joni was talking to, or rather at, a young man. Her eyes did not move from his face. She spoke in her usual low monotone. He shifted uncomfortably as if looking for an opportunity to escape.

"Joni's here" Marianne told Karen, somewhat unnecessarily.

“Don’t I fucking know it” said Karen. “Madam has asked her to help produce these leaflets. Fuck knows why. She knows fuck all about it. Or anything else for that matter.”

“She does seem to be an expert on many things” said Marianne

Karen turned her attention to the councillors. “Right” she barked at them. “I’ll call you one ward at a time. You only need to be in the studio if you’re having your photo taken.”

Marianne’s role was to hold a reflector over the councillors as they were photographed. The photographer clicked way trying to get the best shots. Karen stood back with Pete Samuelson alongside her. Her edict clearly didn’t apply to him. They muttered to each other.

The councillors were photographed in groups of two or three. Most were good humoured and seemed to enjoy the occasion. However, there was one trio who looked spectacularly morose. Karen intervened.

“*Smile* you miserable fuckers!” she bellowed at them.

Marianne almost dropped the reflector on their heads. Pete Samuelson let out a gurgling, asthmatic giggle. It reminded Marianne of the dog in the *Dastardly and Muttley* cartoons. The morose trio twisted their faces into rictus half-smiles.

“They look so fucking depressed” Karen said to Pete. “You’d think they were at a funeral.”

Joni appeared in the studio. Marianne could sense Karen’s hackles rise immediately. She realised that they had stayed well away from each other during the election. Something about Joni made her think Mrs Overall in *Acorn Antiques* if she'd been played by Sienna Miller during her boho phase.

She said to Karen: "We should get individual pictures of the councillors."

"We've been through this, Joni" said Karen, palpably exasperated. "We don't have the time or the budget for it. That's not me being a dictator. It's what we agreed."

This caused Joni to launch into one of her monologues.

"We really need to get beyond this neoliberal paradigm of time and money" she said. "It's this sort of monetaristic thinking that has alienated people from the Labour Party. The Party is changing. Because the parameters of debate are changing..."

"Look!" interjected Pete. "I don't have time to dick about all day having my photo taken, to put it bluntly. We just need to get this done."

The photographer had stopped clicking. The morose trio were staring with fish mouths. Time had been lost.

Karen made an attempt to be conciliatory. She was determined to rescue the situation. "Joni, I am sure if Ana is willing to pay for more photos, we can talk about this some other time" she said.

Joni retreated. Pete exploded as soon as she left the room.

"Why is she even fucking here?" he snarled. "She was in the Green Party until six months ago. Before she decided to jump on Ana's bandwagon."

"I know. I know" said Karen. "She is the bane of my life. But our MP, in her infinite wisdom, seems to think she's useful. I don't know what for exactly. I'm just fucking sick of her telling me how to do my job."

The photo shoot resumed. During a break, Marianne visited the ladies. As she stood in front of the mirror reapplying her lipstick, she heard a toilet flush. Joni came out of the cubicle and washed her hands.

"You see this is why we lost two elections" she said.

"I'm sorry." Marianne was slightly taken aback by the absence of preliminaries. She also had no idea what Joni was on about.

"It's this top-down, top-heavy model of leadership." Joni told her. "It's all about command and control. They don't realise that the tectonic plates of politics are moving, power is shifting. Neoliberalism is in retreat. People want more democracy. Not technocratic arguments about why they should do as they're told."

She said all of this without drawing breath.

"*Okay*" said Marianne. She was unprepared for this.

Joni's eyes were fixed on hers. Marianne had this sense of her personal space being slightly disrespected, if not actually invaded.

"This is why we need a leadership candidate from the left" said Joni. "*To broaden the debate.* They're trying to stitch this up as well, Karen and Pete..."

"Are they?" Marianne was bewildered. She hadn't realised Karen and Pete wielded so much national political influence.

"They will adapt though" Joni said assuredly. "Politicians always do. Because they care about power. And *we* can be the agency in this."

Marianne wondered why Joni assumed she'd be sympathetic. She didn't even know what a neoliberal paradigm was.

Karen banged on the door to tell her she was needed. She was relieved to discontinue the conversation. Joni's monologues felt like an endurance test.

Pete offered to drive her home. It was too late for her to bother going back to the Commons. He seemed to want a chat. They got stuck in rush hour traffic on the way. She learnt a bit about how he had become Leader of Greenwood Council. His predecessor had been embroiled in a financial scandal. She also learnt that he had twin baby daughters and that his wife was a TV producer.

"I'd be a stay-at-home dad if it wasn't for the politics" he said.

Marianne found that a bit difficult to envisage. Still, she reminded herself that she didn't yet know him very well.

They came to a red light. There was a lull in the conversation

After a pause he asked: "Have you thought where you want to go with this?"

"With what?

"Politics. The Labour Party."

It hadn't occurred to Marianne that there was anywhere for her *to* go. She had no plan. She'd fallen into her job pretty much by accident. Still, she was aware that her life had changed profoundly somehow. It now seemed more vivid, more exciting in a way that it hadn't before. She felt connected to events outside her own life. She even seemed to be able to influence them.

"Well, no. Not really" she replied.

"We need some new blood on the Council" said Pete. "To be frank, we have too many fucking useless Labour councillors. I have to be blunt about it."

The light turned yellow. Pete drove off.

He is being frank Marianne thought *and blunt as well. Seems to be a bit of a thing with him*

"I'm not sure I have the experience" she said.

"You have all the right experience" said Pete. "You work for an MP. People say you're good at casework. And you're out campaigning every weekend. Ticks all the boxes. Also helps that you're quite normal."

Marianne laughed at this. "I've never thought of myself as normal. My boyfriend might beg to differ."

She paused for a moment.

"Then again, I've never thought about being a Labour councillor."

"I'm not asking you to decide now" said Pete. "Give it some thought though."

Marianne recounted the conversation to Euan later that evening. They were sat in front of the TV eating a stir-fry

"You're kidding!" he said.

"Are you surprised he called me normal?"

"Obviously. My mind is completely blown at the prospect of you being like elected."

"Why?"

"You've only been involved five minutes" he said. "How long would this be for?"

"Four years" she told him. "Councillors in London are elected for four-year terms."

“That’s a pretty big commitment” said Euan. “What with all the meetings and people hassling you about their bins. Takes a big chunk out of your life. Are you sure it’s what you want?”

“I don’t have to decide tonight! It’s just interesting to know that I could if I wanted to. It had never occurred to me.”

“Might be an idea to see how your job goes. Your boss sounds like she can be a bit of a nightmare.”

Marianne squealed in mild outrage. “Ana? No! She’s lovely.”

“What! Messaging you at 4am?”

“That was *one* time. There were exceptional circumstances.”

“If you say so” said Euan. “Just tell me that you haven’t become so power crazed that you want to be an MP yourself.”

“Fuck no.”

Until he said it, nothing could have been further from Marianne’s mind. She then started to wonder. If she could become a councillor, was it really so crazy that she could be an MP? She knew a fair bit already the work involved.

“It’s certainly a well-trodden path” Ben said to her. “MP’s assistant. Councillor. MP. Plenty of people have done it.”

They were having their regular Friday evening drink in the House of Lords bar. At the end of each week, they’d share a bottle of Sauvignon Blanc. They spoke more freely, more candidly here than they did in their office.

“How does it work exactly?” asked Marianne.

"Well, you'd need to be very active in the Party" he told her. "Really put yourself about a bit. Being a councillor would help. It would give you a bit of a platform. Also helps if you use social media. It means you can be in two places at once. Not *that* is very useful for an aspiring politician."

"Sounds like you have to be very dynamic."

"You have to *give the impression* of being very dynamic" said Ben. "If you want to be an MP, you have to *really, really* want it. It's no use thinking it's something you'd quite like to do. Forget about having a normal existence. It's a way of life, and rather a strange one."

"Were you ever tempted?" Marianne asked.

"Nope" he said firmly. I realised a long time ago that I'm a behind-the-scenes person. Don't get me wrong. I think it's a great thing to be willing to put your head about the parapet. It's just not for me. I'm a political animal but I'm not a politician."

"I never imagined myself as a politician" said Marianne. "But I seem to have a bit of an aptitude for it. You know, I go canvassing every Sunday. I front up to the voters. I defend Labour policy on the doorstep. And helping to sort out Mr Al-Nawazi's case was really satisfying. Maybe I could do some good."

"Christ, I might end up working for you in a few years' time" Ben murmured.

He topped up their glasses and changed the subject. "You know Trudie's leaving?"

"What?"

"Trudie's leaving. She's given her notice. Ana's going to have to hire a replacement for her."

Marianne was more surprised than she should have been. She knew that relations between Ana and Trudie were poor. Still, she'd assumed things would resolve themselves. It hadn't occurred to her that Trudie would leave on bitter terms. She remembered Ben had spoken of the "baton of blame". Batons were eventually passed on.

"Wow, they must really have fallen out" she said.

"I think so."

"Do you know what happened exactly?"

"*Not really*" Ben replied. "Ana is very tight-lipped about it. And Trudie won't talk because of the confidentiality agreement. We've all signed one."

This was true. Marianne had signed hers before her first day of work. She hadn't actually read it. She'd only glanced cursorily at her employment contract. Presumably, the small print wasn't applicable to her Friday night drinks with Ben.

"I guess things don't always work out" she said to Ben, blandly.

On Monday morning, Marianne and Ben opened an e-mail from Ana.

It read: *'Morning team. Hope you had a good weekend. Thought we could have a working lunch in your office. Need to discuss some office changes. I'll bring the sandwiches.'*

Nominations for the Labour leadership were closing that day. There had been much speculation as to whether Jeremy Corbyn, the wild card candidate of the left, would scrape enough support from Labour MPs. Marianne had certainly read many e-mails to Ana about it. Local party members had implored her to nominate him. The reason often given was 'to broaden the debate'. Ana had just laughed when Marianne mentioned it.

Ana appeared just after 1pm bearing a Marks & Spencer bag. She handed them packaged sandwiches as they sat at their desks. Marianne noticed the red 'reduced' label on the one she'd been given. She decided not to look at the sell-by date and opened it.

Ana sat herself at the vacant desk. "Forgive me for the impromptu nature of this" she said. "I just want to run by a few changes I'm going to make to this office. Nothing to worry about."

I hate it when people tell me there's nothing to worry about Marianne thought to herself. *It makes me worry.*

Ana continued. "As you know, Trudie is leaving us very soon. She will be replaced. But her replacement will also be doing the casework. It's a sort of amalgamation of two jobs. They'll be based here and in the constituency. It means we'll have some extra money for a couple of part-timers."

Marianne couldn't easily see the rationale behind this. Still, Ana's retinue of staff would be expanded. Ben had speculated that she would be soon promoted to the front bench. This would be a near certainty if Yvette Cooper became Leader.

"That will mean more work for us" he'd said.

"Do you have anyone in mind for the new role?" Marianne asked Ana.

"No. The job will have to be advertised. There'll be a formal recruitment process. Might need your help drawing up a person spec. My main priority is getting someone who will fit into our little team."

"Bloody hell!" Ben suddenly exclaimed. He was staring at his screen.

Ana looked over at him. "You alright, Ben? I didn't think the changes were *that* radical."

"No, it's not that. Jeremy is on the ballot."

Marianne clicked onto the BBC news website. She saw the headline: *'Labour Leadership: Jeremy Corbyn completes the line-up'*. He would be on the ballot after obtaining nominations from 36 Labour MPs.

"I know" said Ana with a hint of a smile. "I nominated him."

"What!" spluttered Ben. It was unlike him to lose his self-possession.

Ana's mouth expanded into a full smile. "I nominated him. To erm...*broaden the debate*."

"But I thought you were supporting Yvette" said Marianne.

"And I *will* be supporting Yvette. I will publicly endorse her. I will campaign for her and I will vote for her. *But*, you know, I have to give my local members a voice."

Ben looked horrified. "What if Corbyn wins?" he asked.

Ana chortled. "Not bloody likely."

Chapter Four

'GET BEHIND YOUR ELECTED LEADER!' demanded the e-mail.

Marianne blinked at her screen. It was the umpteenth such missive that afternoon. There had been a flurry over the past week. They were mainly from Ana's constituents who all opposed airstrikes in Syria. Many cited the Iraq war. All seemed to be devotees of Jeremy Corbyn.

It was late November. Over two months had passed since Corbyn had seized the Party leadership. This was despite Ana's assurances that this couldn't possibly happen. She'd repeated these right up until the very last moment.

Marianne sighed. "I swear to God all these frigging e-mails are written by the same person" she said to Ben.

"It's Momentum, innit" he said. He didn't look up from his screen. "They are organising big time"

The parliamentary vote was in two weeks' time. Corbyn himself was opposed to airstrikes against Daesh in Syria. Many Labour MPs, however, including Ana, were known to be in favour. The media excitedly predicted a rebellion that would make Corbyn's position untenable. All Marianne knew was that it had added to her already overflowing inbox.

Ben was finally arranging interviews for Trudie's replacement. After over four months, her job was still vacant. Ana had changed her mind several times about the job description. It had therefore gone unadvertised over the summer. She had then become too distracted by the leadership election to deal with it. In October, she ordered Ben to proceed as though *he'd* been the one prevaricating.

Marianne thought Ben was going a little grey around the temples. Dark circles had appeared around his eyes. He maintained his outward calm and showed few obvious signs of stress. Still, he'd acquired a sort of haunted look. It was hardly surprising. Their workload seemed to have multiplied. Between them, they just about managed their casework, their correspondence and Ana's other numerous demands. That was only because they were working later and later.

Her desk 'phone rang. It was Ana calling from her office upstairs.

"I need everything we have on Mr Al-Nawazi" she said. "Now."

"Now?" Marianne couldn't understand this. Mr Al-Nawazi's case had been resolved months ago. Why would Ana be revisiting it?

"Yes. *Now*. That's what I said" Ana replied tersely.

"It's just that we have some stuff in hard copy" said Marianne. "And there are loads of e-mails…"

"Just get me what you have" said Ana. She hung up.

Even by her recent standards, that was abrupt. Marianne didn't know what to do straightaway. Eventually, she decided on a course of action. She e-mailed all of the relevant electronic documents to Ana. This took a few minutes. With Ben's help, she excavated paper files from dusty filing cabinets.

She took them upstairs to Ana's office. Ana was typing away on her computer when she entered. She didn't acknowledge Marianne's presence.

"I have the paper files on Mr Al-Nawazi" Marianne announced.

"Just drop them on the desk" said Ana. "I'll look at them later." She carried on typing.

But I thought you wanted them like now, this very instant Marianne thought to herself. She closed the door quietly behind her as she left.

She supposed that Ana, like her and Ben, was experiencing stress of sorts. This would explain the shortness of her manner over the last couple of months. She knew that the result of the leadership election had been a shock. She now had pressures she wouldn't have anticipated. It probably didn't help that her office was understaffed. Still, she hadn't exactly helped herself, or them, with that.

When Marianne arrived home that evening, she felt lethargic and physically heavy. Earlier that day, she had smoked her first cigarette in months. She had bought a whole packet at lunchtime which she'd then thrown away.

Euan was due home shortly. She regretted offering to cook. It was gone 8 o'clock. They hadn't much in in the way of ingredients. She thought about going to the nearby corner shop or ordering a takeaway. In the end, she microwaved a couple of baking potatoes and heated up a can of baked beans.

"Yum" said Euan when he came in. He dropped his violin case in the hallway.

"It's all we have in" Marianne replied. *And I'm too bloody tired to cook properly* she added inwardly.

"It's alright" he laughed. "Christ, I'll eat anything."

It was true. He wasn't that fussy and he hadn't been getting at her. Marianne immediately felt guilty for being snappy and defensive. She wondered if she'd sounded grumpy.

"Sorry. Long day" she said.

She handed Euan his plate. As usual, they ate on the sofa in their bedroom, in front of the TV. The news was on. There was an item about the Labour Party. Marianne's heart sank but it piqued Euan's interest.

"Jeremy is getting some serious shit from his own side" he said.

"I'm sorry?" Marianne was mildly incredulous. Again, she could feel herself becoming irritable. She got enough of this bollocks at work.

"Syria" said Euan. "Jeremy's MPs are trying to stab him in the back over it, aren't they? What does your boss have to say about it all?"

"They're *Labour* MPs not *Jeremy*'s MPs" Marianne said. She could hear the scratchiness in her own voice.

"There is another side to this" she added. "I should know. I spend all bloody day dealing with e-mails from his fan club."

Euan, to Marianne's surprise, had been enthused by the rise of Jeremy Corbyn. It was the first time he'd really shown any interest in politics. Something about him had clearly resonated. Marianne thought it was probably a good thing. Still, why did he have to say Corbyn's first name like that? *Jeremy*. His fans all seemed to utter it with this strange sort of simper, or even a swoon. Marianne found it rather aggravating.

She hadn't voted for him in the leadership election. Still, she had begun with a relatively neutral view. Her initial feeling was that he'd won the right to lead the Party. She hoped she'd grow to like him. However, the fanaticism of his supporters unnerved her. Their recent e-mail bombardment had given her this sense of foreboding.

"Look, I get it" said Euan. He put down his plate and wrapped his arm around her. "The last thing you want to talk about is work when you get home. And I know you're not exactly feeling it about Jeremy either."

"I'm just a bit tired" said Marianne. She put her aide her own plate and let her head slide onto his shoulder. He smelt of warmth and comfort. "Sorry if I've been a cow. Just been a bit overworked."

He planted a kiss on her forehead. "You don't have to explain" he murmured.

They cuddled up. Marianne closed her eyes. She could feel sleep beginning to envelop her. Euan interrupted her descent into slumber.

"I forgot to mention" he said. "Mum and Dad have invited us over for lunch on Sunday. I said we'd go."

Marianne inwardly wailed. She usually enjoyed visiting Euan's parents. It felt like a treat to go to their rambling house on Hampstead Heath. Still, she'd envisaged a weekend of lying on the sofa watching Netflix. Instead, she would have to put on a dress, heels and make sparkling conversation. It seemed like an unbearable effort.

"That will be lovely" she said.

The next morning, she was drying her hair in the bedroom. Euan was in the shower. She'd overslept and was worried about running late. Her 'phone rang on the dressing table. It was Ana.

Surprised, she answered. "Hello?"

"Where is this bloody café!" Ana barked down the 'phone at her. "I can't find it. I'm supposed to be meeting him in ten minutes."

She was clearly very agitated.

"Meeting who? Where?" Marianne was certain she hadn't been privy to any such appointment. Still, she began to doubt herself.

"The Syrian refugee guy" snapped Ana. "Greenwood High Road."

This didn't ring any bells.

"I'm really sorry" said Marianne. "I have no idea what you're talking about."

"*It's your business* to know what I'm talking about!"

Even in her confused, bewildered state, Marianne thought this slightly unreasonable. Still, she decided against arguing the point with Ana. Instead, she would try to elicit more information from her.

"Can you remind me who you're meeting?" she asked.

"Mr Al-Nawazi!" Ana replied huffily. She sounded as though Marianne was being deliberately stupid.

I'd have remembered that Marianne thought to herself.

She asked: "Do you know the name of the café?"

"I don't know. I think it's something like Deva or Devra. It's a Turkish place."

"I know where that it is" said Marianne. "It's just slightly down from the tube station."

"You know it?" Ana's tone changed. She sounded relieved. Her voice became friendly again. "Can you meet me at the tube station? I could do with someone to take notes."

"Erm…yes" said Marianne. It wouldn't take her long to get there if she ran at Olympic speed.

"Marvellous. See you in five." Ana hung up.

"Shit!" hissed Marianne.

Euan had come back into the room in his old bathrobe. "Everything alright?" he asked.

"Not really" said Marianne. "I have to be on the High Road in about five minutes."

"I thought you were going into work."

"*That* was the original plan."

She pulled back her hair with a scrunchy. She wouldn't have time to do her makeup.

Ana wasn't even at the tube station after Marianne had galloped most of the way there. When she did arrive, she sauntered calmly through the ticket barrier.

"Sorry I'm late" she said breezily.

"No problem" said Marianne. She'd recovered her breath by then.

They found the café. Mr Al-Nawazi himself wasn't yet there. Ana ordered coffee for them both from the counter. They took a table near the front window.

Despite her immersion in Mr Al-Nawazi's case, Marianne hadn't actually met him before. When he arrived, he was rather different to what she'd imagined. She'd pictured him as decidedly middle-aged and paunchy with a drooping moustache and an air of suffering. The cheerful looking, youthful man who bounced in, like Tigger, was a surprise. He was cleanshaven, lithe and wiry with close-cropped grey hair. He wore a shiny green bomber jacket and skinny jeans.

Ana stood up to greet him. "Mr Al-Nawazi" she said, extending her hand. "Thank you so much for coming. Can I get you a coffee or something?"

"Ooh, that would be lovely" he said. "I'll have an espresso if that's alright."

Marianne noticed he spoke with barely a hint of an accent. He sat down next to her facing the window.

After the preliminary exchange of niceties, the purpose of the meeting became clear. He was here to lobby Ana about the airstrikes against Daesh in Syria. Marianne was used to this by now. Mr Al-Nawazi, however, had a different angle. He was passionately in favour.

"You've always been very supportive" he told Ana. "I know many people want you to vote against."

"That is very true." Ana smiled ruefully.

"People seem to ignore what is happening in Syria" he said. "They forget. You know my history, don't you?"

Ana nodded. Marianne looked less certain.

He continued, seemingly for Marianne's benefit. "My wife and I were doctors. Daesh forced us and our children out of our home. Because we spoke out against them.

Because we're secularists. We got near the border with Turkey and they caught up with us. They killed my wife and my children."

He paused, gazing out onto the High Road. "Yet somehow, I am here" he murmured.

There was a silence. Marianne realised she hadn't actually made any notes.

Ana seemed to have tears in her eyes. She spoke slowly and quietly as if trying to stay composed.

"I can assure you that I will never allow people to ignore what's going on in Syria" she said. "I have campaigned against human rights abuse my whole life. Let me be very clear that you, and your community, have my full, unequivocal and unconditional support."

Mr Al-Nawazi nodded and picked up his cup. His focus returned to the present.

"That means a great deal". He gulped the remains of his espresso. "You know, I remember reading this fantastic article you wrote. You made the case for liberal interventionism. Not many politicians have the guts to do that these days"

"That's very nice of you to say so" Ana said. "But I think you give me too much credit. It's your bravery that is really inspirational"

Mr Al-Nawazi smiled. It was a wide, warm smile that suited his open, humorous face. Marianne wondered where he found the strength to persist with his life. She tried to imagine losing a spouse and children in such violent, torturous circumstances. All she could conjure up was an overwhelming sense of powerlessness and despair. Yet he was still here, able to smile and express joy of sorts and his steely determination was palpable. Marianne felt sort of humbled. She had felt sympathy for him as a victim. Now, she felt in awe of something powerful in his character.

After they said goodbye to him, Marianne and Ana took the tube back to Westminster. They spoke little on the way. Marianne wondered why Ana had arranged to meet a constituent like that. As far as she knew, this wasn't something she normally did. It seemed a bit irregular. She wondered if she might tease it out of her.

"It was good to hear the other side of the argument" she said to Ana.

They were sat next to each other on the Central line.

"What do you mean?"

"Well, we've been lobbied *so much* about Syria. And it's been *such* a big issue for the Labour Party…"

"Oh bollocks to that" said Ana. "I came into politics because I'm *against* authoritarianism. I'll tell you something. I'd really like to introduce some of my colleagues to Mr Al-Nawazi. That would put the bloody Labour Party into perspective for them."

Marianne was intrigued. "You're definitely voting for the airstrikes then?"

"Well of course. You have to stand up to fascists."

This explained a great deal. Ana was gearing up to make a stand for her principles in the face of enormous pressure. No wonder she had been so terse and snappy. Marianne felt a proud of her again. She also felt proud of herself and of their work.

When she got into the office, Ben seemed quietly inundated as usual. To her irritation, there was an e-mail from Joni Lessing in her inbox. It was addressed to Ana.

"What does *she* want?" she muttered to herself.

Joni had become even more prolific in the local Labour Party. In fact, she was a big wheel in Greenwood Momentum. Marianne wasn't entirely sure what the purpose of Momentum was. It seemed to be about supporting Corbyn's leadership. The Greenwood branch had held their inaugural meeting a couple of weeks earlier. Marianne nearly went out of curiosity but had been too busy at work.

She read the e-mail.

'Dear Ana,

I hope this email finds you well. On behalf of Greenwood Momentum I would like to express our concerns about your reported position on the upcoming vote on Syria. We would like to formally invite you to a meeting this Saturday to discuss. As you will be aware, the mainstream media are using this vote to undermine Jeremy's leadership and promote their neoliberal imperialist agenda. Momentum which represents the broad mainstream of Labour members who voted for Jeremy would expect our local Member of Parliament to take our views into account. Please RSVP.

In friendship and solidarity,

Joni'

"For fucks sake!" Marianne said out loud. She found Joni's imperious undertone infuriating.

"What's up?" asked Ben looking up from his screen.

"It's this woman from the local Momentum branch. She has just *summoned* Ana to a meeting. To discuss Syria. This weekend! Like she can actually *do* that."

"I'd let Ana know" said Ben. "I doubt she'll go. But she needs to handle Momentum carefully."

"You know she's going to tell them to fuck right off" Marianne told him. "She's voting for the airstrikes."

She felt a sense of elation at hearing herself say this. It felt like a satisfying two-finger salute to those who'd bombarded her with e-mails. Their pomposity was insufferable.

"As I said, she's going to have to tread carefully" said Ben.

"Why?"

Ben frowned in irritation. "Haven't you been reading the papers?"

Marianne thought this unnecessarily snippy. Still, she didn't want to admit that she now avoided media coverage of politics. After all, she was practically living it.

"Of course" she replied.

"Then you'll know that Momentum have been threatening Labour MPs with deselection. If they're disloyal to *Jeremy*."

Marianne found this astounding.

"Can they do that?"

Ben shrugged. "Who knows? Not sure they have the numbers yet. It's pretty hard to deselect sitting Labour MPs. But things have changed. Look what happened in the leadership election."

Marianne thought about this for a moment.

"But Ana is pretty popular in the constituency" she said. "Would people still vote Labour if she was replaced?"

"The risk is they might not" said Ben. "But we're in unchartered territory."

Acting on Ben's advice, Marianne forwarded Joni's e-mail to Ana. Her response came back swiftly.

'*Tell her I'll be addressing the constituency party meeting on Wednesday. They can ask me about Syria then. I don't answer to Momentum (maybe leave that bit out)*'

Marianne composed a diplomatically worded response to Joni. She sent it just before she left work.

On the Sunday, she and Euan took the London Overground to Hampstead Heath. They were on their way to Euan's parents for lunch. As they were climbing up the hill from the station, the heel on Marianne's left shoe broke. She tumbled but Euan caught her wrist just in time. Her handbag dropped to the ground.

"Shit!" she exclaimed. "Flaming cheap shoes!"

She took both off. Euan's parents would probably be amused at her arriving shoeless. At that moment, the 'phone in her bag rang. She reached and pulled it out. It was Bridget. She decided she would answer.

"Hold this" she said to Euan, handing him her bag. "Hi Bridget."

“Marianne” said Bridget in her Edinburgh brogue. “Do you have a moment?”.

“We’re just on our way to Euan’s parents” Marianne told her. Euan was looking at her quizzically. “But yes, very quickly.”

“I won’t take up too much of your time” said Bridget. “I’m just calling to see if you can come on Wednesday.”

“Wednesday?” Marianne knew there was something significant about Wednesday but couldn’t think what.

“The constituency party meeting.”

“Oh that” said Marianne. “Well, I’ll try but I might have to work late…”

“It would be great if you could” Bridget said. “You’ll know that Joni and Momentum are on the warpath over Syria. Ana should have some moral support. They’re going to give her a hard time.”

“When you put it like that…”

“You’ll come then?” Bridget said hopefully.

Marianne found herself thus committed. She couldn’t bear to say no to Bridget. After all, she continued to toil industriously for the Party. This was despite her reservations about Corbyn. Marianne found this reassuring Bridget, for her, personified a sense of decency. It was for this she’d joined the Labour Party in the first place.

She went to the meeting after work on the following Wednesday. Having finished before half six, she took the tube from Westminster. The sweaty rush hour crush was almost unbearable. Her day at work had been particularly irksome. Ana now insisted on standard replies to every e-mail about Syria. Given their sheer volume, this was an insurmountable task.

The meeting was being held in a draughty school hall. Marianne took a bus there from the tube station. As she approached, she noticed a reception committee waiting outside the front gate. They were activists from the so-called Socialist Workers Party which wasn't aligned to Labour. She'd only ever seen them outside tube stations trying to sell their newspaper. Until now, they hadn't bothered Labour Party meetings. It hadn't been worth their while. Few Labour Party members had been willing to entertain them.

"SUPPORT CORBYN. SAY NO TO WAR!" one of them bellowed at her as she passed.

He pressed a tatty leaflet into her hand. Out of politeness, she took it. As soon as she was safely inside the door, she screwed it up.

She made her way, past many classrooms, to the hall. Just before she walked in, she found herself accosted by Joni. She was accompanied by a ruddy faced, grey haired man wearing a beret.

As usual, Joni didn't bother with preliminary social niceties or introduce her companion. She launched straight in.

"Marianne, we were very disappointed by Ana's reply to our invitation. We'd really like to improve communication with your office."

"Excuse me?" said Marianne, stopping.

She wasn't sure how to respond to this ambush. She felt they should really be taking this up with Ana. It was her they'd invited. Marianne also found herself distracted by Joni's bizarre floral headscarf.

"We are in a new political reality" droned Joni in her low monotone. "The Party, under Jeremy's leadership, expects MPs to be accountable."

The man in the beret chimed in. "It is all part of a dialectical process of democratisation" he said. "Party members can't be ignored any longer."

He had a ponderous, self-important way of speaking. He sounded as though he liked the sound of his own voice a great deal. Marianne decided he was an idiot.

"Ana *didn't* ignore your invitation" she said tartly. "I sent you her reply. She wasn't able to make it."

"That's really not the point" replied the Idiot-in-the-Beret.

Marianne could feel her jaw clenching in anger. There was no reasoning with these people.

"There's no need to be defensive, Marianne" said Joni. She fixated on Marianne's eyes with her unblinking stare. "Labour MPs have to recognise that they're there by grace of the Party membership and…"

"That's not quite true, is it?" Marianne interjected.

They were clearly taken aback by this. Joni actually blinked.

"Not quite true?" spluttered The Idiot-in-the-Beret.

"Labour MPs are there by grace of *the voters*" said Marianne. "That is who they're accountable to."

Her point made, she decided to end the conversation.

“I'd love to chat more” she said. “But they'll be starting in a minute.”

She turned on her heel and walked in.

The hall was arranged in rows of chairs, like a school assembly. Party members filed in. Marianne spotted Bridget in a row near the front and sat next to her. She told her about her conversation with Joni and the Idiot-in-the-Beret.

“Good for you” said Bridget. “For some reason, nobody ever challenges that woman. We all know she's a barnpot. *And* she makes the most ridiculous statements.”

“Well, I think I've just told her, in a roundabout sort of way, to fuck off” said Marianne, triumphantly.

The meeting started. Apologies were given. Minutes of previous meetings were discussed at some length. Marianne looked around the hall. There were quite possibly a hundred people in there. The meetings seemed to have quadrupled in size since she joined the Party. This had been accompanied by a marked change in the atmosphere. In the beginning, there had been an almost familial, community feel. Most people who came had been stalwarts for many years.

Now, the meetings were rancorous, acrimonious affairs. In recent months, there had been an influx of new members. Many of them were belligerent and hostile. They seemed to have little interest in the Labour Party beyond *Jeremy*. Quite a few of them had been in the Party long ago. They had left in anger, often over the Iraq war. Many of them looked like retired university lecturers.

There was also another small but distinct group of twenty-somethings. In fact, there were probably no more than ten of them. Most of them were male. They were led by an intense, socially awkward young man, called Ned Critchley-Smith. He was softly spoken with a hint of a Mancunian accent. Marianne gathered from Bridget that they were part of a group known as 'Global Solidarity'. She hadn't heard of them before. Apparently, they shared a house.

"Sounds like a cult" Marianne had said to Bridget.

"Hmm" she replied.

Marianne noticed Karen Giannopoulos standing against the wall at the side. Her arms were folded. She looked like she had come to observe rather than participate. Her countenance gave nothing away. As the paid organiser, she was ever the professional. However, Marianne knew she'd be swearing profusely in private afterwards.

Pete Samuelson arrived and took a seat at the front. As Council Leader, he had to give his monthly report. He sat down and glowered. He seemed positively livid to be there. During recent months, he'd been subject to much baiting on social media. He was regularly denounced as a 'neoliberal Blairite'. His dislike of Corbyn and his followers was no secret. He was equally combative when confronted with antagonism in meetings.

Marianne was aware that Joni and the Idiot-in-the-Beret were sat almost directly behind her. They murmured to each other periodically. Ana swept into the meeting half-way through the Treasurer's report. She sat down next to Pete. There was much droning about procedural matters before she spoke.

When her time came, she stood up before the meeting.

"Comrades" she said. "I know how passionately we all feel about foreign policy. I know how important it is that we get it right. Many of you have written to me about the airstrikes against Daesh…"

"IT'S AN IMPERIALIST WAR!" screeched someone from the back of the hall.

"Sshh" hissed Joni turning around. "Let Ana speak."

Ana carried on: "If you'll indulge me, comrades, I would like to explain my position. I understand why many of you have reservations about military action. In fact, I think you are right to do so. *But* I think these airstrikes are necessary. I will explain why. Let me tell you about a constituent of mine, a refugee from Syria. A refugee from Daesh."

She told Mr Al-Nawazi's story to the meeting. She made, Marianne thought, an eloquent case for intervention. Her argument had a certain humanity to it. When she finished, the floor was opened up for questions and comments. Many people spoke but there was little variation. Opposition to the airstrikes was largely implacable.

Joni stood up. She rambled at some length about the need to rebuild trust after Iraq. There were murmurs of agreement. Still, Marianne noticed, many people seemed to zone out, even people who agreed with her.

The Idiot-in-the-Beret spoke next. "I think it is very important, Chair, that Ana respects the wishes of the members. So we can avoid another appalling folly like Iraq. It is very clear, that under Jeremy, the membership is sovereign! We're not the poor bloody infantry *any more*!"

This was greeted by applause which was positively thunderous in places.

Pompous twat! Marianne thought to herself.

Ned from Global Solidarity stood up. He mumbled something about the working class and imperialism. Some expressed their approval. However, few people seemed able to follow.

Marianne was finding all this speechifying rather tedious. Pete Samuelson put his hand up.

This might be entertaining she said to herself.

Pete stood in front of the meeting. He looked bigger than ever. "Chair, comrades" he began. "As many people in this room know, the Labour Party has a historic tradition of internationalism. We have a tradition of standing up for human rights. For freedom of speech. For rule of law. That is why we supported the creation of the state of Israel."

This caused much consternation. There was furious heckling and murmurs of disbelief.

"Pipe down!" someone shouted at him.

"No, I will not *pipe down*!" bellowed Pete in response. "And I'll tell you why. Internationalism is in the DNA of the Labour Party. It is not the Labour way just to walk on by. That is why we have to make a stand against Daesh and against Jihadism. Because it will affect all of us eventually."

His voice reached a crescendo.

"And I'll tell you this. It's not just about you or Jeremy or even the Labour Party. It's about common humanity!"

There was a moment of silence. He remained standing for a moment, almost as a challenge to the hundred people sat in front of him. For a moment, they seemed almost cowed. When he sat down, a few brave souls applauded. Marianne and Bridget joined in. The heckles and boos were louder though.

Marianne heard someone snarl "Deselect him!"

Ana stood back up. "Thank you for your contributions, comrades. They have been hugely valuable."

"GET BEHIND YOUR ELECTED LEADER!" yelled the same voice from the back of the room.

Marianne was relieved when the meeting finally ended. It had somehow been boring, tense and bad-tempered. She was also annoyed by the rudeness to Ana and to Pete. There was an edge of unreasonable intolerance to it.

She and Bridget made their way out. They were heading to the pub where they could expect to see a few friendly faces. She inadvertently caught Joni's eye as she passed her row. Joni seemed to be about to make a beeline for her. Marianne didn't trust herself to be polite. She fixed her eyes on the exit at the back and quickened her pace.

The day of the vote in the House of Commons came the following week. On the tube to work, Marianne glanced at *the Metro*. About 100 Labour MPs were expected to defy Corbyn and vote for the airstrikes. This would mean the beginning of the end for his leadership. The same article also suggested they would be targeted for deselection.

Marianne's inbox had continued to flood overnight. "There is just no way that I am going to be able to answer all these" she said to Ben. "Like ever."

"Just delete them all after tonight" he suggested. "They'll stop then."

"I don't know" said Marianne. I think Ana is going to have a problem with Momentum. When she votes for the airstrikes."

"Hmm" said Ben. "She might. Still, they're not representative of the voters. She'll be aware of that."

The interviews for Trudie's replacement were taking place that day. Ben was organising. The candidates were being interviewed upstairs in Ana's office.

"Great day for it" Marianne said.

That evening, Euan was performing in a concert. It was a first night and he'd been able to give her a free ticket. She went along and enjoyed it. Afterwards, she met him outside the stage door, and they treated themselves to a taxi home. They cuddled up in the back as the cab snaked through London.

"That was fantastic" said Marianne. "I think it's the first time in ages I've been able to switch off from work."

"Good" said Euan. "I'm glad. Your job sometimes seems like a way of life."

"Tell me about it" murmured Marianne.

She then sat up, agitated by a new train of thought.

"God knows, Ana is not the easiest person to work for" she said. "I find her demanding and frustrating. But you know what? I feel like I'm doing something right. She's taken such a principled stand on Syria. It's hard not to respect her for it. Isn't that what being in politics is all about?"

"But she voted against" said Euan.

"What? What are you talking about?"

"She voted against the airstrikes. I checked online this evening. Just before I met you."

"That can't be right".

Marianne pulled her 'phone out of her bag. She clicked onto the BBC website. 66 Labour MPs had voted for the airstrikes. The rebellion was much smaller than expected. Ana's name wasn't among them.

She checked out another website which listed the Labour MPs who had voted *against*. Ana's name appeared here.

"I don't believe it" she said.

She looked at Euan. He was clearly at a loss as to what to say.

The next morning, she arrived late into the office. There had been severe delays on the Central line. On the way, she tried to rationalise her sense of betrayal. Ana hadn't been under any obligation *to her*. She was elected to exercise her own judgement. Still, Marianne felt as though she had been taken for a ride. She'd been persuaded of the case for airstrikes by the passion of Ana's arguments, and by her sympathy for Mr Al-Nawazi. There was only one plausible explanation.

"Looks like Ana got spooked by Momentum" she said to Ben as soon as she got in.

She dropped her bag and coat on her chair

"I suppose she was under a fair bit of pressure" she added.

Ben didn't engage with this. "I have some news" he said. "We've appointed the new caseworker. She's with Ana now."

"That was quick!" said Marianne.

She hadn't been expecting this.

"She doesn't have to give any notice anywhere" Ben told her. "In fact, I think you know her. She's active in your local party."

There was a knock at the door. Ana walked in smiling. Another woman followed in behind. It took Marianne a moment to register that it was Joni.

What the fuck is she doing here? she asked herself, bewildered.

"Morning team" said Ana brightly. She seemed to be in jovial spirits. "Now I know Joni needs no introduction to you, Marianne. But I'm delighted she's agreed to be our new caseworker. *And* our constituency office manager. She'll be based here. At least some of the time."

She and Joni stood in front of them looking very pleased.

"I just can't wait to get started" said Joni. "I'm very excited about working with you all."

This isn't happening Marianne said inwardly. But she knew it was.

Chapter Five

"The worst thing about my menopause" said Joni "was that my vagina went completely dry."

Ben spat out his tuna sandwich. Marianne would have laughed had she not been so mortified. She was acutely conscious of mouths agape at nearby tables. The three of them were having lunch in the Terrace Cafeteria. This was not the sort of conversation that MPs and their staff expected to overhear at lunchtime.

Joni, oblivious, continued. "As for a sex life, forget it!" she said. It just made penetration too painful. My husband and I almost separated. Besides, I just completely went off sex."

"Sounds awkward" said Marianne. Her mind scrambled for an escape from this conversational abyss. She couldn't understand how they'd even got onto the subject.

It was January 2016. Joni had started work just after Christmas. Marianne and Ben hadn't really had time to get used to her oversharing. Then, there were her other idiosyncrasies.

She was only supposed to be there two days a week. The rest of the time, she was supposed to be in Ana's constituency office. However, she appeared at Westminster nearly every day. That said, she didn't seem to be observing regular hours. She would just casually turn up at odd times without explanation. It had been like this today. Marianne and Ben hadn't invited her to have lunch with them. She hadn't even been in that morning. Presumably, she'd tracked them down after finding neither of them there when she arrived.

After lunch, they went back to their office. Joni, when she was there, occupied the desk opposite Marianne's. Ben sat between them.

Marianne had had one hope of Joni's appointment. That was her inbox would shrink. In that, she was disappointed. The complete opposite had happened. Joni copied her into every e-mail she sent whether she needed to see it or not. Worse still, she was copied into all the replies. She wondered if she should say something. Still, it was early days and she thought she should give her a chance.

There was one thing they'd been working on together. Marianne had drafted a letter, on Ana's behalf, to the Department of Work and Pensions. It had been about a constituent in crisis. Joni was dealing with her urgent case. The letter produced a ministerial reply which had pinged into Marianne's inbox while they were at lunch.

"We've had a letter back from the minister" she told Joni. "About Tracy Kendall. I'll forward it so you can follow up."

"Okay" replied Joni distractedly. She seemed entranced by something on her screen.

Marianne's inbox had had yet another bombardment. The correspondents were familiar. They were the same people who had written to her about the Syria vote. Their tone was exactly the same. They had found something else to rally against; the Greenwood Regeneration Partnership.

It was Pete Samuelson's brainchild. The partnership was supposed to regenerate Greenwood's dilapidated housing estates. It had caused no end of consternation in the local Labour Party. This was because the *partnership* was between the Council and a private developer. Momentum activists had denounced it as "social cleansing" and "privatisation". Pete himself had defended it with characteristic pugnacity. The issue had divided his administration down the middle.

Marianne opened one of her many e-mails about the subject. The sender claimed that the partnership was a 'neoliberal Blairite' project. They said it was 'inconsistent with the values of Jeremy Corbyn'.

"Not this again" sighed Marianne, almost involuntarily.

"Hmm?" said Joni looking up.

"Oh nothing. Just another email about the Regeneration Partnership."

Marianne immediately regretted letting the words escape from her mouth. She knew Joni was directly involved in opposing it. So far, she'd managed to avoid talking politics with her in the office. She was hoping that Joni would try to keep her working life separate from her Momentum activities.

She was swiftly disabused of this notion. Joni had lost interest in her screen and was looking at her intently.

"This regen partnership is toxic" she said. "We have to do something about it. It has huge implications for Ana, and for this office. Pete Samuelson is..."

"Sorry. I have to go the loo" Marianne interjected.

She hurried out the office into the corridor. With any luck, something else would have claimed Joni's attention by the time she came back. She walked into the ladies.

Once inside, she took a moment to check her reflection in the mirror. The door suddenly swung open behind her. Joni had followed her in.

"I need to go too" she said. "I thought it might be a good time for us to touch base about the regen partnership."

Marianne screamed inwardly: *No, no, it bloody isn't.* She'd never understood why going to the toilet should be a communal experience. Besides, she didn't actually need to go.

"Erm, I'm not sure this is the time or the place" she said to Joni. She dived into a cubicle. To her mortification, she realised that she was actually going to have to go through with this whole bloody charade.

"Marianne, this could destroy the Labour Party!" Joni shrieked through the cubicle door. "We *have* to talk about it."

That's a bit dramatic thought Marianne.

She heard Joni go into the cubicle next to her. There was a rustling of clothes. Joni insisted on carrying on talking to her over the top of the partition.

"As you know, we are absolutely committed to stopping it" she said.

There was a tinkling sound as she began to urinate very audibly.

"When you say *we*" said Marianne "You mean Momentum?"

"We are not a neoliberal party any longer" Joni replied.

That bloody word again.

Joni hadn't come in just to relieve her bladder.

"This is just Pete Samuelson's vanity project" she said. He doesn't care about the Party. It's all just about his ego and his Blairite politics."

Marianne heard her expel a puff of wind. Seeing an opportunity to escape, she flushed the toilet she hadn't used and let herself out. She went to the sink to wash her hands.

"This isn't just about ideology for us" Joni called from inside the cubicle. There was a pause before she flushed the toilet. She opened the door, pulling at the top of her elasticated skirt.

"It's not?"

"No" said Joni. She began to wash her hands. "It's about the toxic legacy of the New Labour and Ana would be very wise to disassociate herself. She has to think about her standing in the Party."

Marianne dried her hands quickly.

"I think I'd need to know more before commenting" she said.

She went back to the office without waiting for Joni. It wasn't terribly polite but there was no other way to shut the conversation down. She hoped Joni following her into the ladies wouldn't become a regular thing.

Marianne was unsure of the merits, or otherwise, of Pete's scheme. Instinctively, she felt Ana should try to maintain some neutrality. Still, there was no point Joni lobbying *her*. She had no influence in this. Ana would, as always, make up her own mind, and act accordingly.

That afternoon, she finished work at 4pm. Ana was treating Karen Giannopoulos to afternoon tea in the Pugin Room. This was to mark Karen's recent birthday. She'd invited Marianne to come too as she knew they were friends. Karen and Marianne had texted each other beforehand.

'*This could be awkward*' Karen had written. '*Madam's sporadic acts of generosity can feel more like acts of terrorism*.'

Marianne was looking forward to seeing Karen. However, she was less enamoured of the prospect of socialising with Ana. Their working relationship had a superficial cordiality. There were displays, from Ana, of bonhomie. It was just that it felt like there was no real warmth. After six months of working for her, she had no feel as to whether Ana liked her or disliked her. She had this uncomfortable suspicion it was neither.

Ana and Karen were already ensconced on velvet sofas when she arrived. The Pugin Room never failed to impress her. The red carpet, the hanging paintings, and the chandeliers created an effect of cosiness *and* grandeur. Marianne thought it more beautiful than anything she'd seen on her round-the-world tour with Euan. She sat down next to Karen on a sofa. They faced Ana, who was gracious and smiling.

"I'm so glad we've finally been able to get together" said Ana. "I've been planning a girls' night out for us since the election. Just never happened."

Really? Marianne thought. She wished she and Karen could communicate telepathically.

Their afternoon tea was delivered. Ana insisted on ordering a glass of Champagne each for the three of them. Marianne had been worried their conversation would be stilted and awkward. She needn't have. They were immersed in political gossip straightaway.

"So Nigel has resigned" said Karen. "He texted me earlier to let me know. Just in case I got any calls from the press".

She was talking about Nigel Patel. He was the MP for the neighbouring constituency of Greenwood North and Perivale. Until that morning, he had sat on the Labour front bench as a shadow housing minister.

"Who can blame him?" said Ana.

Nigel Patel had been a rising star in the Labour Party. Only in his mid-thirties and a telegenic barrister, he was often tipped for greatness. He had resigned in protest over the sacking of colleagues for alleged disloyalty. They had publicly criticised Jeremy Corbyn. They'd thought his response to the recent Paris terror attacks inadequate.

"To tell you the truth" said Ana "I can't understand why anyone would want to be on the front bench. Not in the current climate."

"Well, you'd be tainted by association" said Karen.

"Exactly." Ana took a sip of tea. She'd barely touched her Champagne. "I think Corbyn is going to have a job replacing Nigel. Nobody of any calibre wants to know. They've seen the opinion polls. It *is* desperate."

"Do you think Jezza will be gone before Christmas?" Karen asked.

Ana laughed. "Oh, well before then, I think."

The division bell rang about half past five. Ana left. She had been whipped to vote. Marianne and Karen, having drunk their champagne, finished their pot of tea.

"Another drink?" suggested Karen.

"Good idea. We could go to the House of Lords bar" said Marianne.

"Nah. Fuck this place. Let's go to the pub."

Marianne was a little taken aback by this. Surely a visit to the Westminster would be a treat.

"Not your scene then?" she asked.

"I worked here for a Labour MP after university" said Karen. "It was about a hundred years. I'll tell you all about it about it some other time."

Marianne hadn't known this. She thought it sounded intriguing. Still, she didn't probe as Karen seemed reluctant to talk about it.

"What about the Red Lion?" she suggested

"Too crowded. And too full of politicos. I know this place off Victoria Street."

They headed out of the Palace of Westminster. It was a drizzly, dark winter evening. As soon as they were let out of the gate, Marianne lit up a cigarette. She'd bought a packet at lunchtime. She wished she'd worn something warmer than her cotton trench coat. Karen borrowed her lighter so she could light a cigarette of her own.

"We're going to look like a right pair of classy birds" said Marianne.

"Bollocks to classy" Karen replied.

Marianne pictured the pair of them. She was tottering along on her heels, feeling the cold. Karen, impervious to the elements in her bobble hat and fleece, strode purposefully. Both were puffing away like a couple of fag ash Lils. They crossed over Parliament Square, passed by Westminster Abbey, and walked onto Victoria Street.

Karen took them to a pub near Victoria Station. It wasn't too busy and they were able to find a table easily. She bought a bottle of Merlot at the bar and poured them both a glass.

"So what's it like working with Joni?" she asked. "She must be a total nightmare."

"She's more sort of chaotic" said Marianne. "Turns up at odd times. Copies me into endless e-mails. And corners me about her latest obsessions."

"Oh yeah. She doesn't register lack of interest. Some people reckon she might have a touch of Asperger's."

"Well it would certainly explain a lot" said Marianne. "She sort of transmits but doesn't receive. At lunchtime today, she started talking about her menopause and how it dried out her vagina…"

"Fucking hell!"

"Oh my God, you should have seen Ben's face" said Marianne.

Karen snorted.

"And" said Marianne "she followed me into the fucking toilet to talk about the Greenwood Regeneration Partnership."

"What the fuck?"

"Seriously. I didn't even need to go. It was just an excuse to get away from her. She followed me into the ladies and used the cubicle next to me. It was a nightmare. I had to listen to her peeing and farting and well as bending my ear about the regen partnership.

"That must have been a real "Fuck my life" moment" said Karen.

"It was." Marianne took a sip of Merlot. "Tell me, what's your take on the regen partnership."

"Well, the way I see it" said Karen "the Council is broke. We need to improve people's housing. How else are we going to do it? Wait for Jezza to win the next election?"

"I think that is exactly what Joni and Momentum want to do."

Karen was looking distractedly over her shoulder. "Speak of the devil" she murmured.

Marianne turned to see what she was looking at. On the other side of the pub was Ned Critchley-Smith, of Global Solidarity. He was with a woman, in her early twenties, distinguishable by her cropped hair and androgynous clothes. She looked vaguely familiar. Ned saw them and half-nodded awkwardly in their direction.

"Wonder what they're doing here" Marianne said.

"Plotting the revolution probably" said Karen. "Would have thought drinking in pubs would be too bourgeois and capitalist for them."

"Do you want to go over and say hello?"

"Nah. Can't stand the rancid, pizza-faced little Trot."

"That girl he's with looks familiar" said Marianne. "I think she was at the last constituency meeting. When we discussed Syria."

"Quite possibly" Karen said. "Her name's Kate. I think she lives in that house they all share. You know, she didn't used to look like that."

"No?"

"No. She lobbed off her hair and started wearing dungarees fairly recently. Apparently, Global Solidarity have a sort of dress code for their women members. They have to dispense of any *bourgeois capitalist* femininity."

"That sounds very…controlling" said Marianne. "Like..."

"Like a cult. Yeah, that word gets used an awful lot about them."

"I know Bridget is very wary of them" Marianne said. "She thinks they're trying to take control of Greenwood Momentum."

Karen sighed. "Hmmm. It's very hard to know. They operate in such mysterious ways. There aren't very many of them but they're very organised and committed. Makes a huge difference."

"It really is amazing" Marianne said. "The Party has changed *so much*. And so *quickly*!."

"Tell me about it" said Karen.

Marianne bought the next bottle of Merlot. Ned and Kate left, unnoticed by them, at some point. Last orders were announced. Marianne checked her 'phone for the first time that evening. There were a couple of missed calls from Euan. He'd also texted to ask if she'd be home for dinner.

Shit she thought. *I should have let him know.*

She arrived home after midnight. Euan was already in bed. She took her shoes off in the hallway. It was her intention to somehow creep into the bedroom, undress and get into bed without waking him.

The darkness of the flat, and the Merlot, had disoriented her. On her way into the bedroom, she tripped over something and fell. Euan's bedside light snapped on. He stared at her through half-closed eyes.

"Sorry" she said. "I'm a bit squiffed."

She started giggling.

"You're drunk" he said. "And you've started smoking again."

"Yes, but in the morning, I'll be sober! Can't make any promises about the fags though"

She collapsed back on the floor, convulsing with drunken laughter. Euan didn't laugh or look amused. In fact, he looked furious.

"I called you. And I texted you. I wanted to know if you were coming home for dinner."

"Yes, sorry about that" Marianne replied. "I didn't see your messages until quite late."

She hiccupped.

Euan said: "It should have been *you* messaging *me*. Most people in relationships care enough to bother."

Marianne's mirth subsided immediately. "Look, Euan…"

"I'm too tired to argue with you" Euan said, wearily. "I just want to get some sleep."

With that, he switched off his lamp and rolled over.

Even in her inebriated state, Marianne felt stung. She lay there inert on the floor for a few minutes. She reflected that she and Euan had never really argued. This unwelcome development gave her a heart-sinking, nauseas feeling. She decided that she wasn't really in a state to process this. A few hours of sleep would give her some mental clarity.

Euan didn't say anything about it the next day. He seemed sort of coolly pleasant. Marianne weighed up talking to him about it or letting it slide. She wasn't sure how to deal with this tension between them. It simply hadn't happened before. She hoped their argument was just a one-off. She wanted it to recede into the past and be forgotten about.

On the Friday, she had arrived in the office at the normal time. Ben was already in. To her relief, there was no sign of Joni. She might show up later in the morning, in the afternoon or not at all.

Her desk 'phone rang. It was Ana.

"Can you come up and see me please." Her tone was very brisk.

Marianne immediately had this feeling of trepidation. "Sure" she said.

When she went in, Ana regarded her with a cold fury.

"I've had a complaint" she said.

"Oh?" said Marianne. She couldn't think why she would be the subject of a complaint.

"Yes, oh!" Ana hissed.

"Can I ask what about?"

"Tracy Kendall" said Ana. "I got a reply from the minister for her"

"Oh yes, I remember" said Marianne.

"WELL SHE DIDN'T FUCKING GET IT!" Ana screeched at her.

Her face was contorted into this animalistic snarl. She actually looked demonically possessed.

Marianne was so shocked by this explosion that she started shaking. Her heart beat accelerated. She couldn't speak without stammering "I…I forwarded it to Joni. I thought she was going to send it."

"You thought, you thought" said Ana. She banged her palm on the desk. "WELL IT'S JUST NOT FUCKING GOOD ENOUGH!"

After a moment of stunned silence, Marianne took a breath. She felt she needed to regain control of her composure.

"I'm sorry but I really did think Joni was following up."

"*You* should have followed it up" said Ana. "You can see for yourself that Joni is a useless fuckwit."

Inwardly, Marianne said *Why did you fucking hire her then?* However, she kept this thought to herself. Ana's rage did not invite challenge.

"Just don't fuck up like that again" said Ana. "Not if you want to carry on working for me. That's all."

Dismissed, Marianne went back to her office in a state of shock. She was still shaking by the time she sat down at her desk. Ben noticed.

"Is everything alright?" he asked.

"No. No, not really"

"What's happened?"

“I’ve just been screamed at and sworn at by Ana” she told him. “All because fucking Joni didn’t send on that ministerial reply.”

She knew she sounded like she was about to cry.

“That’s hardly your fault” Ben said.

“I know!” said Marianne. She paused for a moment. “You know what? I think I’ve finally inherited that baton of blame.”

“Oh, that comes to us all” said Ben. “I had two months of being sworn at and threatened with the sack by Ana.”

Marianne was appalled.

“You never said. I wish *you had* said something. You shouldn’t have to go through that on your own”.

“I don’t really like to share my stress” said Ben. “Anyhow, I knew it would pass. The good news is that it will be Joni’s turn next.”

This was hugely cheering for Marianne. “Well, I hope Ana tears her a second arsehole when it is her turn” she said.

She was relieved when the weekend came. Euan was playing in a concert on the Saturday and so she saw little of him. Bridget had invited her to a canvassing session on the Sunday for the London Mayoral election. It was a big deal because Sadiq Khan himself was coming. The session would start from the tube station on Greenwood High Road.

Just before she left, she and Euan had a row. She had hoped that things between them would return to normal. However, the coolness had remained like a dense, heavy fog. He expressed extreme irritation when she told him where she was going.

"I don't see what the problem is" said Marianne. "We haven't made any plans for this afternoon."

"That's just it. We haven't. My point is normal couples would."

Something in Marianne snapped.

"Normal, normal, normal!" She could hear her voice rising to a shriek. "What is this *normal* you keep going on about? Does *normal* involve *me* being the little woman by any chance?"

He looked at her intently. "Is that how you see things?"

"Up until now, no" she told him. "I've always gone along with you. I've always fitted in with your plans. You've always worked strange hours, been in and out of work. That's been fine. I haven't minded."

"Why are you getting so angry?" he asked.

His pretence of reasonableness incensed her further.

"You're the one who's angry" said Marianne. "And I'll tell you why. For the first time ever, you've had to fit in with me. You're the one who's being asked to be supportive and understanding. You're pissed off because I have something else in my life besides you and *this* flat."

"Yeah, whatever!" he snarled.

"It's true" Marianne said. "And it's disappointing. Because I always thought you were the sort of man who'd support me. If I found something *that I* really wanted to do."

"Sorry you're disappointed."

Marianne left, slamming the door behind her, without saying goodbye. She stamped most of the way to the tube station. Some unconscious, buried resentment seemed to have physically taken hold of her. How had she not noticed his petulance and selfishness before? Well, she wasn't going to be playing second fiddle any more. She had a purpose and a career of her own.

Her fury had dissipated by the time she got to the tube station. It was a sunny, cold but crisp day. A large crowd of local Labour activists had assembled.

There must have been about 40 of them. Karen was there dishing out clipboards, leaflets and stickers. She was assisted by Bridget. Pete Samuelson was in deep conversation with another councillor. A small huddle of Momentum activists had gathered slightly away from them. They wore stickers and badges emblazoned with Jeremy Corbyn's name. Joni seemed to be holding court amongst them.

Sadiq Khan arrived in a taxi with Ana. He was short, dapper and immediately recognisable. He was greeted by Pete who he seemed to know. There were some more introductions. Marianne noticed a certain froideur between Pete and Ana. They neither spoke nor looked at each other. The session was to begin with a group photo in front of the tube station. Pete and Ana stood either side of Sadiq at the front and bared their teeth for the camera. Karen took the photo on her 'phone to share on social media.

Karen divided the group into teams. This wasn't an easy task as some seemed to wander off in different directions. Others seemed too immersed in conversation to bother with canvassing.

"Honestly, it is like herding cats" Karen said to Marianne. She always said this. She proffered a clipboard in Marianne's direction. "Can I ask you to do the board for Sadiq's team?" she asked

"Erm, yes" said Marianne, taking the clipboard.

Out of the corner of her eye, she noticed Ana introducing Joni to Sadiq Khan. She glanced over at them. Ana had her arm wrapped around Joni's shoulders and was laughing. Nobody would guess, least of all Joni, that only days earlier, she'd described her as a "useless fuckwit".

Just wait 'til she gets that baton of blame Marianne thought to herself.

Ana left shortly afterwards. She did not stay around to go canvassing. Marianne led Sadiq's team out onto the doorstep. Karen had introduced them beforehand. They spent a pleasant hour knocking on doors. There weren't many people in. The candidate himself had this slightly irritating habit of getting into epic conversations with the few who answered their doors. Marianne had to retrieve him on a couple of occasions.

"Thanks, Marianne" he said when they'd finished. He had to dash off across London to another event.

At the end, the remaining canvassers went to a nearby pub. Their stickers and paraphernalia differentiated them from the other lunchtime drinkers. Marianne gathered in a corner with Pete, Karen and Bridget. Joni and the Momentumites sat at a nearby table, safely out of earshot. This meant they had a safe space to discuss the latest local intrigues.

“Momentum don’t really give a fuck about the Regeneration Partnership” said Pete. “They’re just using it as their Trojan horse to take over the local party”.

Karen said: “I think we are just going to have to be very organised.”

“Where does Ana stand on this?” asked Bridget.

Marianne shrugged. She’d assumed the question was directed to her.

Pete had a view. “She’s been absolutely craven and spineless” he said. “She’s shit scared of Momentum. So she’s trying to avoid taking a position. The Regeneration Partnership isn’t something she’d really have a moral objection to.”

At this point, he and Joni exchanged glances across the pub.

“You know why she’s hired that nutjob, Joni?” he said, looking over at her. “She’s using her as a conduit to Momentum. To keep them sweet and find out what they’re up to.”

This made a lot of sense to Marianne. She couldn’t imagine what other use Ana would have for Joni. She’d come to suspect that peoples’ usefulness was always a calculation for her. Still, she decided to keep quiet about this. She did wonder whether this meant Joni had immunity from the baton of blame.

Pete changed the subject.

“Has anybody tweeted the photo with Sadiq?” he asked.

“Oh. Fuck” said Karen. She pulled out her iPhone.

“How does Twitter work exactly?” asked Marianne.

"You're not on Twitter!" Pete spluttered. "Fuck me. You must be the only Labour activist who isn't."

"I'll show you" said Karen. She held up her 'phone so Marianne could see it. "Okay. You just need to attach the photo. Here's the one with us and Sadiq. And you just need to say something really inane and banal like..."

She typed: '*Great response on the #labourdoorstep in Greenwood with @SadiqKhan*'

"And that is all there is too it" she said. "You can follow people, like stuff and retweet other people's tweets."

"Don't forget the labour doorstep hashtag" said Pete. "That's vital. You know, Marianne, you should get yourself on Twitter."

That afternoon, Marianne did create a Twitter feed for herself. She wasn't sure whether she should use a photo or have a bio. She decided these were questions for another day. When she got home, Euan apologised for the scene earlier. She apologised too and the tension between them was diffused. He asked her what Sadiq Khan was like. They laughed when she described the more chaotic parts of her day. In the evening, he cooked a curry which they ate in front of the TV.

In the office the next morning, Marianne had a quiet moment. Ben was in the Library and Joni wasn't there either. She decided to explore Twitter. She followed Ana, Peter and a few others. Then, she came across Joni's Twitter feed. The photo, albeit very flattering, was very clearly her. Her bio identified her as '*Senior Caseworker for @AnaNovakMP*'. Marianne decided to follow her.

She scrolled down Joni's feed. It was mostly retweets of pro-Corbyn news articles. There was one tweet written by her. To Marianne's surprise, it revealed Joni had, at some point, trained as a psychotherapist.

Christ, you'd need therapy after that she thought.

She scrolled up again. The most recent tweet, posted the day before, was also written by her.

It read: '*@CllrPeterSamuelson can lose his toxic Blairite reputation by dumping the Greenwood Regeneration Partnership. #socialcleansing #regeneration*'

"Fucking hell" said Marianne.

She was appalled. Joni's bio identified her as Ana's employee. Surely anything she tweeted reflected on her, despite the usual disclaimers. Calling Pete 'toxic' was unbelievably antagonistic. The reference to 'social cleansing' was just downright dangerous. At best, it was rather unprofessional. At worst, people might think she was speaking for Ana.

Marianne decided the time for politeness had passed. She would have it out with her. While she was at it, she'd mention the Tracy Kendall letter. She'd make it clear that she wasn't going to be blamed like that again. The tweets themselves had all sorts of reputational risks.

As it happened, she didn't have to wait long. Joni turned up in the office that morning. Marianne couldn't remember whether she was supposed to be in or not. She'd lost track.

Once she' d sat down and switched on her computer, Marianne decided to seize the moment.

"Joni, I need to talk to you about something. It's a bit awkward."

Joni looked at her, her eyebrows raised slightly in curiosity.

"I've just seen your Twitter post about Pete" said Marianne. "It's really inappropriate. I think you delete it before Ana sees it."

Joni carried on looking at her, her mouth slightly agape. Her nostrils flared slightly. She sort of looked like a small mammal about to go on the attack. Then, she smiled benevolently.

"It's fine, Marianne, I understand" she said in a voice that was supposed to sound soothing.

"I'm sorry?" Marianne was perplexed by her tone.

"I know you're very close to Pete and Karen" said Joni. "You want to fit in and ingratiate yourself. I get it. But they are the past. Please don't take this the wrong way but I think you need to get with the programme."

Marianne was about to tell Joni to fuck off. She wasn't going to be patronised like that. Her desk 'phone rang before she could open her mouth. It was the office of the Leader of the Opposition. "*Jeremy*" wanted to see Ana that lunchtime.

"Okay, I'll tell her" she told the brusque woman on the end of the 'phone.

She called Ana's office phone. There was no response. She then tried her mobile. Ana answered but sounded extremely irritable.

"Oh God!" she said when told that *Jeremy* wanted to see her. "This really isn't a good time."

She made it sound like the imposition was Marianne's fault but agreed to go anyway. Marianne checked Ana's electronic diary after she hung up. There were no entries for that morning. She couldn't discern why it was such an inconvenience to her.

The business between her and Joni was still unfinished.

"How about we talk about this over lunch?" said Joni brightly.

Just no Marianne said inwardly.

"I really don't have time today" she told her.

Joni had to go to the constituency office. Therefore, Marianne didn't see her again that day. She was very relieved.

After lunch, Ben was back from the library. Ana came into the office positively beaming. Her meeting with *Jeremy* had clearly gone well

"Just wanted you guys to be the first to know" she said. "Jeremy has appointed me to the front bench. I'm going to be shadow housing minister."

She had replaced Nigel Patel.

"Yes, I know" said Marianne. "I saw it on Twitter. Congratulations."

Ana's smile froze. "I'm glad you're so on top of things, Marianne" she said. "Because it's going to mean more work for you all."

Monstrous Member – Chapter 6

"Christ! You've become addicted to Twitter" said Euan.

Marianne looked up from her 'phone. "No, I haven't!" she protested.

She was in mid-tweet: '*Great takedown of Tory housing policy by @AnaNovakMP on #Newsnight.*"

This wasn't strictly true. She and Euan were indeed watching Ana being interviewed on *Newsnight*. However, her performance was far from stellar. In fact, she was floundering. She had, rightly in Marianne's view, criticised housing benefit cuts. Still, government policy was an easy target. She was then challenged to explain Labour policy. In response, she had rambled and blustered for what seemed like minutes. It was painful to watch.

"Yes, you have" said Euan. "You can't seem to watch the news anymore without your 'phone. I don't know how you take anything in with all that tapping and scrolling."

God, you've turned into such a miserable old fart said Marianne inwardly. To Euan, she said "I am just trying to support my boss. She *is* getting a bit of a grilling."

"Well, she certainly needs *support*" Euan said. "She's bloody useless. I thought she was supposed to be like future leader material."

This remark grated on Marianne. She was already irritated enough by his running commentary. "At least she has the balls to front up on TV" she said. "These journalists are like sharks. How would you like to do it?"

Euan looked at her. "It's *her job*. She shouldn't go on if she's not up to it. It does your party more harm than good."

He sort of had a point. Having looked at her 'phone, Marianne knew that Euan was being far kinder than Twitter about Ana. The comments were savage. Respected political journalists slammed her lack of preparation. Others made mean jokes about former newsreaders and autocues. Nobody was defending her. Marianne scrolled down the tweets under the #Newsnight hashtag.

"And what does Twitter say?" asked Euan.

"Oh, you know" she murmured.

She was being deliberately evasive. Being proved right would just make him more insufferable.

Euan, however, clearly wasn't going to let it go. "It's pretty poor really" he said. "When you think how demanding she is and what a total ogre she is to work for..."

"Wait a minute!" cried Marianne. She was really annoyed now. "I have *never* called her an ogre!"

"No, you've never *said* it. I'm just going by everything you've ever told me."

He is just twisting everything Marianne thought to herself. It felt like he was trying to assert ownership over her words, *her stories*.

"We've already had this conversation, Euan" she said. "I work in politics. It's high pressure stuff. It's demanding. But it might surprise you to learn that I can deal with it."

"Is that why you're always jumping down my throat these days?" he asked, resentfully.

Marianne suddenly felt a wave of physical exhaustion. She couldn't be bothered to argue the toss. "You know what" she said. "If my talking about work is such a problem, I just won't talk about it."

Surely this would shut him up.

"What else would you talk about?" he said.

She was too tired to respond to this. He was being a complete knob. They had been so busy arguing they'd missed the end of Ana's interview. She went to bed before *Newsnight* finished. He stayed up for a while longer.

The next morning, Ben was already in the office when she arrived. There was no sign of Joni.

"Whatever you do" said Ben. "Don't say anything Ana about last night."

"I've been wondering how to handle that" said Marianne. "Diplomatic silence it is then."

She had read *the Metro* on the tube. Ana's *Newsnight* interview had made the inside pages. The article was as viciously critical of her as Twitter. It hadn't been like this when she was first elected. Back then, the press coverage had been glowing. She'd been heralded as a rising star.

At 11am, they went upstairs to Ana's office for a team meeting. Joni was also expected. Still, she hadn't yet appeared. They found Ana sat on the sofa next to the office door.

“Morning team” she said effervescently when they went in.

Marianne tried to discern her mood. She was putting on a brittle, determined display of cheerfulness. She clearly wanted to pretend last night hadn’t happened.

“To business.” said Ana. “I’ve called this meeting so we can have a brainstorming session. As you know, I’m speaking from the dispatch box in the housing benefit debate next week.”

That’s brave after last night Marianne thought.

At that moment, Joni burst in, late. She was swaddled in an oversized coat, long scarf and woolly hat. She held a takeaway Costa Coffee cup in her hand.

“Morning” Ana said to her. She regarded Joni coolly.

“Morning team!” said Joni, almost as if in parody of Ana.

They watched and waited as Joni unwrapped her coat and dropped her bag. She took a long, noisy slurp of her coffee. Her hat and scarf remained on as she sank into an armchair. She offered no apology for her lateness.

Ana said “I was just telling Ben and Marianne, before you arrived, that…”

“I *have got to* say” interjected Joni “that I thought you got a really rough deal on *Newsnight* last night.”

There was a silence.

Oh god thought Marianne.

“It’s fine” said Ana.

“No, no.” said Joni. “All those people saying you’re totally incompetent. It just isn’t true. You didn’t seem *at all* out of your depth. Well I didn’t think so anyway.”

Just stop! Marianne screeched inwardly.

Ana's face was completely expressionless. Her eyes seemed to have glazed. Still, Marianne could see a glint of fury.

"That's good to know" she said, after a pause. "Thank you, Joni."

Joni hadn't finished.

"Everybody knows you were a newsreader" she added. "But I wish people would stop saying you need an autocue to speak. It just isn't funny."

Shut the fuck up Marianne wanted to say to Joni. Surely this was the tipping point. There was no way Joni wasn't going to have her head ripped off

Another frosty silence ensued. Marianne waited for Ana to explode like a grenade.

However, sudden death was averted. Ben saved the day with a diplomatic intervention. He changed the subject.

"I think we need to focus on key messages for the debate" he said

This dissipated the tension in the room.

"Yes, that's right" said Ana, visibly defrosting. "The important thing to focus on is young people and the housing crisis. Now *that* is immediate and urgent."

There was a murmur of agreement.

She continued: "It's the rhetoric that's important here. That's what make debates in parliament memorable. So I thought I'd channel Obama and refer to the "fierce urgency of now".

Dear god, no! Marianne implored her inwardly. *You'll never carry that off.*

"I'm really not sure about that" she said hesitantly.

"Why not?" asked Ana. She sounded put out.

Marianne was stumped for an answer. She could hardly tell the truth. Ana simply didn't have the rhetorical skills to emulate Barack Obama. It required a certain deftness that she didn't have. Her disastrous *Newsnight* interview should have made that clear. She would just make a fool of herself.

"Erm…I think it's important to seem grounded, measured" she said, choosing her words carefully. "We have enough facts and figures on our side. I think you need to be…forensic."

"Stop right there!" Joni cried suddenly. "*Grounded. Measured. Forensic.* That is the language of neoliberalism. You've got to get over your addiction to this, Marianne. There has been a paradigm shift and you need to get with the programme."

This caused Marianne to have a fantasy of violence that she'd never experienced. At that moment, she wanted to lean across the table and grab Joni by the nose. With her free hand, she would repeatedly slap the side of her head until it was a swollen, red pulp. Who *the fuck* did she think she was talking to her like that?

She hissed: "I've no idea what you're on about, Joni. What is this programme I should be getting with?"

The fury had risen out of her like steam. She hadn't meant to show temper. She felt she shouldn't have.

Joni paused as if recalibrating. "I am just thinking about the human level" she said in her low monotone. "People are tired of technocratic language. They want to see some actual passion from their politicians."

"I think there is something in that" said Ana

Fine! Marianne said to herself. *Make a tit of yourself if you want to.*

"I think we do need some hard facts and figures though" said Ben.

"How about some comparisons with other countries" suggested Marianne. "Take Denmark. They have a different model. It's normal there for young people to be living independently."

"Not crazy about that" replied Ana. "It sounds like we're saying "why can't we be more like Scandinavia?"

Okay thought Marianne. *I tried.*

"There's an obvious starting point" said Ben. "It's the justification for cutting housing benefit. That's what we need to challenge."

"Agreed" said Ana.

"We need to set out an alternative vision" Joni told them, assuredly. "We need some data about other countries."

"Absolutely" said Ana.

Hold on just a minute! Marianne said to herself. *That's what I just said and you pooh-poohed it!*

The meeting finished shortly afterwards. Marianne and Ben were assigned tasks. She was to help him with the research. He would effectively be writing Ana's speech. Joni left, apparently to go back to the constituency.

Back in the office, Marianne said "I thought I was going to bitch-slap Joni".

“You certainly looked like you wanted to” said Ben sympathetically. “It’s completely understandable.”

Marianne was still seething.

“Not only is she completely bonkers” she said. “She is unbelievably fucking rude and condescending. How does she manage to go through life talking to people like that?”

Ben sighed.

“It wouldn’t be so bad if she occasionally made herself useful” he said. “We could really do with another member of staff.”

This was certainly true. Marianne looked at her e-mails. There were over a thousand unread messages. Ana’s appointment to the front bench had dramatically increased their correspondence. They were supposed to respond within fifteen working days. However, this was becoming increasingly impractical.

That evening, after work, she went to a public meeting at Greenwood Town Hall. It was about the Regeneration Partnership. Bridget had asked her to go. She wanted to lend moral support to Pete and the other councillors.

“We can’t let Momentum hijack everything” she’d said to Marianne. “They’re just trying to intimidate everybody. That’s what I don’t like.”

Marianne arrived just before the start of the meeting at 7pm. She found a seat next to Bridget in a middle row. The room was pretty full. She glanced around. She saw Ned Critchley-Smith and Kate sitting nearby with some of their comrades. There were other Momentumites dotted around the room.

Pete Samuelson sat on the raised platform at the front. As usual, he looked like he meant business. Something about his bearing made Marianne think of a tortoise peering out of a hard shell. He was flanked by three of his senior colleagues.

There was an atmosphere in the room that Marianne found intimidating. She suspected that many had turned up to give Pete a hard time.

Why have I given up my evening for this? she wondered.

She gave it some honest thought and came up with two reasons. Firstly, she felt Bridget deserved some support trying to keep the Party sane and decent. The second reason, however, was rather unsettling. She realised she wanted to avoid going home.

The meeting began. Pete stood up to address the room. Marianne thought he acquitted himself well. As a public speaker, he was professional and engaging. He spoke of the difficulty of funding estate regeneration.

"There is an important distinction to be made" he told them. "The regeneration partnership is about improving our *existing* housing. It's not to be confused with building more. Of course, we'd like to do that too."

He carried on for a few more minutes. Marianne sensed that he'd neutralised some of the hostility in the room. This was no mean feat. His colleagues also spoke briefly. There was a question and answer session at the end.

Bridget asked for clarification of a particular detail. There were a few more questions in a similar vein. Pete fielded these easily enough. Eventually, Ned Critchley-Smith put his hand up to ask a question. Marianne turned to look at him. She noticed Karen Giannapoulos was standing at the back, present but not involved, as seemed to be her modus operandi. Joni had also crept in at some point and was sitting a few rows back.

"I'd like to put it to you, Councillor Samuelson" said Ned in his soft Manchester-inflected voice "that this 'partnership' is about the interests of private developers. You are, in fact, selling out the working class."

His comrades cheered and applauded loudly. Ned seemed to turn red, as if embarrassed by the attention. He quickly sat down and looked at the floor. Pete stared at him balefully.

"I don't even know what *that* means" he said. "Who are these working class people you've been talking to?"

It was, of course, a rhetorical question.

He's about to be frank and blunt said Marianne to herself.

Pete continued. "Some of the most dilapidated, run down estates are in my ward. The ward I'm elected to represent. At every one of my surgeries, there are queues of people turning up to beg for better housing. You haven't talked to them, have you? So I'm not going to be taking any lectures about the 'working class' from *you*!"

This produced a muted round of applause from around the room. Marianne and Bridget joined in. Some of Ned 's comrades jeered and barracked. Ned himself, having turned positively crimson, looked awkward and uncomfortable.

As they were leaving afterwards, Marianne said to Bridget: "I have to say that Pete is pretty impressive."

"Oh yes" she replied. "He can be bullish and obnoxious but he knows his stuff"

They passed through the foyer on their way out. Marianne saw Joni murmuring to Ned and Kate in a corner. They briefly exchanged glances but didn't acknowledge each other. Joni tended to avoid her when they saw each other outside work.

Marianne had had a text from Karen inviting her and Bridget to the pub afterwards. They found her and Pete sat in a snug. Karen was drinking red wine. Pete had a double whisky.

"I didn't think that went too badly" said Bridget.

Pete grunted.

"I thought your slap-down of Ned was brilliant, Pete" said Marianne.

This pleased him. He grinned

"That little Trot deserves a slap" he said, taking a sip of his whisky.

Bridget said: "Global Solidarity worry me. They're just so sort of…fanatical."

"I'm amazed they can find the time" said Pete. "With their drugs-fuelled orgies."

"What!" squealed Marianne. "You *are making this up.*"

"Well, there are enough stories going around" said Karen. "It doesn't mean it's true though."

Bridget had pursed her lips in extreme disapproval. This was not *her* sort of conversation.

"I don't think we should be speculating like this" she said firmly. "It's just gossip."

"There are plenty of stories about that shared house of theirs" said Pete. "From multiple sources. It all sounds very lively."

"Even so…"

"I'm as shocked as you are, Bridget" said Pete. "There must be more wholesome things they could be doing on a Saturday evening. Instead of getting coked up and shunting each other."

He let out his wheezy Muttley giggle at this. Bridget was visibly appalled. Marianne found herself suppressing convulsions of hysterical laughter at the sheer naughtiness of it all. It was like being back at school.

Karen, conscious of Bridget's discomfort, tried to elevate the tone. "I think the key thing is organisation" she said. "That's the only way we're going to beat the entryists."

Sometime later, Bridget visited the ladies'. While she was gone, Karen said to Pete: "I wish you wouldn't talk about those rumours about Global Solidarity in front of Bridget. She finds it very distasteful."

"Oh come on, Giannapoulos" said Pete. "It's not like I'm trying to evoke mental images of Ned 's cum face. You know, when they have their bukkake sessions. I bet he looks all blotchy and constipated. Like this."

He twisted his face into a constipated expression.

This was too much for Marianne

"Oh my God!" she shrieked. She was completely beside herself in a fit of juvenile giggles. "This has to stop!"

"Pete" said Karen sternly. "Behave yourself. *You* are the Leader of Greenwood Council."

"Yes boss" he said.

Karen gave Marianne a lift home. As usual, she drove too fast only just stopping short of jumping red lights.

"How are things with you?" she asked Marianne after they set off.

Marianne sighed. "Oh alright. Mustn't grumble and all that."

"Sounds like you need a bit of a grumble" said Karen. "I bet Madam has been a total nightmare since her promotion."

"It's not so much that" Marianne replied. "There's just more work and only Ben and I are doing it."

"Well, Joni would be no fucking use."

"She just generates more work for us" said Marianne. "And she's just really annoying…and rude."

"Oh, quelle surprise" said Karen. "At least you have your lovely boyfriend waiting for you at home. That must make life more bearable."

Marianne breathed in. She felt a desperate need to unburden herself. "Actually, that is another problem" she said.

"What?"

"We haven't been getting on" Marianne confided. "Things are really tense. We…seem to be drifting apart."

She felt she'd betrayed Euan in some way by vocalising this. Still, it was a tremendous relief to say it out loud.

"Oh!" said Karen.

"I wonder if it's because we live at such close quarters" said Marianne. "Our flat is tiny which probably doesn't help. We're always sniping at each other."

"A bit of cabin fever maybe?" Karen suggested.

"Yes, possibly" said Marianne. "It's just never been a problem before. In fact, it's always been comfortable and easy and cosy. Don't forget that we've travelled loads together as well. He's like my best friend as well as my boyfriend."

"What's changed?"

Marianne gazed ahead at the road. "I don't know" she said. "This job? Me? I now have a life of my own. *My own* reason for existing. It's like he resents it or something."

"Ah" said Karen. "Jealous man syndrome."

She turned into Marianne's street and parked outside her house.

"Well, if you need some time out" she said "you'd be more than welcome to come and stay at mine for a bit. We have a spare home. I don't know how that would affect you in terms of rent and stuff."

"It wouldn't" Marianne told her. "Euan's parents own the flat. They bought it for him when we graduated. We just pay bills."

"I see."

"I really appreciate the offer though" said Marianne. I'll see how things go. Some time apart might do us good."

"Yes, I know that one" said Karen. "My husband and I went through a rough patch a few years back. We agreed to a trial separation."

"What happened?"

"He didn't come back."

The next morning, Ana walked into the office. Marianne was feeling snowed under. She was composing a letter about Japanese knotweed to a constituent who'd been afflicted. Ana had demanded a three-page briefing before responding. As always, she would insist on signing the letter herself.

Ben was doing the research for Ana's speech in the debate. Marianne was supposed to be helping him but she'd got behind. Joni had arrived early for some reason. She'd switched on her computer when she arrived but hadn't used it. She'd spent the morning playing with her 'phone.

It was a Friday. That evening, Marianne was going to the theatre with Euan. They had tickets to see a play called *Absolute Hell* at the Royal Court. They had been given them by Euan's father. Marianne was hoping they could enjoy a relaxed evening together. It might alleviate some of their recent tension.

"Right, guys" said Ana when she came in. "I've been getting some complaints. Apparently, you haven't been sending out letters on time. Remember, we always, always respond within fifteen days."

"Well, there is a bit of a backlog" Marianne said.

"I know! And I want that backlog cleared. Today, preferably. Stay late this evening if you have to."

"We're always here late" said Marianne, almost involuntarily. "Erm, I was hoping to leave on time tonight. Euan and I have tickets for the theatre."

Joni piped up. "I totally agree, Ana" she said. "It's not acceptable. I think it's really important that we are more customer-focussed"

Marianne screamed inwardly at Joni: *I'm going to fucking smash your face in!*

"Yes, that's what we aim for, Joni" said Ana. "Good customer service."

She turned to leave. Marianne realised she hadn't responded to her. Perhaps she hadn't heard.

"Sorry, Ana" she said. "I'm happy to stay late any other night. But I did say that I can't stay tonight as I'm going to the theatre."

Ana stopped. She turned to look at Marianne.

"Can I see you upstairs please?" she said. "Now."

Marianne followed her back to her office. They didn't speak on the way. Once, inside, Ana slammed the door closed.

"How fucking dare you!" she hissed.

"I'm sorry!" Marianne was startled.

They were standing facing each other. Ana's eyeballs seemed uncomfortably close to hers.

"*You* are *deliberately* trying to undermine my authority in this office" she said.

"That's just not true" said Marianne. "I just wanted you to know..."

"I HEARD YOU THE FIRST FUCKING TIME!" Ana screeched. Her face was contorted in an animalistic snarl again. Her red lipstick made her look particularly bloodthirsty.

There was a silence. Marianne could feel herself trembling. Ana was staring into her eyes.

"It's not just here, is it?" she said, her voice dropping to a near whisper. "You're always trying to undermine me. Here. In the constituency. You just can't help yourself. Joni tells me that you're always plotting with Samuelson and Karen."

Marianne felt indignant about this accusation. Did Ana really believe this? Did she actually credit any of Joni's bullshit?

"I'm not involved in any plotting" she said. "If anything, I'm trying to have your back."

"Oh really? How do you work that out?"

"I'm just worried about Momentum" said Marianne. "I think they could turn on you at any time."

Ana maintained her hard stare. "Listen. I can look after myself" she said. "The only thing I want from you is a bit of fucking loyalty. And a bit of commitment. I haven't seen much of either recently."

"Well, I'm really sorry if that's how things seem to you" said Marianne. "But..."

"But nothing" Ana snapped, cutting her off. "I really am going to need to see a big change in your attitude, Marianne. Because it's just not fucking good enough. Now, please go back to your desk and get some work done."

Dismissed, Marianne headed back to her office. She felt angry and tearful. She had this strong sense of having been treated unjustly.

Get some work done!

What exactly did Ana think she did all day? More to the point, what did she think Joni did all day? And why exactly had they been talking about her?

She left work much later than she'd intended. She'd tried to clear as many e-mails as possible. Still, hours of work had barely made a dent. She took the District and Circle line to Sloane Square. The play was starting at 7.30pm and she was cutting it fine. She wouldn't even have time to endure Euan's disapproval while she had a quick cigarette outside. He had embraced non-smoking with the zeal of a convert.

He was waiting for her outside the Royal Court. The curtain would be going up in about two minutes. He was clearly very angry.

"Come on!" he barked when she appeared. "It's starting in a minute". He turned to go in without waiting for her

"Sorry I'm late" Marianne called after him. She was slightly breathless after running up the escalator in the tube station. The cigarettes weren't helping either

She found it almost impossible to concentrate on the play. She was acutely conscious of Euan's fury. He sat beside her with his eyes fixed resolutely fixed on the stage. She knew he wasn't really taking it in either. They barely spoke during the interval.

His mood hadn't improved when they arrived home.

Marianne closed the front door behind them. "What's wrong?" she asked him.

He spun round, his eyes blazing. "You! That's what's wrong" he snarled

"Me?" Marianne was shocked by his virulence.

"Yes, you!" he shouted at her. "I am sick of being messed around and kept waiting and treated like I barely exist. Just because *you* want to feel important."

"I *have had* a mountain of work to get through today!" Marianne could hear her voice rising in fury at his lack of consideration.

"Don't you always?" said Euan. "You're just someone's assistant. The way you bang on, anyone would think you were an MP yourself. I think you're suffering from some sort of false consciousness."

This enraged Marianne further. "I'll tell you what I'm suffering from! I'm suffering from being constantly under the cosh at work. And I'm suffering from coming home and fighting with you all the time. It's like I'm fighting a battle on two fronts and losing. I'm tired! And I'm sick of your constant moods and sulks. I'm sick of having to deal with it."

"Yeah, I can tell" said Euan. He stormed off to bed.

Marianne just stood in the hallway for a few minutes. She felt shaken and exhausted. Eventually, she went into the kitchen to make herself a cup of tea. She wished the flat had a spare room. It felt like she had nowhere to go.

In the morning, she left to go canvassing. The London Mayoral election was less than three months away. However, she didn't make it to the canvassing session. Instead, she went for a long walk before winding up in a pub alone. She nursed a glass of red wine for a couple of hours.

It was mid-afternoon when she wandered out into a deserted beer garden. She lit up a cigarette, took a drag and burst into tears. She had made a decision. After sobbing quietly for a few moments, she composed herself.

She pulled her 'phone out of her bag and made a call. "Karen" she said. "I'd like to take up your offer."

Euan wasn't there when she got home. When he came back, her suitcase was packed.

He stopped in the doorway of their bedroom. "What's all this?" he murmured. He stared uncomprehendingly at her suitcase.

"I'm moving out for a while" she told him. "I think we both need a bit of space."

"What? Why?" He seemed dumbstruck

"You even have to ask?" Marianne said incredulously.

"Are you coming back?"

"I don't know."

"Is there someone else?" he asked. "Is this what all this is all about?"

"No there bloody well isn't!" she spluttered, outraged.

How typical of men to judge women by their own standards she thought.

"I mean, apart from Ana, of course" said Euan. "She *is* like an abusive boyfriend if you ask me."

"For fucks sake, Euan!"

"You're only getting annoyed because you know deep down that I'm right" he said.

"Let's now even go there. Not today."

They looked at each other for a moment without saying anything. Euan puffed out his cheeks. He changed tack.

"Look" he said. "We're not the first couple in the world to go through a rough patch. Arguments are normal in relationships."

"Not for us though" Marianne said. "This isn't normal for us. We've always got on. That's what our relationship has been based on. We've never done the whole mutual antagonism thing. We've never argued. All this fighting makes me feel like something is broken."

"I really don't think it's anything that can't be fixed" said Euan. "Why not stay and try to work it out?"

She almost relented. It would have been easy enough, comfortable enough.

"I'm sorry" she said. "But if I don't get some space, *I will* walk out and I *won't* come back. You're gonna have to trust me on this."

Euan looked at her for a moment as if trying to discern her thoughts

"Okay" he said, conceding defeat. "I can see I'm not going to change your mind. I know I've been a bit of a twat recently and I'm sorry. Wherever you go, let's just keep talking. We can get through this."

Marianne could feel herself beginning to well up. She bit her lip. "Okay" she said.

She wheeled her suitcase out of the flat and closed the front door behind her.

Karen lived in an orange-bricked Victorian semi in the leafier part of Greenwood. She lived there with her teenage son, Daniel. It was early evening when Marianne arrived by taxi. Karen ushered her in through the front door. The hallway was lined by cardboard boxes full of Labour Party leaflets.

"Dan" she called up the stairs. "We need some muscle but you'll do."

Daniel appeared. He was a tall, dark haired sixteen-year old. Marianne could see the family resemblance.

“This is Marianne” Karen told him. “She’s going to be staying with us for a bit.”

“Alright” Daniel said by way of greeting.

“Take her bag upstairs” Karen instructed. “And put it in the spare room.”

“It’s like hotel service here” said Marianne. “I could get used to it.”

Karen led her into the kitchen. There was world music playing on some speakers. A moussaka was baking in the oven and the kitchen table was set for supper. Marianne had the strong sense that this was the centre of their home.

“You have a lovely house” she said.

“We like it” said Karen.

They sat at the pine table. Karen opened a bottle of Chianti and poured them both a glass

“Dan’s off out with some friends tonight” she said. “For once, we’ll be a sulky teenager-free zone.”

Over dinner, they avoided discussing the reason Marianne was there. Instead, they talked more about local party intrigues.

“Of course, things were always going to be difficult between Pete and Ana” Karen said at one point.

“Why?” Marianne was intrigued.

“Well, Pete thought he was going to be the MP here” Karen told her. “Only Ana pipped him to the post when we selected the candidate. Didn’t you know?”

"No." said Marianne. "No, I didn't. But it does explain a few things."

On the Monday, Ana appeared at the dispatch box in the House of Commons. She was speaking on behalf of Her Majesty's Opposition in the housing benefit debate. Marianne and Ben watched from their screens in their office. Joni was elsewhere.

Ana spoke well to begin with. She stuck to the speech Ben had prepared for her. However, it was not long before she was discomfited by the Tory minister she shadowed. At one point, she quoted some facts and figures.

"Bloody hell!" exclaimed Ben. "That's not what I told her. Oh god, this is going to be a disaster. And she'll blame me."

She was duly corrected in the chamber. There was mirth and jeering from the Tory benches. The expressions of Ana's Labour colleagues ranged from glum to mortified. She became increasingly flustered but tried desperately to hide it.

"I'm just going to watch the rest of this from behind my hands" said Marianne. "It's not going to get any better."

It didn't. Ana continued to waffle and prevaricate. Her line of argument was incomprehensible. Marianne checked her Twitter feed. #AnaNovak was trending.

Then, things got much worse. In the chamber, Ana spoke into the microphone. "It is clear that this government is incapable of handing this crisis" she intoned. "It is happening *now*! They need to understand the *fierce urgency of now!*"

There was a brief moment of stunned silence.

"Fuck my life, she didn't just say that" said Marianne.

The jeers resumed and reached a crescendo.

Ben said "Just don't tell me what Twitter is saying. I don't want to know."

Marianne *did* look at Twitter. Within seconds, new memes had been created. They cruelly mocked Ana's attempt at rhetorical flourish. Many involved images of Barack Obama looking scornful. There were tens of thousands of tweets which essentially said the same thing: Ana was no Obama. One high-profile commentator tweeted: 'The only fierce urgency of now is that @JeremyCorbyn shuffles @AnaNovakMP off his front bench.'

Later that afternoon, Marianne's office 'phone rang. It was Ana.

"Get up here now" she hissed.

Feeling enormously apprehensive, Marianne went upstairs to her office. She knocked and went in. Ana was sitting at her desk. She seemed to be reclining as though she had a terrible headache. The only light in the office, on this gloomy February afternoon, came from her computer screen.

"Well thanks for fucking me over today" she snarled at Marianne.

"I don't know what you're talking about" replied Marianne. She said this with a coolness that surprised her.

Ana leaned forward. "You're on Twitter, aren't you" she said. "Are you telling me you haven't noticed that I'm being ripped to shreds?"

"Well, yes but…"

"The *fierce urgency of now*. It's almost like you knew.".

"Yes" said Marianne. "I knew it wasn't a good idea and I advised against it."

"No, you didn't" Ana insisted. "It was *your idea!*

"Hold on" said Marianne "It was Joni who…"

"DON'T FUCKING BLAME JONI!" screamed Ana. "Take some responsibility for once! Stop always trying to deflect blame. It's like Groundhog Day with you, isn't it? I just can't rely on you for anything. Just go. Just get out."

Marianne could see it was utterly pointless to remonstrate. She left and went back to her office in tears.

"Don't worry too much about it" Ben said when she told him. "She's just lashing out. She always does when things go wrong. I've been on the receiving end often enough."

Marianne did worry about it. She barely slept that night. After tossing and turning, she decided to hand in her notice the next morning. She went back to sleep.

She and Karen ate breakfast together at the kitchen table. Marianne told her about the events of the day before and of her decision to quit.

"Just don't do anything too hasty" Karen said. "Madam knows that it's her who fucked up royally. When you work for politicians, you can't take things too personally. Take it from me."

"I'm just not sure I'm cut out for this" said Marianne. "There are easier ways of making a living."

They were interrupted by the doorbell. Karen went to answer. Marianne could hear voices from the hallway. Pete Samuelson wheeled in a double buggy containing his twin baby daughters. He was wearing jogging gear.

"Pete's just come to drop off some forms" said Karen. "While he was out jogging, of course."

"You take your one-year old twins jogging with you?" Marianne asked, somewhat incredulous.

"It's called multitasking" said Pete. "I get the exercise that my Twitter fans tell me I need. And the twins get some fresh air. It's win-win."

"It's efficient" Marianne conceded.

Pete handed Karen some forms which she went through the motions of checking.

"Is it alright if I heat up the twins' bottles?" he asked her.

"Sure" she said. "You know where everything is".

He fished a couple of bottles out of a carrier bag.

"Can you guys to keep an eye on the bairns?" he asked them.

Marianne and Karen took a twin each. Peter heated up their bottles in a pan on the range. This took a few minutes.

"I'm glad I've caught you, Marianne" he said as he handed the twins their bottles. "I've been hoping to have a word."

"Oh?"

He sat down at the table. "We need your help with something."

He and Karen exchanged glances.

"Okay" said Marianne uncertainly.

There was something going on here.

"You're not a big Momentum fan, are you?" said Pete.

"I guess not."

"And you wouldn't want them taking over the local council. Because in your guts, you know their nuts".

He chuckled Muttley-style at this.

Karen cut to the chase. "This is about the regen partnership" she said. "As you know, they're using it as their Trojan horse. We think Ana and Joni are involved somehow. We just don't know *how* exactly."

"But we need to find out" said Pete.

The penny dropped.

"You mean you want *me* to find out" said Marianne. "You want me to spy on my own boss for you."

"Yes" said Pete.

"It's all in a good cause" Karen added.

"I must need my head read" said Marianne. "Because I'm already up to my eyes in shit. But I'll see what I can do."

Chapter Seven

"You have to give Ana some credit" said Ben. "She's certainly raised her game recently."

"True" said Marianne. She took a sip of her Sauvignon Blanc.

They were having their regular Friday evening drink in the House of Lords bar. Three weeks had passed since Ana's disaster at the dispatch box. Since then, she had avoided high profile media appearances. Instead, she immersed herself in her brief. She'd met with people who knew about housing; policy experts, campaigners and property developers.

"That article she wrote was good" Ben said. "The one for *the Local Government Chronicle*. It sounded like she knew what she was talking about."

"Well *you* did the research for that" said Marianne. "So it ought to sound *authoritative."*

Ben swirled the contents of his glass. "I've certainly been kept busy" he said.

This was an understatement.

"At least she's stopped trying to channel Obama." Marianne giggled. "I can't believe she tried to blame me for that."

"Oh, I can."

"She seems over it now though. She's fine with me at the moment."

Ana had bounced back quickly. She hadn't apologised to Marianne for berating her. Still, she just hadn't mentioned it. She had returned to being reasonably pleasant and polite. It was as if nothing had happened.

Ben said: "The baton of blame has passed. To me."

Marianne was aware that Ben had been frequently summoned to Ana's office. He would return looking browbeaten. She could imagine why.

"Does she say stuff to you like "*I can't rely on you for anything*"?" she asked.

"*All the time*. It's like her catchphrase. She has another one which…"

Marianne shrieked "I know the one!"

She and Ben said in unison: "It's just not fucking good enough!"

Marianne performed an impression of Ana. "I can't rely on you for anything. It's just not fucking good enough" she mimicked.

The wine, and the look on Ben's face, encouraged her to repeat it.

"I can't rely on you for anything. It's just not fucking good enough."

They were both hysterical now. Tears of laughter cascaded down their faces. Marianne was feeling lightheaded from the wine. She wondered if they were being a bit indiscreet.

"I feel awful saying this" she said. "But our boss is a bit of a monster, isn't she?"

"Hmmm" said Ben.

Marianne drained her glass. "What about Joni?"

"What about her?"

"Is she immune from the baton of blame? It definitely seems like Ana tries to keep her sweet because of Momentum."

"I think that's the idea" said Ben. "But, I think she might have made a rod for her own back."

"What do you mean?"

Ben put his glass down. "Present company excluded" he said. "I think Ana's wrong to employ local activists. In my experience, it can lead to all sorts of complications…and conflicts of interest."

"In other words, she shouldn't hire people she has to be nice to" said Marianne.

"Well, yes."

They decided against ordering a second bottle. Marianne went home to Karen's house. She was disappointed to find that both Karen and Daniel were out. She opened a carton of soup and heated it up on the range.

Karen and Daniel had made her feel very welcome. She had been there nearly a month now. The space and comfort of the house still felt like a luxury. It was many years since she had had her own bedroom. She enjoyed using the well-appointed kitchen even though cooking wasn't one of her passions.

She ate her soup with bread at the kitchen table. However, she didn't like eating alone in the evening. It wasn't as though she was entirely without companionship. It was more that she missed that sense of a shared life.

She said to herself *I miss Euan.*

After she'd eaten, she pulled her 'phone out of her bag. She gazed at Euan's number for a few moments before calling him.

"Hello" she said when he answered.

"Hello" he replied.

There was a pause. They had spoken many times over the 'phone since she left. Their conversations were punctuated by a strange combination of awkwardness and ease, strangeness and familiarity.

"How are things?" she asked.

"Good. Still missing you though."

They had met up a couple of times since she'd moved out. The first time, they'd had a Sunday pub lunch. A week later, they'd gone to the cinema. Euan had walked her home to Karen's afterwards. She'd kissed him goodnight. It had felt like a date and like a casual night out with an old friend. Their conversation had been light. They hadn't talked about why Marianne had left.

"I miss you too" she said.

"Do you want to do something next week?" he suggested. "I was thinking of dinner at that fish restaurant we went to."

"That would be lovely" she said. "Erm…is next Friday any good?"

"Perfect. I'll book a table for eight o'clock."

"Looking forward to it."

She meant it. A romantic, candlelit meal would be just what she and Euan needed. Time apart had clearly done them both good. She had even stopped smoking altogether. Soon, she could go home and things could return to normal. There was a path back. The prospect made her feel quite elated.

On Monday afternoon, Marianne was in the office with Ben and Joni. She was updating Ana's diary. Ben was trying to concentrate on something. Joni was on the 'phone trying to arrange an appointment with her gynaecologist.

"I don't think you understand" she said to the receptionist. "I work in parliament for a shadow minister."

That doesn't make your cervix special Marianne said inwardly.

"No, I can't come at 6pm" Joni insisted down the 'phone. "My working hours won't permit it."

You are fucking kidding me thought Marianne. *You've never been seen at work after 4pm.*

Ben was frowning in irritation. Joni's 'phone call had broken his concentration. Marianne would like to have exchanged eye-rolls. However, this was too difficult with Joni sat directly opposite.

"But I work in parliament for a shadow minister" Joni told the receptionist again.

For fucks sake! You're not that important. Marianne hissed inwardly.

Her desk 'phone rang. It was Ana.

"Hiya" she said breezily. "I need you to squeeze a meeting into my diary. Preferably late afternoon next week. It's the Greenwood Housing Collective. Thought I'd give them tea afterwards. I'll forward you the e-mail so you can liaise."

"Sure" said Marianne.

She hadn't heard of the Greenwood Housing Collective before. However, the e-mail Ana forwarded explained a great deal. It was from Ned Critchley-Smith. He and other members of Global Solidarity had formed a new group. Ana had agreed to their request to a meeting. She'd also invited them to tea in the Pugin Room.

Pete will be very interested Marianne thought to herself.

She began an e-mail to Ned to offer a date and time. Joni had finished with her gynaecologist's receptionist. Marianne hadn't heard whether she'd got the appointment she wanted.

She was interrupted by her mobile ringing. It was Karen so she answered.

"Hi Marianne" said Karen. "I'm in A&E with Bridget. We've had a bit of an accident in the car."

"Oh God!" said Marianne, alarmed. "Are you alright?"

"I'm fine" Karen told her. "They've checked me out. Just a few cuts and bruises. But they're doing some tests on Bridget and I'm going to wait here with her. I just called to ask if you'd mind feeding Dan when he comes in from football. Just do some oven chips or something."

"Yes. Yes, of course. Are you in Greenwood A&E? I'm going to come down."

"You don't have to do that" Karen said. "I don't want to get you in strife with Madam."

"Don't worry about that" said Marianne. "I'll handle her. I can be there in about an hour."

Marianne called Ana and told her about the accident.

"Do you know what happened?" Ana asked. She sounded very concerned.

"I don't know the details" Marianne told her. "But I think they're okay. I'd like to go down to A&E to see them."

"Yes, of course. Absolutely!" said Ana. "I would come with you myself. But I'm doing a 'phone interview with the local paper."

"Oh, don't worry" Marianne said

"Let me know if there's anything I can do" said Ana. "Tell you what. Get Ben to dig out the office laptop. You can take it with you and do some work while you're there."

Marianne spent over an hour travelling to the hospital by tube and by bus. The accident was hardly surprising, she thought. Given Karen's driving, it was amazing it hadn't happened before. Marianne was worried about Bridget. She was undoubtedly fit and energetic for someone, she believed to be, in her late sixties. She had the litheness of a teenage boy. Still, there was no way of knowing how she'd be affected by a car accident.

When she arrived at A&E, she was directed to a cubicle where she found Bridget and Karen. Bridget was sitting up in bed. Karen was perched on a chair next to her. They both seemed to be in high spirits and pleased to see her.

"What *have* you to been up to?" asked Marianne.

Karen explained. They'd been out delivering leaflets that morning. Karen had been driving them around in her car. Another car had appeared out of nowhere and sped towards them on the wrong side of the road. Karen swerved to avoid it bringing her own car to a juddering halt. Bridget had banged her head on the dashboard. They found out later that the other car had been stolen by teenage joyriders. The police were coming to take a statement.

Marianne felt awful. She'd assumed that Karen's driving had caused the accident. In fact, her quick reflexes had saved them from something far worse.

"It's not all bad" said Karen. "Bridget has enjoyed the ministrations of *Dishy Doctor Sam.*"

"Oh Karen!" said Bridget. "Don't take any notice of her, Marianne. Dr Sam is just a very nice young man."

Karen sniggered. "Yeah, but if you were thirty years younger…"

"Twenty" said Bridget.

They giggled.

Schoolgirls! Marianne said to herself. *I bet he's just some braying public school rugger bugger.*

The curtain opened. Dishy Doctor Sam himself appeared. He was wearing dark blue scrubs and a stephoscope. On first sighting, Marianne thought his sobriquet justified. His close-cropped grey hair was vaguely evocative of George Clooney.

Then she recognised him.

"Mr Al-Nawazi" she said.

His name-badge read 'Dr Sam Al-Nawazi: Senior House Officer'.

He looked at her, surprised. "Yes" he said.

Karen and Bridget exchanged glances.

"We've met before" said Marianne. "Marianne Stuart. I work in Ana Novak's office."

"Oh yes, of course" he said, smiling warmly. "I remember. In fact, I have a great deal to thank you for."

"Really?"

"Yes. You helped with my immigration status. It meant that I could get this job."

"Are you sure that's something to be thankful for?"

They laughed.

"Most days" he said. He turned his attention to Bridget. "Right. Everything seems fine. No sign of concussion. You might have a bit of whiplash. We do want to X-ray you though."

"Fine" said Bridget.

"One of the nurses will take you down there in a bit" he told her.

The curtain opened again. A portly, middle-aged policeman came in. He'd come to take statements.

"If it's a bad time, I can come back" he said.

"No, I'd rather do this now" said Bridget. "If that's alright with you, doctor?"

"Of course. I'll get them to hold off with the X-ray."

He left the cubicle.

"I'm going to go away for an hour" said Marianne. "I'll go and have a coffee and do some work. Ana gave me the office laptop to use."

"Madam is all heart" said Karen.

Marianne found the hospital canteen. It was almost empty and brightly lit by late afternoon sunshine. She bought a coffee and found a table. Opening up the laptop, she tried to find a wi-fi connection.

"Mind if I join you?" said a voice.

She looked up to find Dr Sam Al-Nawazi standing in front of her holding a coffee cup.

"No, not at all" she replied.

"Thanks." He sat down opposite her.

Marianne felt there was something she needed to say. "Mr Al-Nawazi…sorry, *Doctor* Al-Nawazi…"

"Please, just call me Sam" he said.

"Okay, *Sam"* said Marianne. "I'd just like to say that I am really sorry about the way the Syria vote went."

"Don't be. You didn't vote in it."

"Yes, I know" said Marianne. "But you were led to believe Ana was going to vote for intervention."

"Yes, that was disappointing" he said. "Still, it's very hard to hold a grudge against Ms Novak. Not after all her help. It's because of her I'm here…and you of course"

"That I *am* pleased about" Marianne said. "It's great that the NHS benefits from having you. You have all the right language skills too. In fact, you speak English with barely a hint of an accent."

"I was at boarding school over here" he told her. "And I read medicine at Imperial College."

Marianne was intrigued. "What made you go back to Syria?" she asked.

"Good question" he said. "Lots of reasons, I guess. Family was a major one. And, I wanted to use my skills in my own country."

Marianne knew his wife had also been a doctor. She wondered where they'd met. However, she felt she couldn't probe.

He really is rather hot she thought to herself. *Amazing I didn't notice before.*

Her mobile rang. It was Ana. She pressed the 'decline' button. Whatever she wanted, it could wait.

"Hope that wasn't important" said Sam.

"It wasn't" she said. She took a sip of her coffee. "You know, you are probably one of our great casework successes."

Sam laughed.

"That's good to know" he said. "As it happens, I now do quite a bit of casework myself. Outside of work."

"Really? How come?"

"I'm involved with a local Syrian refugee group" he told her. "I make all sorts of representations for them."

"Well, if there's anything we can do to help" said Marianne "you should let us know. I say *we* but I really mean Ana."

Sam breathed in. "That's a bit awkward" he said.

"Oh?" said Marianne. "Because of the Syria vote?"

"No, not at all" he assured her. "I approached your office a couple of months ago about something else."

"And?"

"And I dealt with Mrs Lessing."

"Joni?"

"Yes, Joni." He was clearly uncomfortable relating this.

What the fuck had Joni done?

"Was she helpful?" asked Marianne although she already knew the answer.

"Not *exactly*" he said. "She invited me out for a drink. I only went because I thought she was interested in my casework."

"And wasn't she?"

"Hard to tell. We never got around to discussing it. She insisted on just talking about her marital problems. Her very *intimate* marital problems."

"Yes, she does rather overshare sometimes" said Marianne. "What did you do?"

"I made my excuses and left" he said. "I thought that was it. Then she started bombarding me with text messages."

"About what?" Marianne was appalled.

"Mainly trying to get me to go for another drink with her. Then she started complaining about a rash on her chest. She wanted *me* to examine it! I told her to go to her GP. She then told me she would send a photo."

"Christ almighty!" Marianne spluttered. "That's a bit forward. Even for her."

"That's what I thought" said Sam. "So I blocked her number."

"I am so sorry" said Marianne. "I don't know *why* I'm apologising for her but…"

She was interrupted by her mobile ringing again. Ana had called back. The ring tone had a nagging, plaintive sound. She'd decided she'd better answer.

"Hi Ana" she said.

"Marianne! This is the fifth time I've tried to call you." Ana sounded like she was spitting with fury. "You're not on holiday. It's just not fucking good enough."

"I'm just here talking to Mr Al-Nawazi, Ana" said Marianne.

There was a silence.

"Oh" said Ana. She didn't know what to say.

Sam could hear all of this. He smiled his warm open smile. However, there was a conspiratorial gleam in the corners of his dark eyes. Marianne smirked back.

Ana clearly wanted to change the subject. "I'm calling about the Japanese knotweed letter" she said. "Have you done it?"

Shit, shit, shitty fuck! She'd forgotten all about it.

"Yes" she said. "I'll bring it up to you to sign first thing in the morning".

"Okay, see you tomorrow" Ana said briskly.

"Before you go, Ana" interjected Marianne before she could hang up.

"Yes?"

"Bridget and Karen are both fine, by the way."

"Thank God!" said Ana. "I've been so worried".

She hung up.

Marianne and Sam looked at each other and laughed.

"Important call from the boss" she said.

"So I heard."

Marianne shut her laptop. She wasn't going to be doing any work that afternoon.

"Is Ms Novak a Remainer?" Sam asked.

He was referring to the upcoming referendum. In a few months, the British people would decide whether to stay in the European Union.

"I believe she is" said Marianne. "I know that I am. In fact, it's something I feel very passionately about. I love having an EU passport. I did French as part of my degree."

"It's a passion of mine too" said Sam. "I'm also involved with an organisation called 'Doctors for EU'. We're having a fundraiser this Friday. Why don't you come along?"

"Oh I..."

"I have some free tickets" he told her. "You can bring your two friends. There's a buffet, free drinks and karaoke. But we have a band rather than a karaoke machine."

"Are you going to be singing?" asked Marianne.

Sam smiled. "One way for you to find out" he said. "I can e-mail the tickets to you."

"Okay" said Marianne. "I will see if Karen and Bridget are up for it. I'll let you know."

The next morning, Marianne got into the office early. She dashed off the letter about Japanese knotweed and gave it to Ana to sign. She then finished and sent her e-mail to Ned Critchley-Smith. Joni arrived about half-past ten. Ben was spending the morning in the House of Commons library.

Shortly before lunch, Marianne's mobile beeped. She'd received a Twitter notification. Joni's phone had also beeped. They both looked at their screens. A feed called 'Greenwood Trot Watch' had tagged them into the same tweet.

It read: '*Hope @AnaNovakMP realises that partying with the Global Solidarity Group involves serious *group participation**'.'

Marianne knew exactly what they were referring to. Still, she was disconcerted. Who was behind this? Since joining Twitter, she'd learnt the Greenwood local politics was a vipers' nest of cyber activity. Anonymous feeds would spring up and snipe on behalf of their faction. Each side strived to outdo each other in their viciousness.

She and Joni looked at each other.

"Is this a friend of yours?" asked Joni.

"I beg your pardon!" Marianne said indignantly

She could feel her body tightening with outrage. This accusation was unfair and arbitrary.

"Well, it's clear whose side they're on" said Joni

"I don't like anonymous Twitter trolls" Marianne told her firmly. "I don't know who it is and I don't have any sympathy with them."

“It’s utterly disgraceful” said Joni. “They’re trying to ruin the reputations of young, idealistic activists.”

“Well, the rumours are out there” Marianne heard herself mutter

She immediately wished she’d stopped the words escaping from her mouth. She should have just agreed with Joni. It would save a lot of hassle.

Joni fixed her unblinking stare on her.

“You know, Marianne” she said in her low monotone. “Rumours are manufactured. When one discusses *rumours*, one becomes complicit in their dissemination. Wouldn’t you agree?”

“Absolutely” said Marianne. She was going to shut this down.

Joni, however, wasn’t going to let this slide. “I would like to tell you the facts about those *rumours*.”

Now who’s gossiping? Marianne said inwardly.

“Global Solidarity are just like any other group of young people” said Joni. “They like their drinking and their partying. They invite their mates round to drink with them and maybe they’re a bit loud sometimes.”

Christ, she’s not going to give details about the orgies, is she? Marianne wondered. *I don’t think I can cope with that.*

Joni carried on: “They had a party at their house last summer” she said. “They invited people on Facebook. Anyhow, they were gate-crashed by people they didn’t know. A whole load of 18 to 30s showed up and invaded the house. They’d come back from Faliraki or Malaga or somewhere and were tooled up with alcohol and

God knows what else. That's when you got people misbehaving in the back garden in front of the neighbours."

"I see" said Marianne.

She thought Joni's version of events had a certain plausibility. Try as she might, she couldn't really imagine Ned and the others involved in drugs-fuelled orgies.

"I just thought you should know the facts" said Joni.

"Thanks, Joni. I agree with you about discussing rumours. I won't be mentioning it again to anyone."

Joni seemed pleased by this. Finally, there was peace. They carried on working in an almost companionable silence.

A new e-mail pinged into her inbox. It was from Sam. The tickets to the fundraiser were attached. Marianne knew she wanted to go. There was just one problem. It was on the same night she'd agreed to have dinner with Euan.

The next evening, Marianne went to a local party meeting. In the pub afterwards, she and Pete Samuelson had a chat by the bar. He'd been given a rough ride over the Greenwood Regeneration Partnership. Marianne told him about the meeting Ana had arranged with Ned .

"Any chance you can get in on it?" he asked.

Marianne looked at him. "Might be a bit obvious" she said.

"I suppose" he conceded.

She changed the subject.

“Have you come across a Twitter account called ‘Greenwood Trot Watch’?” she asked.

She really wondered if he was behind it.

Pete chuckled Muttley-style. “No, but I like the sound of it though. Why? What have they done?”

“They’ve only tweeted Ana about the *alleged* Global Solidarity orgies. Joni and I were copied in too.”

“No! Fuck me!” Pete was clearly delighted by this.

“The worst part about it” Marianne said “is that Joni insisted on explaining what she says are the *facts*. Apparently, they had a perfectly innocent party which was gate-crashed.”

“She would say that” said Pete “Joni’s not exactly a reliable source. She’s way too pally with them. In fact, she probably goes round to their house to hang out…smokes a reefer…gets her tits out…”

Well, she sort of has form for that Marianne said to herself. However, she decided not to share this with Pete.

“You *are* going to go the Hell” she told him.

“Eventually” he said, with a hint of triumph.

On Friday evening, Marianne was in her bedroom at Karen’s getting ready to go out. She had opted for a little black dress. Her makeup was done. She was undecided between a red pair of high-heels or a black pair. She tried on the red pair and inspected her full-length reflection. Karen knocked and came in.

“Can I ask your honest opinion?” Marianne asked her.

“That’s all you’re going to get.”

“Do these shoes look a bit…slutty?”

“They are definitely “fuck me” shoes” Karen told her. “Still, if that’s the signal you want to give Dishy Doctor Sam…”

“It really isn’t” said Marianne. She put on the black pair instead.

They were going to the fundraiser. To her surprise, Karen and Bridget had been keen to go. However, she’d had to endure merciless ribbing from Karen about Sam.

More uncomfortably, she’d had to call Euan to cancel their dinner date. She gave him some vague excuse about a work do. She said it had been in the diary for weeks but she’d overlooked it. He’d made a valiant attempt at being understanding but his disappointment was palpable. She felt sad and guilty. Still, she found it surprisingly difficult to dwell on it for very long.

“Hope you’re nearly ready, Cinderella” said Karen. “Bridget is about five minutes away in the Uber.”

The taxi delivered the three of them to the venue. It was the same hotel Marianne had been with Ana months earlier for the Greenwood Polish Business Guild function. She felt she was infinitely better dressed this time.

A much bigger room was being used for the fundraiser. There must have been about a hundred people milling around when they arrived. Many were already seated around tables draped with white table cloths. A podium had been set up for the band in front of an empty dance floor. Above it, a banner emblazoned with

'Doctors 4 EU' hung like a flag. Once again, there were teenage waiting staff proffering glasses of Champagne.

Marianne's eyes sought out Sam. She soon spotted him talking in a small crowd on the other side of the room. He looked dapper in a navy blazer, white shirt and dark grey jeans. When he saw them, he came over, smiling. He kissed Marianne on both cheeks and shook hands with Karen and Bridget.

"Delighted you could make it" he said. "If you feel the urge to sing, there's a sheet next to the stage. You just need to write your name down and the tune."

"I'm not sure I've quite recovered enough for *that*" Bridget said.

"Might need a bit more alcohol" said Karen.

The three of them had been allocated to a table. Marianne was a little disappointed to find Sam wasn't on it. The crowd on their table were older, pleasant if a little reserved. Bridget, however, got on like a house on fire with the woman sat next to her, a doughty looking oncologist. She'd grown up in Edinburgh too. They were soon immersed in conversation about their home town.

Both Marianne and Karen drunk a lot rather quickly. This was in contrast to Bridget who'd had only a few sips of wine the whole evening. Karen helped herself to food from the buffet. Marianne wasn't hungry. The band started up. Different guests took to the microphone to give renditions of their favourite songs. The quality varied considerably but the dance floor quickly filled.

"Fancy a boogie?" Karen suggested to Marianne.

Bridget was deep in conversation with her new friend about Edinburgh property prices.

"Yeah, why not" said Marianne.

They got up and ventured onto the dance floor. The last act was just finishing. Sam then appeared onstage. He'd taken off his jacket.

"Oh look" said Karen. "Dishy Doctor Sam has come to serenade you."

"I've never been serenaded in my life" said Marianne. "Well, not by anybody who can actually sing."

"Go Sammy!" someone yelled.

The band began playing. Sam sang into the microphone.

"*Well she was an American girl,*

Raised on promises,

She couldn't help thinkin',

That there was a little more to life somewhere else,

After all it was a great big world,

With lots of places to run to"

He was covering 'American Girl' by Tom Petty and the Heartbreakers. Marianne and Karen swayed along on the dance floor.

"He is actually rather good" Karen said at one point.

Marianne agreed. Sam's singing voice was tuneful. However, it also had a raw, spirited quality which added something to the song. Marianne found it particularly affecting. That was because she knew his story.

How can he get up there and sing like that? she asked herself. *He's endured so much pain.*

The others on the dancefloor were clearly enjoying it. Some energetically sang along.

"*Oh yeah, all right,*

Take it easy, baby,

Make it all last night,

She was an American girl"

Sam seemed to glance over at her at one point. When he finished, the dance floor loudly expressed its appreciation with claps, cheers and whoops.

"Right, I can't dance anymore" said Karen. "I'm getting too old."

They headed back to their table. Marianne became conscious of a presence behind her. She knew it was Sam.

"Would you like to dance?" he murmured in her ear.

Marianne stopped and looked at Karen.

"You go" Karen said.

"Erm, yes. Sure" Marianne replied to Sam.

She followed him back onto the dancefloor. A moustached consultant was on stage. He was singing 'Smoke Gets In Your Eyes' by the Platters. Marianne didn't really know how to dance properly but she let Sam lead. They danced slowly. She could feel his body under his shirt. For such an ostensibly wiry man, he was surprisingly sinewy and muscly.

When the song finished, Marianne felt someone touch her shoulder. It was Karen. She could see Bridget standing at the edge of the dancefloor.

“We’re heading off” Karen told her. “Bridget and I are way past our bedtimes. Unlike you young people. Make sure you get a taxi home.

“Oh, I will” Marianne said.

Karen was not sufficiently reassured by this.

“If I find out you’ve walked, I will properly lose my shit with you” she said.

“Don’t worry” said Marianne. “I know better than to incur your wrath.”

She and Sam danced to another song. At one point they took a break from the dance floor. He introduced her to a boisterous group of junior doctors he worked with. They were knocking back Champagne. Marianne helped herself to another glass.

She found the junior doctors noisy but fun. They teased “Sammy” for being in their ranks at the age of 40. Still, he was clearly more than capable of dealing with med school banter.

Marianne dragged Sam back onto the dancefloor when she heard a song she liked. They carried on dancing through many more numbers, energetic and slow. Eventually the band stopped playing.

“What time is it?” she asked.

He looked at his watch. “About half-past three in the morning.”

“Bloody hell!” said Marianne. “I had no idea it was that time.”

The lights in the function room went up. The stragglers slowly began dispersing. Marianne and Sam went with the junior doctors to an all-night café nearby. A few of them ordered fry-up breakfasts. They were still noisy and high-spirited. Sam just drank black coffee.

"Won't the caffeine keep you awake?" Marianne asked him.

"I hope so" he said. "I'm back on duty at 9am."

"You *are* kidding me?"

He shook his head.

"Will you be alright to work?"

"Yes" he said. "I'm quite used to sleepless nights. It's good training for A&E."

He looked at his watch.

"My car is nearby" he said. "I can drop you home or..."

"Or?"

"I like to go for a drive early in the morning" he told her. "I go to Richmond Park and see the deer. It clears my head. Would *you* like to come?"

Marianne considered this for a moment.

"Okay" she said. "That would be nice."

They slipped away from the café. He offered his arm to her and walked slowly because she was tottering along on heels. His car was parked a few streets away. It was a black convertible jeep with a left-hand steering wheel.

"Wow! The Sam-mobile is quite something" said Marianne.

"It gets me around." He opened the passenger door, on the right-hand side of the car, for her.

It was unseasonably mild for an early morning in late March. Sam wound down the roof of the jeep. He fiddled with his iPod. Music started playing on the speakers and they drove off. Once they were outside Greenwood, he drove much, much faster. Marianne found it exhilarating. She felt the wind blow in her face and through her hair.

The iPod began playing 'Dakota' by the Stereophonics.

"*Thinking back, thinking of you,*

Summertime think it was June,

Yeah think it was June"

"I love this song!" said Marianne.

Sam was tapping his fingers against the steering wheel. "Me too" he said.

They sang along to the chorus together.

"*You made me feel like the one,*

Made me feel like the one"

They exchanged glances. Marianne raised her arms euphorically into the air.

"*The one,*

You made me feel like the one,

Made me feel like the one

The one

I don't know where we are going now

I don't know where we are going now"

They sped towards Richmond Park as the sun was rising. The world seemed very vivid and colourful.

Chapter Eight

"I've met someone else" Marianne told Euan.

"But you said there wasn't anybody." He looked at her accusingly.

They were sitting in a greasy spoon near the flat. Marianne had wanted to meet somewhere neutral. It was a Friday evening. Three weeks had passed since Marianne had cancelled their dinner date.

"There wasn't" she said. "Not at the time."

"*When* did you meet them then?" he asked.

He looked at her for a moment waiting for a response.

"Who is it anyway?"

There was a part of Marianne that desperately wanted to tell him about Sam. She wanted him to be happy for her. Still, this was probably a bit unreasonable under the circumstances. It might also be unwise. She had discussed the case of Mr Al-Nawazi with him months earlier. He might think the whole thing improper.

"It doesn't matter" she said.

"It does to me."

Marianne sighed. "I don't want to get into it, Euan. The point is...the point is I'm not coming back."

"Is that it? Is that all you can say after ten years? After everything?"

Marianne could feel the hurt and the incomprehension in his voice.

"This hasn't come out of nowhere" she said. "We've been growing apart for a while now. You know that."

They sat in silence for a moment. Marianne found their surroundings bleak and oppressive. The grey gloominess of the evening seeped into the café. She wanted to escape.

"I'll come over to pick up my stuff" she said. "Just let me know when. I'm still at Karen's."

"Fine. Whatever" he replied. "Thanks for the coffee. I'll see you around."

He got up to leave and did his best to saunter out coolly.

Marianne waited before leaving herself. She felt sadness but no regret. She tried, out of loyalty, to reflect on her years with Euan. However, they seemed to recede faster and further into a hazy past. She was on her way to meet Sam. They were going to Ronnie Scott's Jazz Club in Soho. All she wanted to think about was the future.

The next morning, she woke up in Sam's flat. She had spent the night there. He was already up and in the kitchen. The smell of baking and fresh coffee pervaded. She reached for her 'phone on the bedside table. It was after 9am. She supposed she ought to get up.

Sam's flat was small, spartan and monochrome. It was also conveniently near the hospital. He seemed to have little in the way of personal effects. However, he did keep a framed photo of his wife and two children on the bedside table. Marianne picked it up and studied it.

She had the impression it was from a holiday. They were outdoors, smiling and casually dressed. Sam's wife was very slim, in her mid-thirties and wore her hair in a ponytail. Marianne imagined her to have the brisk confidence of an accomplished professional woman. His son, who must have been about ten, looked like a miniature version of him. They had the same easy smile. The daughter, who was younger, seemed to resemble her mother.

Marianne put the photo back and got out of bed. Her clothes were strewn over the floor. She couldn't be bothered getting dressed. Instead, she put on the blue shirt Sam had worn the night before. It still smelt of his aftershave.

In the open plan living area. Sam pulled a tray of baking out of the oven. He was wearing a white towelling robe.

"I hope you're hungry" he said when she came in. "I've made breakfast."

"It smells absolutely wonderful" said Marianne. "Whatever it is."

"Blueberry muffins. I used to do them for the kids sometimes" he told her. "They used to love them."

It was the first time he had mentioned his children. Marianne thought about the photo on the bedside table. She wanted him to talk more about them but she was instinctively reluctant to push it.

He'll open up to me in time she told herself.

"Help yourself to coffee" he said. "The Saturday papers are on the table."

"Lovely. Thank you".

She poured herself a mug of coffee and sat down at the little round table. She opened up *the Guardian.* The first story she read was about the London Mayoral election.

“This is absolutely outrageous” she said, scowling at the page.

“What’s that?”

He handed her a plate and fork.

“It’s the Tories” she said. “They’re trying to paint Sadiq Khan as some sort of terrorist. It just reeks of Islamophobia, if you ask me”

Sam sat down at the table. “Well, it’s desperate stuff” he said. “It won’t work though.”

“I’m not so sure. The Tories have done well out of negative campaigning. They’re really good at using Facebook. That’s why they won the election last year.”

“Yes, but I think they’ve got it very wrong this time” he said. “One thing I know is that London *isn’t* England. It’s a liberal city. I think you’re right about the Islamophobia but I think it’s backfiring on them.”

“I hope you’re right” said Marianne.

“There’s no question in my mind. Sadiq *will* win. It’s just a question of by how much. Obviously, I want it to be *this* much.”

He held his hands very far apart to demonstrate the point.

“Do you?” asked Marianne.

“Of course” he said.

“Really?”

"Absolutely" he assured her.

Marianne smiled at him sweetly. "You know that you can help make that happen, don't you?"

He raised his eyebrows. "You mean I should go canvassing with you?" he said.

"*Only* if you feel strongly."

He thought about this for a moment.

"I can't do tomorrow because I'm working" he said. "When are you next going?"

"Thursday evening."

"Okay, I'm not working then so I can't get out of it. Consider it a date."

"Who says romance is dead?" said Marianne.

On the Monday, she had another vexing, irritating day at work. She arrived in the office at 8am. Ana had demanded a three-page briefing about badgers. This was because of a letter from an obsessed constituent.

"She's literally badgering me about badgers" Marianne said to Ben.

Joni appeared around 9.30am. She was carrying multiple bags, as was her habit.

"Morning team" she trilled.

She sat down at her desk and switched on her computer.

"I've come in early for a special reason" she told them, looking very pleased with herself.

It might be early for you Marianne said inwardly *but some of us have to work for a living. So don't take the piss.*

"Sounds intriguing" said Ben.

"Ana and I have been working on a statement over the weekend" Joni said. "I'm going to upload it to her website now."

She was clearly excited about this.

"What's it about?" Marianne asked.

"The Greenwood Regeneration Partnership" replied Joni. "I'll tell you when it's up."

What fresh hell is this? Marianne wondered.

Joni hammered away at her keyboard for about half an hour.

"Right" she said when she'd finished. "Check. It. Out."

Marianne and Ben were both curious. Almost in tandem, they accessed Ana's website. Marianne's mouth dropped slightly open when she read it.

It was an open letter from Ana to Pete Samuelson. She was imploring him to pause the Regeneration Project immediately. The letter was lengthy with numerous clauses. However, the last paragraph summarised its purpose.

'*I do not believe the legitimate concerns of the local community have been adequately addressed. In addition to reiterating these concerns, I write today with the utmost urgency to urge caution and call on you to pause and reflect further on whether entering into a public-private partnership is the correct decision for the Borough and its residents.*'

Marianne was certain Ana hadn't raised this with Pete privately. She was also conscious that she was now challenging him publicly and directly. Relations between them were already frosty but this was a declaration of war.

Joni seemed positively gleeful. "Please help get the message out on Twitter" she said. "Ask your friends to retweet."

Like fuck! Marianne said inwardly.

She wondered what Pete's initial reaction would be. She found out that evening when he came over to Karen's.

"Ana is a fucking cunt!" he thundered.

"Yes, we know" said Karen.

Pete was pacing up and down the kitchen. He was deeply agitated. Karen and Marianne were sitting at the table, sharing a bottle of red wine. Pete had declined their offer of a glass.

"I'll tell you what this is about" he said. "She's trying to take me out."

"Possibly" said Karen. "But I think this is about her trying to curry favour with the activists."

"Well if she wants a fight, she can have a bare knuckle one" he hissed.

Karen looked at him. "What are you going to do, Pete?"

"I'm going to call her out. She's in cahoots with the far left. And I'm going to publicly call her out on it."

Karen and Marianne exchanged glances. Pete paused for a moment before turning his attention to Marianne.

"What about you, Marianne?" he said. "I thought you were going to do some digging for us"

"And I did" she replied.

"You've found about one shitty little meeting" he snarled. "With Global Solidarity. Big whoop! Is that the best you can do?"

"Pete!" snapped Karen. "You really need to calm down. There's no point having a go at Marianne…"

"No, it's fine" Marianne said. "Pete, two things. Yes, I'll help but I draw the line at getting myself fired. Secondly, Ana doesn't trust me. It limits what I can find out"

Pete looked exasperated by this.

Marianne added "She thinks I'm too close to you and Karen."

He rolled his eyes.

"Pete" said Karen firmly. "You need to listen to me. If you go head-to-head with Ana on this, *you will* lose. She has the support of the Party and you don't."

"The Party has been taken over!" he bellowed.

"Yes! Yes, it has!" Karen cried. "I know! I'm the paid bloody organiser. I work with the members, day in and day out."

"So what are you saying? That we just surrender to these people!"

"No, that is not what I'm saying" said Karen. "I'm saying we can't pick battles we can't win. We have to get smarter. You won't like me saying this but we have to find a way of working with them."

"Sounds like surrender to me." He puffed out his cheeks. "Anyway, I've got to go. It's my turn to bath the twins."

He saw himself out, somewhat huffily. The tension followed him out the front door.

Karen topped up their glasses. "I had to be straight-up with him" she said after he'd gone.

"Yes, you did."

"Pete really doesn't help himself" said Karen. "He *is* a bruiser and he has absolutely no fear of confrontation"

"No kidding".

"It hasn't always been a bad thing" Karen said. He's managed to get a tight grip on the Council. Greenwood used to have a terrible reputation for being a loony left borough. He's put an end to a lot of nonsense."

"He is fundamentally decent, I think" said Marianne. "Underneath his bullish exterior. Why else would we put up with him?"

"Well quite." Karen took a sip of her wine. "The problem is that the dynamics of the Party have changed. He can't call the shots like he used to or get all aggro if he doesn't get his way."

"You mean we need to use more *soft* power" said Marianne.

"Exactly."

"And *information* is power."

"Indeed" said Karen. "Do you have a cunning plan?"

"I'm just thinking about what I said to Pete" said Marianne. "Things are difficult because Ana doesn't trust me."

"And?"

"I need to regain her confidence, rebuild her trust. To do that, I'd have to become more of an employee and less of an activist. I need to step back a bit from the Party"

"I see you're where you're going with this" said Karen.

In the office, the next morning, Marianne took the 'badger' letter upstairs for Ana to sign. It was overdue. She hoped she wouldn't notice.

As Ana glanced over the text, Marianne said: "I thought your letter to Pete was absolutely bang-on."

"Oh?" said Ana looking up. She scrutinised Marianne's face for a moment.

"Yes, I've always had doubts about the regen partnership" Marianne said.

This seemed to please Ana. She gestured at the chair in front of her desk.

"Sit down" she said.

Marianne sunk into the chair.

"I'm glad that we're on the same page about this" said Ana. "It's important that our little team functions as one."

Wowzers, that was easy Marianne thought. *She fell for it. Hook, line and sinker.*

"I totally agree" she said to Ana. "When things change, we have to change with them."

Ana smiled. "Exactly. I think Greenwood Council is in a bit of a rut. There's no innovation. It would benefit from…some new leadership.

So she does want to get rid of Pete Marianne said to herself.

"You know, Marianne" said Ana. "There's a reason I hired you. You're very perceptive and you can see the bigger picture."

Marianne didn't know how to respond to this. She wasn't used to such praise.

"Oh, well" she said bashfully.

"I think it's time I started making better use of you" Ana said. "Are you free on Thursday afternoon?"

"Erm, I'm sure I can be." Marianne knew full well this wasn't really a question.

"I'm doing a pop-up surgery" Ana said. "On one of the estates earmarked for regeneration. A BBC news crew is coming. It would be good to have you with me."

This is new Marianne thought.

"I'd love to" she said to Ana.

When she went back to her office, Ben was at his desk. Joni was elsewhere.

"You're looking pleased with yourself" he told her.

"I've had a bit of realisation" she said.

"Oh, really? Do share."

"Our boss is a bit of a monster and a nightmare to work for."

"I'm not sure that can be a fresh realisation" he said.

"No. The point is how to deal with it" said Marianne. There is only one thing you can do when you have a boss like her."

"And what's that?"

"You have to always be one step ahead!" she said triumphantly.

Ben looked at her. "If you can."

Later that afternoon, Marianne checked her Twitter feed. She saw that Ana was being lavishly praised by Momentum. Her letter to Pete had endeared her to them.

That evening, Karen had invited Sam to join them for dinner. Marianne was late home because of delays on the tube. When she got in, Karen was in the kitchen cooking. Sam was outside in the garden kicking a ball about with Daniel. She could see them through the French doors.

"Sorry I'm late" she said. She flung her bag and coat over one of the kitchen chairs.

"You're alright" said Karen. "Can you do me a favour?"

"Sure."

"Can you snap these asparagus stalks for me?" She handed Marianne a silver colander with the asparagus in.

"No problem." Marianne sat at the kitchen table, breaking the stalks one by one.

"I have to say Dishy Doctor Sam is multi-talented" said Karen. "He was even doing headers for Dan earlier."

"He can sing and he can bake as well" Marianne said

"You can't really ask for much more in a man."

Marianne watched Sam outside in the garden with Daniel. He would make a good father and husband, again. It was entirely conceivable that *they* could have children. She'd never be able to change the past but she could give him a whole new future.

She imagined taking him to meet her parents. He would easily charm them. They still lived in the house she grew up in in Leamington Spa. She imagined the four of them, on a summer's evening, sitting outside in the garden. Her mother would light a citronella candle and they would drink gin and tonics. Maybe she and Sam would buy a large, rambling house nearby.

Karen joined her at the table. "I guess you haven't said anything about Dishy Doctor Sam at work" she said. "What with him having been casework."

Marianne shook her head. Something then occurred to her.

"It's funny you should mention that" she said. "Because Sam had dealings with Joni."

"Bet she buggered up his casework."

"It's worse than that" said Marianne. "She invited him out for a drink under false pretences. And then, she bombarded him with text messages."

"What! You mean she stalked him?"

"Pretty much."

"Fuck me" said Karen

"It gets worse" Marianne said.

"How?" Karen was incredulous.

"Well, she claimed to have a rash on her chest. She wanted him to examine it and she even threatened to send a selfie. That's when he blocked her."

"Oh my god!" said Karen. "I'll tell you something. It's a good thing he didn't see her saggy baps. It would have traumatised him for life. He's been through enough horror already."

Marianne squealed in appalled mirth. They became convulsed by hysterical giggles. They didn't notice when one of the pots on the range boiled over.

On Thursday afternoon, Marianne went with Ana to her pop-up surgery. It was to be held on a housing estate off Greenwood High Road. They took the tube from Westminster. It was the middle of the day so they were easily able to find seats.

As they sat on the train together, Ana asked: "How is…Evan…is it?"

"Euan" said Marianne, correcting her. "Erm…yes…he's fine."

She realised that Ana didn't know that they'd split up. This also meant she didn't know that she was living at Karen's. She'd had no reason to mention it to her. Still, she'd assumed it was quite widely known and that Ana would have heard about it somewhere. This clearly wasn't the case. She thought about the implications of Ana finding out, which she would eventually. It might not be conducive to gaining her trust.

They'd been given a community room, in one of the blocks, for the pop-up surgery. It had been advertised by posters. When they arrived, there was no sign of the TV news crew.

"Strange" said Ana. "Joni said they'd be here now."

"Joni arranged it?"

Marianne was surprised by this.

"Yes" Ana replied.

A number of residents dropped by. Some of them reported problems with drains or graffiti. Others wanted to discuss the state of the world. Marianne diligently took notes. Ana was charming to each of them. Not one would have sensed any distractedness or absence of sympathy.

Marianne, however, knew that she was deeply agitated. The absence of the TV cameras was vexing her. She'd been planning a major public relations coup against Pete in his backyard.

After an hour passed, the residents stopped trickling in. Only Marianne and Ana were left in the room. Ana then allowed her discomfiture to show.

"Where the fuck are they?" she said angrily.

They waited for another half hour before Ana pulled her iPhone out of her bag. She called Joni but there was no response. Her face was white and clenched with fury.

"Right!" she barked at Marianne. "We're going over there now."

She meant the constituency office where Joni was based some of the time. It was a five-minute walk away. Ana marched off at high speed. Her rage was visible for all to see. Marianne found herself running and skipping to keep up.

Christ Almighty thought Marianne. *She's forgotten she's supposed to be the local MP.*

She hoped that they wouldn't be seen by too many people.

Ana's constituency office was just around the corner from the tube station. It had been a shop before she'd taken it over. The windows were adorned with her election posters. When they got there, Ana banged furiously on the door.

After what seemed like an age, Joni answered, surprised. She looked like she had just woken up. Ana pushed past her. Marianne followed closing the door discreetly behind her.

"What *the fuck* are you playing at!" Ana roared at Joni.

"Sorry?" Joni looked confused.

Marianne looked around the room. It looked dirty and chaotic. There were open box files everywhere. Joni's own desk used was covered by piles of paper.

Ana loomed over Joni. "Where's the fucking TV crew?" she screeched. "That's what we fucking came here for."

Marianne realised that she was completely possessed by her rage and out of control.

"Oh yes" said Joni.

"Oh yes, what?" hissed Ana.

"They came yesterday. I think there was a mix-up."

"Why *the fuck* didn't you tell me?" Ana growled

Joni shrugged. "I just assumed they'd come back today" she said

"You fucking stupid bitch!" Ana snarled.

She raised her hand and slapped Joni hard across the face, not once but twice.

"I can't rely on you for fucking anything" she said with venom. "It's just not fucking good enough!"

With that, she stormed out slamming the door behind her. Marianne found herself left alone with Joni.

"Joni, are you okay?" she asked, desperately concerned

Joni stood there with her hand clutched to her cheek. She seemed to be in some sort of shock and unable to communicate. Marianne was horrified to see blood pouring out her nostrils.

"Oh my God, you're bleeding!" she said. "Sit down."

She pulled over a chair and eased Joni into it.

"It's nothing" murmured Joni. "I get these nose bleeds all the time."

"It's not nothing" said Marianne. "Here."

She handed her some paper tissues she kept in her bag. Joni pressed them to her nose. Eventually, the blood started to clot.

Marianne had long anticipated Ana turning on Joni. She'd always imagined getting a visceral thrill from it. Instead, she found herself feeling appalled, even hurt, by the ugliness of the scene. It was as though she had been demeaned and humiliated by it as much as Joni.

She fetched a glass of water for Joni and sat down beside her. She noticed her hands were shaking but her face was expressionless. She seemed to be looking into the distance in a classic thousand-yard stare. Marianne knew that she was ill-equipped to process trauma.

"Joni" she said. "What just happened is not okay. It's not normal."

"I'm fine. Really" Joni said. "I sometimes overstep the mark with people. I guess I did today."

“I can’t accept that” said Marianne. “If she did that to you, she’ll do it to me. It’s just a matter of *when* not *if*. And I’m not prepared to be assaulted at work.”

“No” said Joni. A single tear cascaded silently down her face.

“If you need me to be a witness to what happened” Marianne said. “I’m won’t hesitate. It’s up to you.”

“Thank you, Marianne” said Joni. “I’ll give it some thought.”

It was now late afternoon. Marianne encouraged Joni to go home and shut up the office for her. There was no point her going back to Westminster. Besides, she really couldn’t stomach seeing Ana.

She almost forgot she was due to go canvassing at six. Sam had said he would be going. She took a westbound bus to the meeting point. The session was taking place on a newbuild development a couple of miles away. Bridget was leading.

The canvassers were meeting on a street corner. There were five or six of them when Marianne arrived. Bridget presided with her clipboard. Sam wasn’t there yet

“Did you say there was someone else coming?” Bridget asked her.

“Yes” Marianne replied. “Sam. Oh, here he is.”

Sam drew up alongside them in his jeep and got out. He was wearing his shiny green bomber jacket. Marianne remembered he’d worn it the first time they’d met.

“Sorry I’m late” he said.

“Not at all” said Bridget. “Have you canvassed before?”

“Never” he replied.

“Not a problem” said Bridget. “I don’t think you’re the only newbie here. I’ll give a bit of a briefing and explain the basics and you can shadow an old hand…like Marianne, if you like. Or you can go off on your own if you’re happy to.”

Bridget gave her spiel to the canvassers. Marianne helped out by dishing out leaflets and stickers. As it was, Sam was happy to go off on his own. Marianne didn’t mind a bit. If anything, she was pleased by his confidence.

They canvassed a row of townhouses. Marianne could hear Sam’s laugh from a few doors away. He was a relaxed and engaging canvasser. People seemed to like him. Occasionally he, like all canvassers, was met with uninterest and low-level rudeness. Still, he seemed perfectly able to shrug it off.

“He’s an absolute natural on the doorstep” Bridget told her at one point. “You have found yourself a lovely young man there.”

“I like to think so” said Marianne.

They came to a block of flats. Sam pressed the buzzer and persuaded a resident to let them in. The block seemed to be L-shaped with three storeys and a confusing layout. Bridget stayed in the foyer next to the front door, dispatching the canvassers to different flat numbers.

Marianne trudged up to the second floor to knock on a door. There was no answer. She made her way back to the stairs but found herself disoriented by the labyrinth corridors. The exposed brickwork made her think of *Prisoner Cell Block H,* a TV show she and Euan had watched when they were students.

“Excuse me” said a man’s voice. “Are you the Labour Party?”

Marianne turned to find the man standing behind her. He was perhaps in his late fifties, bearded and tidily dressed.

"Yes" she replied.

He stared intently at her for a moment. "Don't come here again" he said.

She decided this wasn't worth responding to and turned to go.

"Don't turn your back on me!" the man roared. "I haven't finished with you yet."

He grabbed her arm. Marianne tried to pull it way.

"Let go!" she exclaimed.

"Why?" he said. "So you can spread your legs for some terrorist!"

He tightened his grip.

"It's because of stupid little slags like you that the Muslims are taking over this country."

At that moment, Sam appeared from around corner.

"Oi!" he shouted. "Let her go!"

He advanced towards them. There was murder in his eyes.

"Didn't you hear what I said? Let her go."

The man said to Marianne "Is this your boyfriend?"

Sam grabbed him by the throat, lifted him into the air and pushed him against the wall. Marianne later thought this was quite a feat given the other man was much heavier.

"Didn't you hear what I said?" he hissed.

He looked at the man dead in the eye. Their faces were very close together. He placed his thumb on the man's windpipe.

"Tell me something" he murmured. "Is this worth dying for?"

He pressed his thumb harder. The man began to cough, splutter and writhe, desperately panicked.

"Sam" said Marianne, pleadingly.

"Go on, tell me" Sam whispered to him. "Are you prepared to die for this?"

"No!" wheezed the man.

He was choking now.

"Sam, please" said Marianne. She tried to sound calm. "That's enough."

Sam flung his arm away and the man dropped to the floor, hyperventilating.

"No. Didn't think so, big man" he said.

He turned to go.

The man sat up, gasping

"I'm going to call the police!" he cried.

Sam swiftly spun back around and strutted menacingly towards him.

"What, what? You're going to call the police? You can borrow my 'phone if you like. Do you want to borrow my 'phone? No? Well, they probably wouldn't believe you."

"Look, let's just go" Marianne said.

The man gingerly picked himself off the floor. He was visibly relieved to see the back of them.

"I wasn't really going to hurt him" Sam said later that evening.

"Oh, I *am* pleased!" said Marianne. "A little light choking never hurt anybody."

They were having dinner in an Italian restaurant on Greenwood High Road. Their table faced out onto the street. Sam sat with his back turned to the big glass window.

"I *am* a doctor" he said. "I know how far to push things."

Marianne supposed this was true. Still, she wasn't entirely mollified.

"You seemed to enjoy it a bit too much" she told him.

"I just hate seeing men violently bullying women" he said. "Just because they have the temerity to have an opinion. I've seen a bit too much of it in my time."

"I know" Marianne said. She took a sip of water. "I appreciate you defending me but I feel like I've had a day of violence."

"What do you mean?"

Marianne breathed in. "I don't know where to begin with this" she said. "Today, I witnessed an assault in my workplace."

"What happened?"

"Ana slapped Joni's face. Twice and pretty hard and gave her a nose bleed."

"Oh my God" said Sam, appalled. "That is horrendous."

"Yes, it is" said Marianne. "Totally uncalled for. Look, you know Joni a bit. She's as mad as a box of frogs and she's a total nightmare to work with. But she doesn't deserve *that*. She was pretty distressed. And so was I."

“What are you going to do?” he asked

Marianne sighed. “All depends on Joni” she said. “But I’ve told her that I’ll be a witness if she makes a formal complaint.”

“You’d lose your job” he told her.

“Yes, I know” said Marianne. “And I really don’t want to lose my job. But I can’t turn a blind eye to this. I just can’t. The whole reason I’m in the bloody Labour Party is because I believe in decent working conditions *which* includes not being assaulted at work.”

“You’re brave” said Sam.

“No, I’m not brave” she said. “I just have the occasional moment of courage.”

“That’s why I love you” he said.

He leaned over and kissed her on the lips.

Marianne closed her eyes briefly. When she opened them again, she could see a figure standing outside the window, watching them. She drew back from Sam to get a better look. It was Joni.

“What the fuck?” she said looking over Sam’s shoulder.

“What’s up?”

He turned his head around. Joni had scurried off.

“I just saw Joni” Marianne told him. “She was just standing there, staring at us.”

“Are you sure?”

“Yes, I’m sure. It was definitely her.”

“Hmm. Strange” said Sam. “Oh well.”

Marianne instinctively felt it was a portent of trouble ahead.

When she arrived at work the next morning, Joni and Ben were already there. Joni greeted her casually enough, but she seemed withdrawn, subdued and said little. A certain quietness pervaded on the office.

Marianne had felt sick with dread since waking up. She was absolutely determined to support Joni if she made a formal complaint. Still, she knew it would be at a personal cost to her and her own life would become very uncomfortable. Part of her hoped Joni wouldn’t pursue it.   There was also another problem. Joni now knew about her and Sam.

This could get very complicated she said to herself. She felt in dire need of a cigarette.

They worked in silence for the whole morning. Marianne noticed Joni kept furtively looking over at her and then looking away. Marianne suspected she wanted to initiate a conversation which she wouldn’t want Ben to be privy to. Besides, it wouldn’t be fair to involve him anyway.

Before lunch, she went to the ladies’. As she was flushing the toilet, she heard someone come in. She opened the cubicle door to find Joni standing in her way.

“Marianne, we need to talk” she said. Her tone was urgent

“Yes, Joni, we do.”

She brushed passed her and went to the sink to wash her hands.

"About yesterday" said Joni. "There's something you really should know. I don't know whether you already know it."

"No. No, I don't."

She could see Joni in the mirror, standing behind her.

"Marianne" said Joni. "I know we've had our differences. But I have got to tell you this."

"Tell me what?"

She turned to face her.

"That man" said Joni. "The man you were with last night, Samir Al-Nawazi."

"What about him?"

Marianne had a distinctly uneasy feeling about this.

Joni looked at her intensely. "He's a war criminal" she said.

"What!"

"He committed war crimes. In Syria."

Marianne looked at her in a mixture of bewilderment and disgust.

"You're fucking nuts, Joni" she said and stormed out.

Chapter Nine

"The biggest issue in politics" said Pete Samuelson "is parking. It inflames passions like nothing else."

"Well, it certainly inflames *my* passions" said Karen.

They were in Sam's jeep with Marianne. Sam was driving with the roof down. It was the day of the 2016 London Mayoral election. The day was bright and warm.

Sam said: "I've never understood why the British are so bloody precious about parking. Why can't people just park where they want?"

"Man after my own heart" said Karen.

"I'm glad you two have found something to bond over" said Marianne.

A few days earlier, Karen's car had been clamped by Greenwood Council. This meant that she was without her car on election day. Sam had stepped into the breach by volunteering to be her driver for the day. They were taking Marianne and Pete to a committee room.

"The problem with this country" Karen said "is our interfering local councils. They're always trying to make a quick quid at our expense."

This was directed at Pete to whom she had already expressed her displeasure.

"What you have to understand about parking revenues…" began Pete.

"Stop!" interjected Karen. "I already know that parking is like your specialist subject. That and waste."

"I could talk for hours about waste" Pete said.

"Please don't."

Marianne giggled.

Sam pulled up outside a 1930s semi-detached house. This was one of the local committee rooms. There was a placard in the window emblazoned with 'Campaign Centre'. The front door was open.

"Here we are" he said.

Marianne and Pete got out.

"Remember, Pete" said Karen from the passenger seat. "It's election day. So play nicely with the comrades."

Pete grunted in response.

The engine roared as Sam and Karen drove off. Marianne watched the jeep zip down the street. Sam was as observant of traffic regulations as Karen.

Inside the house, they found Bridget directing operations from the dining room. The owner seemed to be elsewhere. The dining table was covered by sheets of paper. A young woman was perched on a chair with a laptop. Bridget, efficient as always, was dispatching volunteers out onto the doorsteps.

This was just like every other committee room Marianne had ever been in. There were throngs of volunteers arriving and leaving again just as quickly. However, there were also others sat around in the front room eating and drinking. It often seemed to be the same people, all day.

"The cavalry has arrived!" said Bridget when they walked in.

"We've only popped in to use the loo and have a cup of tea" Marianne told her.

Bridget gave her a meaningful look. "Well, you wouldn't be the only ones."

At that moment, about half a dozen newcomers arrived. They included Ned McGady and Kate of Global Solidarity. The temperature of the room cooled when they saw Pete. He looked at them without speaking. The Regeneration Partnership hung in the air.

This is going to be awkward thought Marianne.

Bridget was quick to take charge of the situation.

"Hello folks" she said. "Ned, you're an old hand. Would you mind running a board?"

"Sure" Ned murmured.

"Pete, I'd like you to go out with Ned 's team." said Bridget.

"Fine by me" said Pete.

"And Marianne, can you hang on for a bit? I'll send you out with another group."

Pete, Ned and the newcomers were duly sent out. Marianne could only imagine the atmosphere between them would be icy. Still, the furore over the Regeneration Partnership seemed to have died down. Pete had written back to Ana and thanked her for her letter. He said he respected her views and welcomed her input. Karen had described it as an "act of nuclear passive-aggression".

Marianne thought the Party had become more united because of the Mayoral election. Sadiq Khan had proved to be a candidate they could all get behind. This was because of the campaign he had run, and because of the campaign that had been run against him.

It's like we're all on the same side again Marianne said to herself.

Ana and Joni arrived together. Marianne was almost startled by their companionableness. Nobody would guess about the slapping incident a couple of weeks earlier.

I don't think anybody would believe it thought Marianne. *Not even if Joni and I both told them.*

This was highly unlikely. Joni had shown no sign of wanting to take up her offer of support. To her shame, Marianne felt relieved. They hadn't seen much of each other since Joni ambushed her in the ladies. She had spent most of her time in the other office. Therefore, they hadn't needed to speak much to each other much. She suspected this suited Joni too.

Marianne hadn't mentioned anything to Sam because Joni's claim was so patently ludicrous. She supposed she *could* go online to investigate further but there was just no need. Sam was a doctor and the sanctity of human life would be sacrosanct to him. As for the choking incident, it wasn't entirely unprovoked. The man was a fascist and a thug. Sam had probably saved her from being assaulted.

Her train of thought was interrupted by Bridget. "Would you mind running a board, Marianne?" she asked.

Marianne groaned inwardly. She'd actually been looking forward to talking to voters.

"Not at all" she said brightly.

"Great. You can take Ana and Joni...and I'm sure there must be a couple of others next door."

She went into the front room to evict a couple of volunteers. They reluctantly finished slurping from mugs and dragged themselves off the sofas. Marianne was given a clipboard.

"We have a crack team" said Ana, smiling.

Marianne wasn't sure if she was being jovial or sarcastic.

They were sent to some nearby streets. On the way, they passed a lone Tory canvasser and there was an exchange of glassy smiles. Marianne felt certain that Sadiq Khan was going to win overwhelmingly. The Tory campaign had elicited very little enthusiasm.

Wielding her clipboard, Marianne gave the volunteers a door to knock on each. Their job was to remind Labour supporters to vote. She was left with Ana and Joni hovering by her. Ana seemed to be in a convivial mood, or at least was giving a display of being.

"Anyone seen Karen today?" she asked. "I made a bet with her that she couldn't get through an election day without a parking ticket. She never does."

"She will today" said Marianne. "Her car's been clamped."

Ana forced out a squeal of laughter that was undecided between mirthful and regretful. "Oh dear. Poor thing. What's she going to do without a car?"

"Sam's driving her around today."

"Sam?" said Joni, taking an interest. "You mean Samir Al-Nawazi?"

There was a moment of silence.

"Yes" said Marianne, looking Joni straight in the eye.

"*Mr* Al-Nawazi?" said Ana. "*Our* Mr Al-Nawazi?"

"That's right."

"Oh" said Ana.

Marianne decided it would be wise to change the subject. She looked down at her clipboard. "Ana, can I send you to Number 20? Mr and Mrs Hedges. They're both very strong Labour supporters."

"Erm..sure" said Ana.

She seemed disappointed to have to discontinue this juicy conversation.

Joni waited for Ana to go before turning to Marianne.

"Are you really still seeing him?" she said.

"Yes" replied Marianne, turning to face her. "Not that it's any of your business."

"Marianne, I would never involve myself in other people's relationships. But doesn't it bother you what sort of man he is? The guy is a psychopath. He ethnically cleansed..."

"Shut the fuck up!" Marianne hissed. "It has absolutely fuck all to do with you. I don't know where you've got this bollocks from but..."

"Google him!" shrieked Joni. "Google him if you don't believe me! Google 'Samir Al-Nawazi', 'People's Protection Unit' and 'Aleppo'."

"Like fuck I will. I'm not entertaining this shit."

There was a pause. Joni changed tack.

“I understand, Marianne” she said, putting on her soothing voice “You don’t want to face facts. It’s a common reaction.”

This was like red rag to a bull.

“How fucking dare you patronise me like that!” exclaimed Marianne.

She could feel her entire body clench with rage. She wanted to puncture Joni’s air of self-satisfied certainty. She wanted her to feel stung and doubting of herself.

“Listen” she said. “I know you are a sad, menopausal old biddy who doesn’t have much of a life. People *tolerate* you because you sometimes make yourself useful. Like. A. Doormat. But they laugh at you behind your back. Sam laughs at you. He thinks you’re a joke. Is that why you’ve made up all this shit? Because Sam didn’t want to know.”

This certainly seemed to have an effect. Joni bit her lower lip. There was a hint of wateriness in the corners of her eyes. However, her gaze remained hard. She breathed deeply and audibly through her nose to calm herself. When she spoke, her voice was icily, resolutely steady.

“Well at least I’m not sleeping with a killer” she said.

Marianne took a sudden step towards her, her eyes blazing.

“Ladies! Please!” cried a voice behind them.

It was Ana. Marianne and Joni turned to find her standing behind them. She was with the two volunteers who were gawping like goldfish. How long had they been there and how much had they heard? Marianne was mortified.

Ana took the clipboard off her. She sent the two volunteers to knock on other doors. When they'd gone, she handed it back to Marianne.

"I would like to ask you both to calm down" she said. "I am aware there have been tensions between you."

Not helped by you bitch-slapping your staff Marianne wanted to say.

Ana continued: "But today, I just want us to focus on getting Sadiq elected. That said, I don't want any more bad blood in our little team."

You'll be telling us to give peace a chance next Marianne said inwardly.

"As your employer, I feel it is my duty to mediate" said Ana in a grave, statesmanlike tone. "I have always been very good at resolving conflict. I'd like to see you both in my office at 1pm on Monday."

Fuck my life thought Marianne.

The result of the election was declared at lunch the next day. As expected, Sadiq Khan easily defeated his Tory rival. London had elected the son of a Pakistani bus driver as its Mayor. Marianne felt elated. She felt like her values had been validated at the ballot box.

That evening, Sam had asked her over to his flat. He'd said he would cook dinner. When she arrived, he looked tired and bleary eyed having worked a 14-hour shift. Marianne was feeling pretty fatigued herself. She had walked for hours day before.

"Dinner *will be* served tonight" he said as he led her into the kitchen.

"Lovely."

Sam opened the fridge door. "I just haven't had time to cook it yet."

He pulled out a Tesco oven pizza box and a bottle of Veuve Clicquot.

Marianne laughed. "You know what. That is absolutely perfect" she said.

They had their pizza and Champagne in front of the TV, watching the coverage of the election. Various commentators and pundits had their say.

"It really does feel like a victory" said Marianne. "For things I've believed in my whole life. Like liberalism. And multiculturalism. It sounds silly but I sort of feel like I've got my country back."

"Indeed" Sam said. "It's a good sign for the referendum next month."

"I hadn't thought of that. But you're right." Marianne took a sip of her Champagne. "I'm going to talk to Karen about organising some street stalls and some canvassing."

"Does it just have to be a Labour Party thing?"

"What do you mean?" Marianne asked, slightly confused

"I don't know how *you* feel about this" said Sam. "But I think the referendum is about something bigger, something more profound than political parties. I'd really like to work with the cross-party Remain campaign."

Marianne considered this. "Yes, I suppose I agree" she said. It's something I feel unusually passionate about. As you say, it is bigger than normal party politics."

Sam topped up her glass. Another thought occurred to her

"It would be nice though to have a break, just a mini-break, from campaigning" she said, longingly.

"I wanted to talk to you about that" said Sam. "Are you free next weekend?"

"Yes. Yes, I think so."

"Excellent. I hope you don't mind. But I took the liberty of booking us into a hotel for the weekend. It's a country house hotel in Sussex with four poster beds and a Michelin-starred restaurant. I think we both deserve it."

"Wow" said Marianne. "I don't think I've done anything to deserve that. But it sounds amazing."

They watched more of the news. Marianne found herself struggling to keep her eyes open. She noticed Sam seemed to be nodding off too. They went to bed early. The last couple of days had been tiring for them both. They were asleep within seconds of climbing under the covers.

As she slept, Marianne dreamt of being submerged in water under a black sky. She could hear sirens and helicopters overhead. There was a man shouting in agitation and distress. She couldn't discern the words because she didn't recognise the language. It sounded like Arabic to her.

She woke up with a start but the shouting had got louder. It was Sam. He was writhing furiously next to her in the bed. He was clearly having a nightmare. She put her hand on his shoulder and shook him.

"Sam! Sam! Wake up""

His eyes flicked open. He looked disoriented. His forehead was damp.

"What?" he mumbled.

"I think you were having a bad dream" she told him.

He looked at her wide-eyed for a moment before sitting up in bed.

"Sorry" he said. "I didn't mean to frighten you."

"You didn't. What were you dreaming about?"

"Oh, I can't remember" he said dismissively. "I never remember dreams."

"Is everything alright?"

"Yes, everything is fine" he replied. "I've just had a stressful few weeks at work. It's very common for doctors. Some deal with the stress by drinking too much or taking drugs. I just have the odd nightmare. It's not a big deal."

"If you're sure" said Marianne. She wasn't the slightest bit reassured by this. However, something in his manner discouraged her from probing.

"Absolutely" he said.

He kissed her on the forehead and drew her closer. She let her head fall onto his shoulder. He soon went back to sleep but she stayed awake for a while longer.

On Monday afternoon, Marianne went upstairs to Ana's office for her mediation with Joni. For once, Joni had arrived early. They sat on chairs in front of Ana's desk.

"I have taken advice from HR" said Ana. She read tonelessly from a page of instructions in front of her. "This is an opportunity for you to say how you feel. We can the identify the key issues and work together to resolve them."

Fuck me, you should get a job at the UN Marianne said inwardly.

"Joni, why don't you go first?" Ana suggested

Joni sighed as if she were about to unburden herself.

"I think it is reprehensible" she said in her low monotone "that Marianne is pursuing a relationship with Samir Al-Nawazi when..."

"What?" Ana spluttered. She looked directly at Marianne. "You and Mr Al-Nawazi? What happened to whatshisname…Evan?"

"Euan" said Marianne. "We split up."

"Really?" said Ana, sounding very interested. "When did this happen? Did you have to move out?"

You are one fucking nosey bitch thought Marianne.

She didn't get a chance to answer as Joni ploughed on.

"I think it is reprehensible of Marianne to pursue a relationship with a constituent we have done casework for…"

"Well, she sort of has a point" Ana said rather unhelpfully.

Marianne screamed inwardly *You're supposed to be fucking mediating!*

"*And!"* said Joni like she'd found the smoking gun. "With a man who is a *war criminal*. A man who has been involved in *ethnic cleansing*."

"Well he kept *that* quiet" said Ana.

"It is total bollocks!" cried Marianne.

"Sshh" said Ana raising her palm. "Let Joni finish. Then you can have your say."

"Samir Al-Nawazi" said Joni "was a member of the People's Protection Unit in Syria."

She sounded like she'd memorised a newspaper article.

"They are aligned to the Syrian Democratic Forces. In 2012, they were criticised by the international community for an ethnic cleansing at Aleppo."

"Where's your evidence that Sam was involved?" said Marianne.

Joni's slow, serious monotone was really grating on her now.

"It is a matter of *public record* that Samir Al-Nawazi was aligned to the People's Protection Unit" said Joni.

"Where?"

"There's an article on the the Stop the War Coalition website"

"Stop the War!" shrieked Marianne. She began to laugh mirthlessly. "You're fucking kidding me. They have zero credibility."

"Marianne, please!" protested Ana. "We must all try to be civil."

Happy to follow your example Marianne said inwardly.

"As you know" said Joni. "I have had extensive dealings with the local Syrian community. There is *sustained* and *extensive* anecdotal evidence linking Samir Al-Nawazi to the Aleppo massacre."

"*Anecdotal evidence*!" exclaimed Marianne. "You mean speculation, gossip and rumour. That's all you've got isn't it?"

"If you would just listen..." snapped Joni. She was losing her composure now.

"I am really curious, Joni" said Marianne. "Why have you taken such a close interest in Sam? Seems a bit unusual."

Joni seem to blanch. She was clearly discomfited by this. "Well, I...."

"Yes, go on."

"Just a moment" said Ana. She looked down at her advice from HR. "At this point, I would like to ask if either of you would like to take a break?"

"I think that would be good" said Joni.

"Thank you, ladies" said Ana, deciding the matter. "Going forward, I would like to speak to you both individually. Marianne, can you come and see me after lunch? Joni, I know you're in the constituency office this afternoon. We'll catch up later in the week."

Marianne felt like slamming the door behind her but didn't. The whole thing was outrageous. Surely, her personal life was her own business. The intrusion made her wanted to hiss with resentment. She stamped back to her office, her face taut with fury. Ben looked at her as she sat down.

"Everything alright?" he asked.

"I can't even" she said.

"I think we all have days like that in this office" he said understandingly.

Ben knew there was something going on. Joni's absences from the office had made that obvious but he was too diplomatic to ask. Marianne had desperately wanted to tell him about Ana slapping Joni. However, she decided against it. She would also have to tell him about Sam, and about Joni's crazy allegations. His discretion could be assured. She was just worried that he might judge her.

"Can we have our drink on Thursday evening instead?" she asked him. "It' just that I'm going away for the weekend on Friday."

"Sure" he replied.

After lunch, Marianne went back to Ana' office.

"I just need to nip out to the loo" said Ana as soon as she went in.

She left Marianne alone. Her personal laptop was open on the desk. Marianne looked at the screen. It was a live CCTV image of the constituency office.

Fucking hell, she has a camera rigged up in there she thought. *Why?*

She could see Joni working in there. Presumably, she was oblivious to the fact that she was being observed from some 8 miles away.

"Sorry about that" said Ana when she came back. She closed her laptop and sat back down. "Right. Where did we get to?"

Marianne's irritation returned. She quickly forgot what she'd just seen.

"Ah yes" said Ana. "So you and Mr Al-Nawazi have been seeing each other."

"That's right" Marianne said tightly.

"Well Marianne, please tell me if you think it's none of my business…"

Happy to Marianne said inwardly.

Ana continued. "I just think you have to be a little careful mixing business and pleasure" she said. "But I've checked with HR and there are no rules against you having a relationship with a constituent. Even one we've done casework for."

"I *am* pleased" said Marianne.

She realised this had sounded sarcastic. There was a silence. Ana looked at her witheringly but decided to ignore it.

"*However"* she said. "I think we should always be mindful about conflicts of interest. We are, after all, in a privileged position. And we deal with some very vulnerable people."

Marianne said: "I didn't start seeing Sam until long after we finished his casework. He's not what you would call vulnerable. He's working as in the NHS as a doctor."

"I get that" said Ana in a tone of utter reasonableness. "My worry is the tension this is causing our little team."

"Joni has got the wrong end of the stick about Sam" said Marianne.

"Oh, I have absolutely no doubt" said Ana. "She does sometimes get a little carried away."

Marianne was pleased to hear this. Ana, was of course, a bit of a monster. Still, she could at least recognise certifiable insanity when she saw it.

"I think I can resolve this" Ana told her. "I have a contact at the Foreign Office. He specialises in Middle East affairs. I can run this by him and I'm sure we can put all of this to bed."

"I would really appreciate that" said Marianne.

She meant it.

Ana smiled graciously and leaned across the desk towards her, matily.

"I just want to put your mind at rest" she said. "Mr Al-Nawazi is *such* a patently decent, caring man. And I'm very impressed that he's campaigning for the Party now."

Marianne could feel herself softening towards Ana. Perhaps she was occasionally monstrous because of a determination to get things right. That would make people difficult to deal with.

"He has been really good" she said to Ana. "Especially with the way he drove Karen around on election day. He's also a passionate Remainer. As am I."

"Is he?" said Ana. "Karen's organised a Referendum canvass this Saturday. I said I'd go along. Will you guys be coming?"

"We can't this weekend" Marianne told her. "We're going away for a mini-break."

"Oh, how lovely. Where are you going?"

"A country house hotel in Sussex. Near Arundel, I think. Sam's booked it."

"That sounds absolutely wonderful" said Ana. "I'm so glad you're treating yourselves. You deserve it after working so hard."

Marianne was unsure of what to make of Ana's solicitousness and concern for her welfare. Still, she decided, as she left the office, she wouldn't look a gift horse in the mouth.

However, the image on the laptop returned to haunt her. She mentioned it to Ben when they met for drinks on the Thursday.

"What? You mean she has a camera in there?" he asked incredulously.

"Well she must do" said Marianne.

"Are you sure?"

"Yes! It was definitely the constituency office. It was definitely Joni. And she was definitely wearing the clothes I last saw her in."

"Weird" said Ben. "Why would she do that?"

"I don't know. I thought you might have a theory"

He didn't. Ben was usually very insightful about Ana but this clearly eluded his powers of explanation.

On Friday evening, Sam picked up her up outside the Palace of Westminster. They were heading down to Sussex. She had waited for him on the pavement opposite Parliament Square wheeling her suitcase She had meant to use her overnight bag but it hadn't been big enough.

Sam stopped his jeep in the road and leapt out. There was much outraged beeping from the traffic behind. He hauled Marianne's suitcase into the boot.

"Travelling light?" he said.

"Just the essentials" she replied.

"You clearly learnt a lot from backpacking, didn't you?"

They drove down the Chelsea Embankment. Sam had wound the roof down. Marianne felt the breeze from the River Thames on her face. The saltiness was invigorating. They sang along to Belle and Sebastian's 'Mornington Crescent' which was playing on Sam's iPod.

Their drive out of London was smooth. The traffic was surprisingly light for a Friday evening. After they had been travelling for an hour, Marianne heard her 'phone vibrate in her bag. She pulled it out and saw it was Ana calling. With great reluctance, she answered.

"Hello?" she said.

"Marianne, it's Ana" said Ana, somewhat unnecessarily. The breeze made her sound faint. "Sorry to trouble you when you're going away."

You bloody well should be thought Marianne.

"No problem" she said.

"I just want to check when you're sending out the letter about badgers" said Ana.

"The letter about badgers? I sent it a couple of weeks ago. You signed it."

"Oh. Really?" said Ana. "I must have done. You know you are far too efficient, Marianne. Thank you so much for all you do. I hope you and Mr Al-Nawazi have a really lovely weekend."

"You too, Ana" said Marianne.

She hung up.

"Badgers!" Sam roared with laughter. He'd heard the conversation. "She called you to talk about badgers?"

"Welcome to my world."

"I thought I had to deal with some crazy stuff in my job" Sam said. "But you have top trumps."

They arrived in Sussex after 7pm. The hotel was at the end of a long gravel drive. Marianne saw from the car that it was a castle rather than a country house.

"Wow, this is grand" she said.

When they checked it, their luggage was carried upstairs by uniformed porters. Their room had the four-poster bed promised. Childishly, they jumped up and down on top of it. Marianne thought back to her 18 months of backpacking with Euan.

This sure beats youth hostels and tents she said to herself.

The next morning, they went for a long walk on the South Downs. They ate lunch in a pub in the local village. As they were about to leave, Marianne's phone rang.

"Oh my God, it's Ana again" she said. "I'm not going to answer it today. Whatever it is, it can wait."

"No, you really should answer" said Sam.

"You're kidding me. Why?"

He was positively giggling now.

"Because I want to know what could be more important than badgers."

Marianne answered, if only for Sam's amusement.

"Hi Marianne" said Ana breezily. "Sorry to call. Hope you and Mr Al-Nawazi are having a lovely weekend."

"We are, thank you."

"I've just done a campaign session for the referendum" Ana told her. It was really inspiring."

"Fantastic" said Marianne

"Anyhow, I am only calling because I know you're as passionate about this as I am. I'd like you to set up an urgent meeting meeting with the Greenwood Remain campaign."

"Absolutely" said Marianne. "I will do that first thing on Monday morning."

"Thanks, Marianne" said Ana. "You're a doll."

When the call was over, Marianne looked at Sam in askance. He was beside himself.

"Maybe next time, we'll invite her to come with us" he said.

"Suggest that to me again and you will be summarily dumped" said Marianne.

They had a dinner reservation in the hotel restaurant. Marianne wore the same black dress she'd worn to Sam's fundraiser. This time, she put on the red shoes she'd decided against that night.

When they were getting ready, Sam had had to take an urgent call from the hospital. Marianne was sat at the dressing table applying her makeup when Ana called her again.

The sight of Ana's name on the screen gave her an inexplicable sense of foreboding. She declined the call and switched her 'phone off. She decided to leave her it in the room when they went down to dinner. Some instinct prevented her from telling Sam about it.

Their meal in the Michelin-starred restaurant was truly sumptuous. Marianne managed to forget about her unease for a while. After their main course had been cleared, Sam proposed a toast.

"To us" he said. "Here's to many more weekends like this. Without your boss, of course."

Marianne laughed. "To us" she said, clinking his glass.

In the morning, Marianne switched her 'phone back on. Sam was in the shower. They were heading back to London after breakfast. Ana had called about a dozen times so she decided she had to call her back.

"I'm just returning your calls" she said when Ana answered.

"Oh yes" said Ana. She sounded half-asleep. "Is this a good time to talk?"

"I suppose it is."

"This is a difficult subject, I'm afraid. I have heard from my contact in the Foreign Office."

Marianne felt sick. "Oh yes?" she said.

"He's seen the intelligence" Ana told her. "Mr Al-Nawazi was involved in that massacre."

"Are you sure?" said Marianne.

"Yes, Marianne. I am sure" said Ana. "He's had it confirmed from a few sources."

There was a pause.

"Thank you, Ana" said Marianne.

Sam came back into the room in a hotel bathrobe. "Everything alright?" he asked.

"Fine."

It was a drizzly, wet morning. Sam had put the roof of the jeep up. As they drove up the motorway, Marianne looked ahead at the rain.

"You've been very quiet this morning" Sam said. "Are you sure everything is alright?"

Marianne decided she had to broach the subject. This couldn't be ignored

"There is something bothering me" she said. "I've been having some problems with Joni at work."

"I didn't realise. I can imagine she's a erm…challenging colleague."

Marianne inhaled deeply. "Yes, she is. Particularly where you're concerned."

"Oh?" said Sam. "Sounds interesting."

Marianne looked at him. "She says that you were involved in an ethnic cleansing at Aleppo."

Sam didn't respond immediately. He just carried on driving. After a while, he said: "Well, you know she's crazy."

"Yes, I do know that" said Marianne. "The problem is that she's not the only one saying it."

Sam suddenly pulled into a layby and turned to face her. "It wasn't an ethnic cleansing. I promise you."

"What?"

He held her gaze for a moment. "Are you sure you want to hear this?" he asked.

"Yes, I do" said Marianne. "I want to know the truth."

He turned back to face the windscreen. His hands were clasped on the steering wheel.

"The truth is what I've always told you" he said. "My family were killed when we tried to cross into Turkey."

"Tell me what happened" said Marianne.

"We passed through Aleppo on the way" Sam told her. "We had contacts there who arranged a safehouse for us to stay there a couple of days. I went out to get some supplies for the journey and when I came back, I found them…"

His voice broke. He paused, swallowed and then turned to look at her again.

“I found the bodies my wife and our children. Daesh killed them.”

Marianne tried to block out the mental images. She remembered the family photo on his bedside table

“My contacts knew the animals responsible” he said.

Marianne steeled herself for the rest of the story. “Then what?” she asked.

“We waited a couple of days” he told her. “Then we ambushed a convoy. We took them to the basement of a house and we forced them to kneel. I had a revolver. I shot every single one of them in the back of the head, execution-style. It was all very clean and clinical.”

“Oh God” breathed Marianne, appalled.

There was moment of silence.

“You wanted the truth” said Sam, after a pause. “And I’ve told it to you. But you have to know that the ethnic cleansing stuff is total bullshit. It’s been made up by fucking idiots.”

Marianne didn’t know what to say.

“I’m really sorry you’ve had to hear this” he said.

“Don’t be” Marianne murmured.

They drove back to London in silence. The journey had an unreal dreamlike quality. Marianne felt numb. The future she’d pictured with Sam, with a house, children, family and friends, shimmered away like a mirage.

When they got back to Greenwood, Sam parked outside Karen's house and got Marianne's suitcase out of the back.

"Look, I understand" he said. "You may not want to see me again. It' s probably all just too much."

Marianne just nodded.

Karen was in the hallway when she wheeled her suitcase in.

"Hello" she said. "How was your dirty weekend away?"

Marianne forced herself to grin. "Oh, utterly filthy" she said. "I'll tell you all about it later over a bottle of vino."

"No, spare me the details" said Karen. "I can't cope with TMI today. We'll drink the wine though."

Once upstairs in her room, Marianne closed the door behind her. It was a relief to be alone. She slid onto the floor and wrapped her arms around her knees. She sat like that for hours unable to think or feel anything.

Sam called her a couple of days later when she was at work. She was busy trying to arrange Ana's urgent meeting with the Greenwood Remainers. She looked at her 'phone while it rang but didn't answer. He didn't leave a voicemail.

She saw Ana only briefly on the Monday morning. She asked if Marianne was alright and told her that she was sorry to have to share that news. She did look genuinely concerned. Still, Marianne had seen her use the same look on constituents. It annoyed her to be on the receiving end of it.

She did manage to arrange the meeting. However, she ended up going in Ana's place. It was held in someone's flat early Thursday evening. She said little but took copious notes as Ana would want a briefing document. The Remainers didn't let her leave emptyhanded. She was given a pile of leaflets to deliver.

Bridget had invited her over for supper that evening. She took a bus to the mansion block where she lived. On the way, she received a text message from Sam.

'*Would really like to talk. Call me. Sx*'

Marianne was unsure how to respond or even if she should. She would decide later.

Bridget was pleased to see her when she arrived. It was the first time Marianne had visited her at home. Her flat was decorated in cool greys and creams. They sat at the kitchen table and ate Tuscan sausage stew with green salad.

"You seem a bit down" Bridget said. "Are things alright between you and Sam?"

Marianne put down her fork. "No. No, they're really not."

"What's happened?"

"I found out something about him" said Marianne. "Something really quite awful. From bloody Joni, of all people."

Bridget sighed. "Well, he does have quite a life story."

"No kidding" said Marianne. "I guess you know about his wife and children being killed. By Daesh."

"Yes, I knew that" said Bridget

"Well, he hunted down the people responsible."

Bridget raised her eyebrows.

"And executed them" Marianne added.

Bridget inhaled deeply as she took this in.

"I see" she said. "And how do you feel about that?"

"Shocked" said Marianne. "And a bit disgusted. He described the way he killed them. You should have heard him. He called it 'clean' and 'clinical'."

"Have you decided that you don't want to see him again?" Bridget asked.

"No" said Marianne. "I can't decide anything."

"Well, you're going to have to" Bridget told her. "I can give you the benefit of my experience, if you like."

"Please do."

"Sam is a lovely, decent young man" she said. "He obviously loves you. But there is one thing you have to understand. He is very, very damaged. There's no getting away from that. He has the most terrible demons to live with. If you were to have any sort of future together, you'd have to live with them too. It's a big ask. If you can't deal with it, you have to walk away, now."

Marianne could feel herself shaking. She failed to stifle a sob. A tear cascaded down her face. Bridget squeezed her hand.

"Sorry" Marianne said. "I really don't know what to do."

"Well" said Bridget. "The one thing you can't do is judge. You and I have never been in Sam's situation and I hope to God we never are."

"No. I know." Marianne wiped a tear away with a tissue and blew her nose.

“I remember reading an article years ago” Bridget told her. “It was by a woman who covered the Rwandan genocide. She said perfectly decent, ordinary people will kill their neighbours if put under pressure. The point is that we just never can know what we’d do if pushed.”

Marianne looked at her. “Could you imagine doing what Sam did?” she asked.

“What? If someone hurt my children like that?”

Marianne nodded.

“Yes” said Bridget. She fixed her grey-green eyes on Marianne’s. “Yes, I could.”

Chapter 10

"*Oh* fuck off, you cunt!" shouted Karen.

She threw a cushion at the TV. The target of her ire was Nigel Farage, the Leader of the United Kingdom Independence Party. He was being interviewed on a Sunday morning TV show about the referendum. She and Marianne were watching it in their dressing gowns in Karen's sitting room.

Karen glanced upwards at the ceiling. "I hope Dan didn't hear that" she said. "I told him off for saying "bloody" the other night."

Fortunately for Karen, her teenage son had heard nothing in his slumber

Farage was particularly bumptious this morning. One poll had put the Leave campaign ahead. This was a huge boon for him. He brayed at them triumphantly from the TV. His tweed jacket and mottled complexion reminded Marianne of Mr Toad in *the Wind in the Willows*. She found herself strangely transfixed.

"I really don't get why people find him so persuasive" she said. "I wouldn't buy a used car off him."

"Well, I suppose people think he's a bit of a lad, one of them" said Karen. "He likes his fag and his pint. Or pretends to. It's all about the *authenticity* these days. That's why we've got frigging Corbyn."

"True" said Marianne.

“Speaking of Dear Leader” said Karen. “You know he went on holiday last week? In the middle of the fucking referendum! He’s been about as much use as a vibrator without batteries.”

“Can I quote you on that?” asked Marianne.

“No, please don’t.”

Marianne checked her ‘phone ostensibly to check Twitter. She tweeted a disparaging comment about Farage. It might earn the odd retweet or like. She really wanted to see if she’d had any messages from Sam. She hadn’t.

She’d last seen him a couple of days after supper with Bridget. She’d gone over to his flat and they’d sat awkwardly next to each other on his sofa. Marianne had given the situation a lot of thought. She’d decided what she wanted from him.

“I really don’t want us to stop seeing each other, Sam” she’d said.

“Good. I’m glad.”

“But there is something I want to suggest to you.”

“*Okay…”* Sam said, uncertainly.

“Well, it’s things like the nightmares. And the erm…occasional loss of temper. Like with that guy we canvassed.”

“You think I’m post-traumatic, don’t you?” said Sam

“Well, it would be bloody strange if you weren’t. After everything that you’ve been through.”

“I know quite a bit about PTSD” he told her. “I regularly treat people who’ve got it. I’ve written a peer-reviewed journal article about it.”

"Have you had any counselling?" asked Marianne. She was no longer prepared to skirt around this.

"No" he said. "I haven't."

"Well I think you should" said Marianne

"Look, I don't deny I have PTSD" said Sam. "But I know there is more than one way to deal with it. I deal with it by immersing myself in things that matter to me in the here-and-now."

"Physician, heal thyself"

"Exactly."

"I'm sorry, Sam" said Marianne. "But that's not good enough for me. I don't want this to always be there, like the proverbial elephant in the room. I'm not prepared to deal with you pretending everything is fine when it isn't. I can't bear the denial."

Sam looked down at his lap as he contemplated this.

"I understand" he said.

"I'm asking a hell of a lot of you, I know" said Marianne.

"And I of you. And we haven't known each other that long."

"Just think about it." said Marianne. "Call me if you want to."

She left. Two weeks had passed, and she'd heard nothing. She wondered if she'd been too blunt. It must have sounded like an ultimatum. Still, she'd resisted the urge to contact him.

Back in the present, Karen said "I suppose we'd better get a wiggle on".

She switched off the TV. Reluctantly, they hauled themselves off the sofas. They were expected at a canvassing session. There'd been little time between the Mayoral election and the referendum. Karen had lamented the timing more than once

"It really is unbelievably fucking inconsiderate" she would say.

The next morning in the office, Marianne discussed the referendum with Ben.

"Surely no-one is going to believe that bollocks on the side of the bus" said Marianne. "Extra money for the NHS sounds good, superficially. But where's the evidence?"

Ben shrugged. "It might be bollocks" he said. "But it's a clear, simple message. Like it or not, it resonates with people."

They were interrupted when Ana breezed into the office, beaming. "Morning team!" she said.

Why are you in such a good mood? Marianne wondered. *Has someone died?*

"I've been asked to go on *Question Time*" said Ana. "Four weeks on Thursday."

Don't do it! Marianne thought. *You'll be fucking useless.*

"How exciting" she said.

"Yes" said Ana. "Anyhow, I've asked the BBC to liaise with you. Just tell them that you need to check my diary."

Marianne looked at her screen. "But you are free that evening" she told her.

Ana's smiley countenance faltered. "Yes, I know" she said. "I just haven't decided if I want to do it yet. If I do, you guys will have to help prep me."

Marianne and Ben exchanged glances after she left.

That evening, after work, Marianne went to a 'phone bank for the Remain campaign. It was being held in the offices of some mysterious charity off Victoria street. She had persuaded Bridget to join her. They met outside just before six and took a lift to the fifth floor. A friendly intern greeted them on arrival. They were led through a maze of dusty smelling rooms heaving with volunteers.

"We're a bit inundated today" said the friendly intern. "So, I'm going to put you in the overflow room. We have headsets and laptops for you."

"I prefer pen and paper" Bridget muttered to Marianne.

They were seated at a bench in an anteroom, which had probably been a stationery cupboard at some point. There were only the two of them in there. The friendly intern gave them their instructions after they put on their headsets. They began making calls.

"Oh hell!" exclaimed Bridget after a few minutes.

Her screen had frozen as had Marianne's.

The friendly intern put her head around the door. "System's crashed" she told them. "We'll have it back up in a few minutes."

"I thought it was just me being a Luddite" said Bridget.

During the interregnum, they were joined by another volunteer. She was a slightly built woman with light brown hair, perhaps in her late thirties, dressed in cycling gear.

"Hi, I'm Jo" she said, introducing herself. She spoke with a Yorkshire accent.

Marianne recognised her. She was Jo Cox, the Labour MP for Batley and Spen. Ana was known to be on friendly terms with her.

"Hi Jo" said Marianne, extending her hand. "I'm Marianne Stuart. I work for Ana Novak."

"Oh, right. I know Ana well. She's lovely, isn't she?"

If only you knew said Marianne inwardly.

They had to wait a few more minutes for the system to be restored. To pass the time, they chatted about the referendum.

"The atmosphere is truly sulphurous" said Bridget. "I've never known anything like it in this country. My family and friends in Scotland have told me all sorts of horror stories about the independence referendum. But this feels worse. There is this real sort of...*visceral edginess*."

"It's all probably amplified by social media" Marianne suggested.

"It's funny you should say that" said Jo. "I have been getting the most insane abuse online. You expect a bit of that as a politician. But it has really got out of hand."

The friendly intern reappeared. "System's back up" she told them.

Afterwards, Marianne and Bridget walked to Victoria tube station together.

"I did like Jo" said Bridget. "There is a warmth about her. She seems very genuine and committed."

Unlike certain other MPs I could mention thought Marianne.

After lunch, the next day, Joni walked into the office. She hadn't been in for a while. Her appearances at Westminster had become very infrequent.

"Afternoon, team" she said to Marianne and Ben. She seemed to be in good cheer.

As usual, she was lumbered with several different bags but today, she was also carrying a tray covered by tin foil.

"I baked some Lamingtons last night" she told them. "I've brought some in for you."

How awkward thought Marianne.

"How sweet" she said. "Thank you, Joni."

"It's my pleasure" Joni said. She dumped her tray and bags on her desk and produced a couple of paper plates from a carrier bag. She gave them one each.

She had come in for a one-to-one with Ana. This was not unusual. However, Marianne suspected this meeting might be less than cordial.

"I think Joni might be in a bit of a trouble with Ana" she said to Ben after she went upstairs.

She took a bite out of the Lamington that Joni had given her. It tasted good if a little overly sweet.

"Why's that?" Ben asked.

"You haven't heard about the latest controversy?"

"No." he replied

Marianne explained. Hostilities had resumed in Greenwood over the Regeneration Partnership. It was the subject of bitter dispute on Twitter. Opponents to the Partnership had held a meeting the previous week which Joni had gone along to. It had been intended as a cross-party affair. Joni, however, had managed to cause outrage during a heated discussion by likening Tories to Nazis.

“My god” said Ben. “That is pretty crazy even for her.”

“The worst part about it” said Marianne “is that everybody there knew she works for Ana. It was all over Twitter within seconds.”

“I bet Ana was thrilled” said Ben

Joni came back to say goodbye before she left. If she had been viciously admonished by Ana, she showed absolutely no signs of it. Marianne thought of Trudie, Joni’s predecessor. She would always leave Ana’s office with a haunted, harried look.

“Hope you enjoyed the Lamingtons” Joni said she went out the door.

Marianne marvelled at Joni’s ability to bounce back. The memory of the Mayoral election day had made her feel uncomfortable. Her words to Joni had been vindictive and hurtful. Still, Joni seemed genuinely incapable of holding grudges.

I don’t think I would ever have spoken to me again Marianne thought.

In some ways, Ana’s mediation between them had proved very successful. There had been absolutely no follow-up. Ana had quickly lost interest after she’d extracted the information she wanted. Still, the whole subject of Sam had been dropped. Neither Ana nor Joni had mentioned him again. Perhaps they’d just assumed she’d stopped seeing him.

On Thursday evening, Marianne went to a meeting at the Greenwood Labour office about the referendum campaign. Karen had organised it. There were about a dozen people there including her, Karen, Pete Samuelson, Joni and Ned Critchley-Smith. Much to everyone’s surprise, Global Solidarity were enthusiastic Remainers.

"I want to do more canvassing sessions" Karen briskly told the meeting. "Marianne, are you happy to take this forward?"

"Erm…sure" said Marianne.

"Excellent. We also need to get a leaflet out…"

"Sorry, Karen" injected Marianne, awkwardly putting her hand up. "I just want to float an idea about canvassing."

Everyone looked at her.

"Go on" said Karen.

"I've been thinking" said Marianne. "This is one of the biggest questions facing the country in my lifetime. So, I'm wondering if we could organise some *cross-party* sessions."

The room fell completely silent. Marianne later imagined gasps of shock when she remembered it.

"Absolutely not. Not ever" said Joni from the back of the room.

Karen said: "I think it would be very complicated to organise."

Pete said: "I'm not against the idea in principle. But like Karen, I don't think it's feasible this late in the day."

"Well, I *am* against the idea in principle" declared Joni. "It is an absolutely terrible idea. How could you suggest colluding with our political enemies? People would just think we're offering up the same old neoliberalism."

Ned Critchley-Smith mumbled something about showing solidarity with "the working class."

That's a resounding no then Marianne said to herself.

The meeting carried on for a while longer. During a short break. Marianne went to the kitchen to make herself a hot drink. The kettle had just boiled when Pete came in.

"Have you seen this?" he asked showing her a screengrab on his iPhone.

The image was of a tweet by an anonymous individual. They had tagged Pete.

It read: 'Bet @CllrPeteSamuelson is already counting the pieces of gold and silver he's gonna sell greenwood for.'

"Charming" said Marianne.

"It's blatant antisemitism" Pete said.

"Well, there are an amazing number of tropes in one tweet. Who is this creep anyway?"

"No idea" said Pete. "Point is that it was retweeted by the 'Great Greenwood Giveaway'. They deleted it pretty quickly though."

'The Great Greenwood Giveaway' was a new Twitter feed set up supposedly to oppose the Regeneration Partnership. Its tag was @GWoodGiveaway. Many speculated it was run by Global Solidarity or Momentum. Ned Critchley-Smith's name was frequently mentioned in connection. It tweeted personal, vituperative remarks at local councillors on an hourly basis. However, Pete himself was the main target.

"It's almost like retaliation" said Marianne. "For all the snide references on Twitter to the Global Solidarity house parties."

Pete chuckled Muttley-style. “Ah yes, the great Global Solidarity gang-bang” he said. “I might say something in front of Ned. Just to see how he reacts.”

“You are awful” said Marianne. “I have to say I tend to believe Joni about the orgies.”

“What!” Pete exclaimed. “Bollocks were they gate-crashed!”

“I’m not so sure. Sounds plausible enough to me.”

“I smell bullshit” said Pete. “I’ll tell you something though. If those “gate-crashers” were misbehaving on the lawn in front of the neighbours, I bet there are some embarrassing photos online. Imagine if *someone* tracked them down.”

Marianne began to giggle at the thought. She stopped abruptly when she noticed Joni standing in the doorway. She was looking at them like a perturbed hamster, her mouth slightly open.

Fuck! I hope she didn’t hear that Marianne thought.

“We’re ready to start again” said Joni, staring at them unblinkingly.

The meeting resumed. Practicalities were the main topic of discussion. It seemed as though the meeting would end on a cordial, consensual note. However, Joni had other ideas.

“Before we all go” she said. “I have to say how tired I am of seeing Jeremy being demonised. He’s doing what the Party wanted by campaigning for Remain.”

Pete snapped at this. “Just a shame he went on holiday in the middle of the campaign” he hissed.

“That is totally unfair, Pete” said Joni. “Jeremy has travelled the length and breadth of the country and made over a hundred speeches. Some people are just looking for any excuse to attack him. It makes things worse when people talk about colluding with our political enemies and…”

She was interrupted by Marianne slamming her hand down on the table.

“For fucks sake, Joni. Not everything is about frigging Corbyn!”

Another silence. For the second time that evening, Marianne found herself being stared at by a roomful of people. She’d been so incensed by Joni’s dig at her that she’d reacted involuntarily.

After the meeting had finished, Marianne decided she needed a walk. She declined Karen’s offer of a lift home. Some fresh air would clear her head. She set off from the office.

As she walked, her mind turned to Sam. She wished she was meeting him for dinner or going back to his flat. There was nothing she would have liked better than to be cuddled up with him on the sofa. They would watch *Newsnight* and climb into bed afterwards. Marianne acutely felt his absence from her life. Still, she had at least resisted the urge to start smoking again.

Her train of thought was interrupted when she heard someone running to catch up with her. It was Joni, who was out of breath.

“I want you to know, Marianne” she gasped. “That I think you are a good person.”

As usual, she hadn’t bothered with preliminaries.

“Oh, hi Joni” said Marianne, stopping.

It took Joni a few breaths to restore her equilibrium. “I just think you allow your prejudices against Jeremy to get in the way” she said.

Marianne turned to face her. “I don’t have any ‘prejudices’ against Jeremy” she told her coolly. “I just don’t think he’s the Messiah. That’s all.”

“I heard you and Pete talking in the kitchen.”

“And?”

“You were talking about those rumours again. About the Global Solidarity house.”

“Yes. And you would have heard me say that I believe what *you* told *me*.”

“I’m just very concerned” said Joni, sighing. “I think Pete’s going to hunt for incriminating material. For evidence of this so-called ‘orgy’ so he can embarrass them.”

“I’m sure he’s got better things to do, Joni” said Marianne.

They began walking again.

The next day was a Friday. Marianne and Ben had their weekly drink in the House of Lords bar.

“Joni seems to be getting really paranoid” said Marianne.

Ben agreed. “She is definitely more erratic” he said. “You’re right about the paranoia. On the other hand, she’s always unnervingly friendly and cheerful to us.”

Marianne took a sip of her wine. “We should probably just stop trying to apply any sort of logic to her.”

“Well, we already know she’s bonkers” Ben said. “Still, it does make you wonder what Ana says to her in their one-to-ones.”

"What? Do you think she's like gaslighting her or something?"

"Who knows" said Ben. "But she'd be in a good position to. She has a camera in the other office and one thing Ana is good at is playing people."

"True" said Marianne. "I just don't see what purpose is served by driving Joni madder."

"It's just divide and rule" Ben said. "Ana's used her to get Momentum onside but she won't want to have to carry on relying on her. It gives Joni too much power. Therefore, it makes sense to isolate her."

"Sounds elaborate" Marianne said. "And has the potential for unintended consequences. You know what? I think she's almost as erratic as Joni."

They had had a trying day with Ana. The BBC had e-mailed Marianne. They wanted to know if Ana had yet decided whether to appear on *Question Time*.

When pressed, Ana said "I am eighty percent decided I will."

She had then summoned Marianne and Ben upstairs for a practice run. She insisted they pose questions that might be asked. Ben raised the Leave Campaign's promise of more money for the NHS. He challenged her to explain *why* this was inaccurate. She couldn't, not clearly and coherently, and became visibly frustrated with herself.

"It's just not fucking good enough" she groaned.

"At least that wasn't directed at us for once" Marianne said to Ben later in the bar. "To be honest, I didn't realise she was capable of anything resembling self-criticism. She *almost* seemed human."

"She works hard to overcome her limitations" said Ben. "I'll give her that."

Marianne topped up their glasses. "You know" she said. "I don't really understand why Ana wants a political career. She can mouth platitudes and she is, as you say, good at playing people. But there doesn't seem to be any real passion for anything."

"It's mainly about the power" said Ben. "That said, I think she believes some of her own hype. She's convinced herself that she has some sort of mission in life"

"Hmm" said Marianne. "I just think politicians at her level should be able to think on their feet. She should be able to make an argument in public."

That weekend, Marianne spent most her time campaigning. She canvassed, delivered leaflets and ran a street stall. There was a less than a fortnight to go before the referendum and the polls were all over the place.

"How are things?" Bridget asked her when they were out canvassing on the Saturday.

"I'm really missing Sam" said Marianne candidly.

Bridget squeezed her shoulders. "I know things haven't been easy for you" she said.

The next week, Joni started working in the Westminster office again. She was there in the afternoon of Thursday 16th June 2016, a day that she, Marianne, and many others, would never forget.

That morning, the BBC had e-mailed again. They told Marianne they could wait no longer for Ana to make up her mind. Therefore, they had booked Nigel Patel instead. Marianne called Ana upstairs to let her know.

"Nigel Patel?" said Ana. She sounded incredulous.

"That's right" said Marianne

"Well, I didn't want to go on anyway" Ana sniffed. "The only people who watch that show are political nerds."

She slammed the 'phone down. Marianne sniggered to herself.

After lunch, she, Ben and Joni were at their desks working. As usual, Joni seemed transfixed by something on her screen.

"Oh my God!" she suddenly said out loud.

Marianne and Ben looked at her.

"A Labour MP has been attacked" she told them. "She was out campaigning for the referendum in her constituency. She's been shot and stabbed."

"Christ!" said Marianne. "What's happened to her."

Joni read from her screen. "She's been taken to hospital" she said. "They say she's in a stable condition."

Marianne checked the BBC News website and gasped. The MP in question was Jo Cox.

"I met her!" she cried. "Last week at a 'phone bank. She seemed really nice. Oh god, this is just horrendous."

For the rest of the afternoon, they were unable to work. Instead, they looked at news websites and Twitter. There were many contradictory reports. The extent of Jo Cox's injuries was unclear. The motives of her assailant were even more opaque. There were suggestions she'd been targeted but there was no confirmation of anything. Later in the afternoon, her husband tweeted a photo of her.

"There's going to be a statement at 5pm" said Ben.

Marianne thought this sounded ominous.

At five, they gathered in front of Ben's screen to watch the BBC News. An announcement was made: Jo Cox MP had died of her injuries earlier that afternoon.

“But she had two children” said Joni, her voice quivering.

Marianne bit her lip and put her arm around her. They watched the coverage in silence for a while.

A few minutes later, Ana came in. She was pale and very red-eyed.

“I think you should all go home” she said. “No-one should be working here late tonight.”

Marianne went with Ben and Joni to the Red Lion on Whitehall. They felt some profound need of each other's company. The pub was busy but the atmosphere was subdued. They took their drinks outside onto the street.

It was now very clear that Jo Cox had been murdered. She had been chased and hunted down. Marianne thought of the slightly built woman she'd met the week before. She shuddered. Her murderer was thought to be politically motivated. It was the first political assassination in Britain for twenty-five years.

Joni seemed especially disturbed. She was mumbling a great deal, often repeating herself. “Are they coming for us?” she would murmur.

Marianne thought about the last time she and Sam had canvassed together. She had been accosted by that angry man. He sounded like he had far-right sympathies. He'd grabbed her arm, stopped her from moving. What would have happened if Sam hadn't been there? How far would a man like that go?

She stayed at the pub for about an hour before heading home. The tube was busy. The world felt like a more dangerous place somehow.

You can never really know what people are capable of she thought.

When she got home, her 'phone vibrated. It was a text from Sam.

'Just heard about Jo Cox. Can't stop thinking about you. Hope you're okay. Sx'

For the next few days, the murder of Jo Cox dominated the news. Marianne went to the vigil in Parliament Square on the Friday. As a mark of respect, campaigning in the referendum was suspended over the weekend.

On Monday evening, Marianne led a canvassing session in Greenwood. This had originally been for Labour supporters. However, Marianne had taken the unilateral decision to make it cross-party and spent the weekend publicising it on Twitter. Karen hadn't been best pleased. Still, she decided to allow special dispensation this once.

Marianne arrived at the meeting point just before six carrying clipboards and rolls of stickers. Ana had let her leave work early. She was amazed by the turnout. There must have been forty or fifty people there, including Bridget who made a beeline for her.

"There's a lady from BBC London News" she told her. "She'd like a word."

"Oh really?" said Marianne, surprised.

Before she knew it, she found herself in front of a TV camera.

"Marianne Stuart" said the reporter. "Can you tell us why you have organised this event?"

Fucking hell thought Marianne. *I didn't realise this was a speaking part*

"Well, I met Jo Cox before she died" she said. "And I can say she inspired me. Her murder is not just an attack on pro-Europeanism. It is a vicious assault on freedom, democracy and decency. In this country, we settle things at the ballot box and not down the barrel of a gun. It doesn't matter which party you support. I felt it was important for us to come together in the spirit of Jo Cox to send a message. We won't be cowed. We are not afraid and *we will* have our politics free from violence!"

She wondered if she'd overdone it. She hadn't meant to make a speech. Her fluidity surprised her.

"That was fabulous" said Bridget, who'd been watching.

"They really put on the spot there" said Marianne. She felt rather elated like she'd just come off stage.

She then had to turn her attention to the volunteers. Organising such a number was no mean feat but she was helped by Bridget and a couple of others. Between them, they dispatched the volunteers onto the doorsteps. Her 'phone kept vibrating and buzzing in her bag. She decided she had to ignore it.

The session lasted no longer than an hour. Bridget helped her gather up all their things afterwards and they went to the pub. Some of the volunteers joined them. To her irritation, her 'phone continued to buzz and vibrate. She switched it off without looking at it.

She was exhausted by the time she got home. Karen was watching *Newsnight* in the sitting room.

"Marianne, is that you?" she called out. She sounded uncharacteristically excited.

"Yes" said Marianne putting her head around the door.

"Oh my God!" cried Karen. "You've gone viral!"

"What?"

Karen looked at her, slight exasperated.

"You don't know what's been going on?"

"Well no, actually."

Karen gestured at the TV. "You've been on every news item about Jo Cox" she said. "*And* you're trending on Twitter."

Marianne couldn't comprehend this

"Why?" she murmured.

"It's that interview you gave tonight" said Karen. "It's gone down a storm. Check your 'phone, you silly cow!"

Marianne pulled her iPhone out of her bag and switched it back on. It seemed extremely slow. This was a very good reason for this. She had received tens of thousands of different notifications. These were from Twitter, Facebook, her e-mails and text messages. It was amazing the 'phone hadn't crashed.

"Oh my God" she said. "This is insane."

She looked at her Twitter feed. That morning, she'd had only a few hundred followers. Now, she had over twenty thousand. She'd had even more mentions on Twitter. She began to scroll through them.

A famous actor said she was 'a true heroine of the Remain campaign'. Many MPs from all parties tweeted lavish praise. She was told repeatedly how proud Jo Cox would be of her. Some suggested she should stand in the forthcoming Batley and Spen by-election.

This was the constituency Jo Cox had represented. At some point, her constituents would have to elect a new MP.

"This is utterly ridiculous" she said to Karen. "All I did was say a few words on telly."

"Well, you're like the new Messiah now" said Karen. "Jezza had better watch out."

She was also scrolling though her 'phone.

"Fucking hell!" she shrieked. "Listen to this."

"What?"

"I've just come across this Facebook page" said Karen. "It's called 'Marianne Stuart for Prime Minister."

She roared at this.

"Fuck me! It's got nearly twelve *thousand* members!"

"That's it!" said Marianne. "I'm going to bed. I can't cope with this anymore."

"Sweet dreams."

Marianne meant to switch her 'phone off when she got into bed but she couldn't resist looking at it. Her mother had left a very excitable voicemail. She'd had messages from people she hadn't heard from in years. There was even a text from Euan.

'Saw you on TV. Thought you were fab. Hope you're well. X'

She was delighted the warmth of his tone. Perhaps she and Euan be friends again. She hadn't wanted them to be irretrievably estranged. He'd been too bigger part of her life.

She was about to switch her 'phone off when it vibrated again. It was a text from Sam.

'*You are a total star. So proud of you. Sx'*

Karen woke her early the next morning with a mug of coffee.

"You might want to get your best face on" she said. "You're going to get papped when you leave the house."

"What?" Marianne muttered. She sat up in bed, bleary eyed.

"The media are outside" Karen told her. "Waiting for you."

"Fucking hell!" said Marianne.

"You'll have to try to be more articulate now you're a celeb" Karen said. "It's probably best if I drive you into work today."

Marianne drank her coffee but she didn't bother with breakfast. She wasn't hungry. After showering, she took particular care with her makeup.

When they were about to leave, Karen said: "Whatever they say, don't react. Don't answer any of their questions. Just keep smiling even if it makes your face hurt."

As soon as she opened the front door, there were calls of "Marianne!". The clicking of cameras pervaded the air.

Karen put her hand on Marianne's back and propelled her through the scrum. "Excuse us. Can we get by please? Thank you. No, she's not giving interviews today. Thank you so much."

A reporter shoved a recording device in Marianne's face.

"Marianne, is it true you're going to stand in Batley and Spen?"

Christ almighty! Marianne thought. *This just isn't real*

She ignored the question and kept smiling as instructed. After a while, it felt like her face had frozen into a rictus.

Karen drove her all the way to Westminster. When she got into the office, she was surprised to find Ana perched on the end of Joni's desk. This wasn't normal. Ben surreptitiously gave her a meaningful look.

Ana smiled and stretched out her arms, as she had on Marianne's first day. "Marianne!" she said. "I wasn't sure if we'd see you today."

I don't see why not Marianne thought to herself. *Some of us have to work for a living.*

"Oh, there was no real reason for me not to come in" she said.

"I was just saying to Ben how incredibly proud we are of you" said Ana. "I thought you were absolutely amazing last night. I didn't know you had it in you."

"To be honest, neither did I."

Ana stood up. "Well keep up the good work" she said.

She patted Marianne on the shoulder. Her smile was gracious although Marianne thought it had a glassy quality to it.

After she'd gone, Ben said: "You've just had publicity she would kill for. I think she's a bit put out."

"Probably" said Marianne. "But I think it's all going to die down very quickly. Especially after the referendum on Thursday. That will overshadow *everything*."

She opened her work inbox. There were dozens of requests for interviews. The BBC had e-mailed to ask if *she* would like to go on *Question Time*. She declined straight away but agreed to do an interview with *the Guardian* that evening.

The day of the referendum finally arrived. The British people were asked to decide whether to remain in the European Union or to leave. Marianne spent the day knocking on doors in Greenwood.

The weather was fine, as it had been on the day of the Mayoral election. Marianne thought this was a good portent. The polls had been close in the final days but Remain seemed to have the edge. That morning, *the Guardian* had published their interview with her. They described her as 'the unlikely poster girl of the Remain campaign'.

Well, it was pretty bloody unlikely Marianne said to herself. I *won't argue with that.*

Turnout was tepid during the day. Marianne spent a long, slow afternoon knocking on doors that weren't answered. Still, those she found in had either voted or seemed quite enthused about doing so. Back at the committee room, the atmosphere was languid.

From the early evening onwards, the pace rapidly accelerated. People started coming home from work and seemed to need little persuading to vote.

"I'm getting a really good feeling" Marianne said to Bridget.

It was shortly before 7pm. They were standing on a street corner wearing their 'Labour In' stickers. Bridget was leading a team of canvassers.

"Well, it looks like West London has turned out for Remain" she said. "We'll just have to see what happens elsewhere."

A familiar black jeep drew up alongside them and Sam got out. It was the first time Marianne had seen him for weeks.

"Hello!" she said.

"I just had to come and help" he told her. "I hope you don't mind."

"Of course I don't mind!" Marianne hugged him, briefly burying her head in his shoulder. She inhaled the scent of his crisp white shirt and his aftershave.

"And *I* certainly don't mind" said Bridget. She kissed him on the cheek. "It's always good to have someone who knows what they're doing."

The next couple of hours were made more agreeable by Sam's presence. As far as canvassing went, it was an easy sell. Marianne had never seen such willingness to go out to vote.

Just before 9.30pm, Bridget said "I think we can wrap this up now."

Most of the other volunteers had tailed off. More importantly, there were hardly any Remain voters left to call on.

A terrible thought then occurred to Marianne. "Fuck, fuck, shitty fuck" she said.

Bridget and Sam looked at her, questioningly.

"I haven't voted" she told them. "I forgot to go."

"But you've just spent the whole day reminding *other people* to vote" said Sam.

"I know! Oh Christ! What am I going to do?"

"You still have time" said Bridget. "Where's your polling station?"

"At the church hall, just around the corner from my house."

"I can drive you there" said Sam. "We'll have to be quick though."

His jeep was parked a few streets away.

"Go, go!" Bridget told them.

Sam grabbed Marianne's hand.   He began running, with her in tow. Marianne found herself becoming breathless very quickly.

"Buggery, shit, bollocks, fuck" she said. "I'm not fit enough for this."

"Focus on breathing rather than swearing" said Sam, as he pulled her along the street.

"Easy for you to say!" Marianne gasped

"In through the nose and out through the mouth."

They made it to the polling station with ten minutes to spare. Sam waited outside in the jeep while Marianne voted.

"Thank fuck for that" she said when she came back. "I would never, ever have forgiven myself if we lost this referendum by one vote."

"It won't be that close" said Sam as he started up the engine. He then looked at her. "I'm just wondering if you'd like dinner before I drive you home. I'd really like to talk."

"Okay" said Marianne. "That would be nice."

He took her to a kebab shop at the less salubrious end of Greenwood High Road.

"Last time we had dinner together" said Marianne "it was in a Michelin-starred restaurant."

"I know" he said. "This place is the most disreputable, disgusting health hazard in West London. My junior doctor colleagues love it."

"They won't live to your age if they don't change their habits" said Marianne

"That's what I keep telling them."

They sat on plastic chairs near the counter. An awkwardness descended as they were about to eat.

"There's something I want to tell you" said Sam. "I started seeing a counsellor a couple of weeks ago."

"That *is* good" said Marianne. "How are you finding it?"

"Awful!" he said. "I hate. It's like the emotional equivalent of a colonoscopy."

"When you put it like that..."

"But I recognise I need to do it" said Sam. "For myself as much as anyone else."

Marianne said: "Sam, I didn't want to sound like I was giving you an ultimatum. I just need to live in some sort of truth. I don't judge you for what happened but it's too big just to ignore."

"I understand" he said. "Anyhow, the subject of *relationships* has come up."

"Oh yes?"

"The counsellor advises against what he calls 'accelerated' relationships. Or too much, too soon."

"It sounds like sensible advice" said Marianne.

"Well, this is what I want to talk to about" he said. "I want to ask if you'd like us to start seeing each other again. We'd take it a bit slower than before. One day at a time."

"Yes, I absolutely would" said Marianne, smiling. "I have really missed you."

He took her home. They coincided with Karen who was just parking. Marianne kissed Sam goodnight before he drove off.

Karen was unlocking the front door when Marianne approached. "Are you and Dishy Doctor Sam back on?" she asked.

"Might be" said Marianne, smiling coyly.

She hadn't told Karen the full story.

They dropped their bags in the hallway. Karen opened a bottle of Merlot in the kitchen and poured them both a glass.

"What sort of day have you had?" Marianne asked.

"I've been running around like a blue-arsed fly" said Karen. "But I managed not to slap anyone or shout at them."

They went into the sitting room to watch the results of the referendum come in. Karen switched on the TV.

Early indications suggested a narrow Remain win. Nigel Farage was interviewed at one point and conceded defeat.

"Haha! Wanker!" said Karen.

They clinked their wine glasses.

Their mood changed, however, when more results came in. After about an hour, it became clear that the North East of England had voted to leave.

"That's not very encouraging" said Marianne.

The following results were even less encouraging. A clear divide had opened between Britain's cities and provinces

"Fucking hell" said Karen. "This isn't looking good."

Marianne scrolled through Twitter. She was struck by a post from a commentator she rated.

He'd tweeted: *'Something feels off.'*

They were glued to the TV for hours. Eventually, reality dawned. Britain had voted to leave the European Union, albeit narrowly. Marianne was numb with disbelief. She hadn't been expecting this.

In the early hours, Nigel Farage spoke at a rally. He gloated at them from the TV.

"And we will have done it" he intoned. "Without having to fight, without a single bullet being fired."

Marianne sprung up from her seat.

"What the fuck!" she hissed. "Did you hear that? *Not a single bullet being fired*. He actually said that. After what happened to Jo Cox."

"I know". Karen shook her head disbelievingly.

Marianne stared at Farage on the screen. "You fucking bastard" she said. "You total, utter fucking bastard."

Chapter Eleven

“I think Corbyn will be gone by Friday” said the young intern.

It was the Monday after the referendum.

“Do you think?” said Marianne.

They were in the kitchenette used by staffers in the surrounding offices. Marianne was in there making coffee for her and Ben. The young intern worked for another MP.

“Leaders *have to* have the support of their MPs” he said, knowledgeably.

He was a slightly built young man, perhaps about nineteen or twenty. He seemed to be wearing his dad’s suit. Marianne thought him rather sweet. His manner suggested a particularly youthful combination of ambition and naivety.

She smiled at him. “We’ll just have to see” she said.

Westminster was feverish with speculation. Jeremy Corbyn was engulfed in a leadership crisis. The day after the referendum, he had called for the triggering of Article 50 to hasten Britain’s exit. This outraged Labour MPs who’d campaigned to remain. A weekend of tumult followed with a succession of resignations from the frontbench.

Marianne’s own attitude to Corbyn had hardened. After the referendum, she could no longer maintain a neutral opinion. She felt betrayed. His leadership of Labour’s Remain campaign had been deliberately tepid.

Now we’re landed with Brexit she thought. *It’s a disaster.*

She and Ben had spent the morning speculating. Ana had not yet joined the mass exodus from the frontbench. They wondered what she would do.

Ben said: "She's trapped between a rock and a hard place. She won't want to jeopardise her relationship with Momentum. On the other hand, she won't want to be seen to be propping up Corbyn either."

"I can't say I'm wildly sympathetic" said Marianne. "I just hope that she doesn't drive us mad with her indecision."

Marianne's hopes were dashed. She and Ben received an e-mail from Ana summoning them upstairs for a meeting at 2pm.

"Afternoon team" she said briskly when they went in.

She motioned at them to sit at the sofa next to the door.

"I want you to draft a statement" she told them. "I want it published on my website and all my social media platforms by the end of the day."

Fuck me! She's resigning! Marianne thought.

She and Ben nodded encouragingly.

Ana continued: "I'm suspending work on my frontbench portfolio. Until the question of the party leadership has been resolved."

"Might writing to the Leader be more appropriate" suggested Ben, gingerly.

"No, Ben. This is not a resignation." She said this with a certain firmness.

What? Are you going on strike? Marianne said inwardly. *That's taking the piss a bit if you ask me.*

“We’ll need to be careful with the wording” she said to Ana. “It might be…*interpreted* as a resignation.”

She had tried hard to be tactful. Still, Ana seemed to bristle at this.

“Resignation! Is that what you both think I should do? Resign from the frontbench. Make a martyr of myself. Is that why you’re both being so resistant?”

There was a palpable note of anxiety in her voice. On one hand, she seemed to be berating them. On the other, she sounded like she was asking for advice.

“I think that is a matter for you” said Marianne.

Ben nodded in agreement.

Ana sighed wearily. “Okay. Fine” she said. “All I want you both to do is show a bit of initiative for once, if that’s not too much to ask. Just draft something and send it over before five. Okay.”

Charming as ever Marianne said to herself.

She and Ben went back to their office. They spent about an hour working on this non-resignation statement. It was a torturous process. They debated each paragraph.

“She won’t like that” said Ben at one point. “She’ll think it’s too critical of Jeremy.”

“But she thinks his leadership sucks” said Marianne. “Isn’t that why she’s erm…*not* resigning?”

“She didn’t exactly *say* that” said Ben. “It’s more that she has concerns…about the concerns about his leadership.”

“Yeah, makes perfect sense.” Marianne felt grumpy and irritated.

Between them, they crafted a suitably bland statement. They did their best to make it coherent, glossing over any contradictions. When they'd finished, Marianne e-mailed it to Ana.

Later that afternoon, Marianne was going through Ana's diary for the week. She noticed some rather interesting entries that Ana had made herself. She was extending a great deal of hospitality to local Labour councillors in Greenwood. She was having drinks with some that evening. A couple more were coming for tea in the Pugin Room the next day. The more influential ones had been invited to dine with her.

Curiouser and curiouser Marianne said to herself.

Most of these councillors were Momentum supporters. A couple, she knew, were deadly political rivals of Pete Samuelson. Something was clearly afoot. Ana would have a reason for entertaining them.

Marianne and Ben were about to leave for the day when the office door suddenly flung open. Ana steamed in. She was brandishing a printout of the statement they'd written.

"Is this really the best you can do?" she hissed at them. "This has to be the most vacuous, meaningless piece of drivel I've ever read."

"We thought that's what you wanted" said Marianne.

Ana slammed the printout down on her desk. "Really poor effort. It's just not fucking good enough."

"Would you like us to do it again?" asked Ben.

"Don't bother" said Ana. "Just put it up on the website and get it over with."

She turned on her heel and slammed the door behind her.

Marianne and Ben exchanged glances.

"You get off" said Ben. "I'll post this online."

He sat back down at his desk and restarted his computer.

That evening, a 'Keep Corbyn' protest had been organised outside Parliament. Marianne saw it as she left. The Labour leadership crisis had excited a great deal of interest. Seemingly thousands of Corbynistas had converged on Parliament Square. Their enraged chants must have been audible for miles.

"Blairites out! Corbyn in!" seemed to be their mantra.

Many were holding up Socialist Worker Party placards. There were quite a few homemade efforts too. All proclaimed devotion to the great man himself. Some of the protestors reminded Marianne of people she'd known at university. She thought a few of them might even be there this evening. They would have aged but with their adolescent world view intact and consumed by this snarling fanaticism.

"It's been a bloody long day" Marianne said to Karen when she got home.

She dropped her bag on a kitchen chair. Karen was cooking dinner

"Every day with Madam must seem like an eternity" said Karen.

"Well, some days are hell. Others just seem like purgatory."

"I bet" said Karen. "Just bangers and mash for supper tonight. Hope that's alright."

"That sounds perfect" said Marianne. "I'm just happy to have someone else cook for me."

"Well make yourself useful and pour us a glass of vino" said Karen.

Marianne did as she was told. Karen took a break from cooking and sat down with her at the kitchen table.

"Big vote tomorrow then" she said taking a gulp of her wine.

"Yep" said Marianne.

The Parliamentary Labour Party were to have a vote of confidence in their leader. Corbyn was widely expected to lose.

"Has Madam said how she's voting yet?" Karen asked.

"Nope. She's playing her cards very close to her chest."

"Fucks sake" said Karen. "She always tries to ride two horses."

"Yes, I know."

They silently contemplated Ana's mendacity for a moment.

Karen said: "Corbyn's not the only Labour leader facing a confidence vote this week."

"Oh?" said Marianne

"Pete has one coming up. It's happening on Thursday night at the Greenwood Labour Group meeting."

"Really" said Marianne. "Why?"

"Things have come to a head with the Regeneration Partnership. Some people think he's lost control."

"What are his chances?" Marianne asked.

Karen pondered this for a moment. "It's going to be tight" she said. "He's has been working the 'phones like a bastard. But some of the councillors are really spooked by Momentum. And they're sick of being trolled by that account Ned Critchley-Smith runs."

"The Great Greenwood Giveaway?"

"That's the one. Pete is absolutely convinced Ana is behind it all."

"It's funny you should say that" said Marianne.

Karen raised her eyebrows.

"I was looking at Ana's diary earlier" Marianne told her. "She's definitely on some sort of charm offensive. She's seeing a whole load of Greenwood councillors this week for drinks and dinner."

"Really?" said Karen. "That is *very* interesting."

"I think Pete is probably right" said Marianne. "I don't know for sure. I just know she's not motivated by kindness."

"That reminds me" said Karen. "Speaking of parliamentary hospitality, are you coming to Nigel's drinks on Thursday? You can bring Dishy Doctor Sam if you like."

They had been invited by Nigel Patel to his summer drinks party. He held it each year on the House of Commons terrace, weather permitting, and invited local worthies and supporters.

"I'll see if Sam wants to come" said Marianne. "I'm seeing him tomorrow night. He'd probably enjoy it. I'm not that fussed myself."

"I'd really appreciate it" Karen said. "I'm a bit worried about numbers. I think Nigel feels people have been boycotting him."

"People are very paranoid at the moment" said Marianne.

In the office, the next morning, she and Ben speculated about the confidence vote later that day.

"There's no question Corbyn's going to lose" said Ben. "It's a matter of by how much, and what he does about it."

"Surely, he'll have to resign" said Marianne. "Margaret Thatcher was finished when her MPs lost faith in her."

"You'd think."

Joni arrived. As always, she seemed to be keeping her own hours. Still, it was unusual for her to be in this early. She looked dishevelled and unkempt and was deeply agitated.

She looks like a bag lady Marianne thought.

She didn't bother saying hello or good morning today. Instead, she said: "I just can't believe the scale of this betrayal!"

"I'm sorry" said Marianne although she knew exactly what Joni was talking about.

Joni dropped her bags behind her desk. "It's the complicity in this neoliberal deep state conspiracy against Jeremy" she said. "People don't seem to realise they're being manipulated by the mainstream media. There is a vast coalition of vested interests involved. But Jeremy has the support of the people…"

She rambled on in this vein. Marianne had become increasingly concerned about Joni. The death of Jo Cox seemed to unsettle her. In some ways, she had become increasingly withdrawn. She was very pale and had lost weight. Still, her very limited self-awareness had diminished altogether. Her monologues were longer and less coherent. Marianne wondered if she was having some sort of breakdown.

Joni settled herself behind her desk and switched on her computer. Her agitation subsided and she stopped rambling. Shortly afterwards, Ana came into the office.

"Morning team" she said.

They never found out what she wanted. Joni immediately sprung up from her seat and invaded her personal space.

"Ana" she said breathlessly. "You're going to support Jeremy, aren't you? Your statement was very disappointing. But at least you didn't resign. This is about the will of the membership."

There was a moment of stunned silence. Ana stepped back away from her.

"I appreciate you sharing your thoughts, Joni" she said icily. "I am always interested in the views of my *employees*."

Her coolness didn't deter Joni.

She said: "It is very important that you listen…"

"No, you LISTEN!" Ana roared.

Her eyes were black with fury. Her frostiness had given way to molten rage.

"I don't answer to you" she said. "You're here as a member of my staff. It's time you remembered that. Unless you're thinking of leaving of course."

She turned to go.

"But you *are* going to support Jeremy aren't you!" cried Joni.

She grabbed Ana's arm.

Christ! That's dangerous! Marianne thought.

Ana spun around, snarling like cobra. "Get *the fuck* off me!" she hissed. "How fucking dare you touch me like that! Who the fuck do you think *you are*?"

Joni took her hand away and stepped back. She seemed to realise she'd gone too far.

Ana pointed at her desk. "Pack up your shit" she said. "And go and work in the other office. I don't want to see you here for the rest of the week."

She left, slamming the door behind her as had become her habit.

Later, after Joni had gone, Ben said "I actually thought Ana was going to hit Joni for a moment."

She certainly has form for that Marianne said to herself. *But I'll tell you that story some other time.*

That afternoon, Marianne took a late lunch. She went to a café off Victoria Street. She was grateful it wasn't too busy. Her 'phone rang as she was eating her sandwich. It was Pete Samuelson. She answered.

"Hi Pete" she said.

"Hi Marianne. How's things?"

"Good. Thank you."

"Excellent. You know I have this bollocks confidence vote on Thursday night."

"Yes."

"I hear Ana is entertaining some of the councillors."

"That's right" said Marianne. "And I'm guessing you want me to tell you who they are."

"That would be tremendous" he said.

"I'll send you a text" said Marianne. "In the strictest confidence as always."

"Of course" said Pete. "Really appreciate it."

Marianne said: "You're going to do one of two things, aren't you? Persuade them or kneecap them."

She heard his Muttley-style chuckle down the 'phone.

"Maybe both" he said. "But I have another trick up my sleeve. It *will blow* Ned Critchley-Smith and his little pals out of the water."

Marianne was intrigued, but she didn't ask him to elaborate.

That evening, she met Sam at a cocktail bar. It was in a basement beneath a furniture shop on the edge of Holborn and Covent Garden. She knew it from her student days. It was something of a 1980s institution with distressed, minimalist décor that had barely changed in thirty years. They sat on stools sipping mojitos.

"How are you are coping with fame?" Sam asked her jokingly.

Marianne laughed. "I don't have to anymore" she said. "All that media attention has just dried up, as I knew it would."

This was true. Marianne had expected the referendum to eclipse everything. Still, she was a little surprised by how quickly she'd been forgotten. The interview requests had stopped instantly, and her 'phone was no longer buzzing with notifications.

"That's instant celebrity for you" said Sam.

At that moment, Marianne's 'phone vibrated. She wondered if they'd spoken too soon. She pulled it out of her bag and looked at the screen. It was a text from Ben about the confidence vote. Corbyn had lost by 172 votes to 40. An overwhelming majority of his MPs had expressed no confidence in him. She related this to Sam.

"I can't see how he can hang on now" she said. "Surely he's going to have to resign."

"I don't think he's going to" said Sam. "If anything, he's going to stare down his MPs and appeal to the members. He'll force another leadership election."

"That could be dangerous for him" said Marianne

"I don't think it is. I think he'd win it easily. And probably win even bigger this time. The really interesting thing is the implications for the Labour Party."

"What do you mean?" Marianne asked

"It would fundamentally change what the Labour Party is" he said. "Until now, it's been all about the elected representatives, the MPs and the councillors. They have the power. If Corbyn gets his way, it will be transferred to the party members."

"I can see that" said Marianne. "This isn't just about who the leader is or what our policies are."

“Exactly.”

Marianne stirred her mojito with a straw.

“Well” she said. ”It would interesting to see how that would play out locally. Pete Samuelson would be in a lot of trouble.”

She told Sam about Pete’s latest travails, and about her conversation with him earlier that day.

“Hmmm” said Sam, meaningfully.

“Is that a disapproving “hmmm”?” Marianne asked.

“No. It’s not disapproving. It’s just that… You know what? It’s not my place to say.”

“No, I’d like you to say what you’re thinking” Marianne said. “I find your interest quite refreshing.”

Sam paused so he could choose his words carefully.

“It strikes me that there is this epic power struggle between Ana and Pete” he said.

“Understatement of the century” said Marianne. “You’re not telling me anything I don’t already know.”

“Well, you’ve been caught right in the middle of it” Sam said.

He paused again

“How can I put this? I think that they’re both using you for their own ends.”

Marianne felt unsettled by this, and a little defensive. Surely Sam would realise that she and Pete were friends. They were on the same side. She wasn’t naïve or a fool either. She would be able to tell if she was being played.

"I don't think that's quite true, Sam" she said. "I don't think Pete would intentionally misuse me…"

"It might not be intentional" said Sam. "Or malicious. I just know how people behave when the stakes are very high. They lose their moral compass, and they can become very manipulative."

"I don't think I'm exactly easy to manipulate" said Marianne.

"I don't think you are either" he said. "Maybe I shouldn't have said anything. I don't want to come over like the overly protective boyfriend. I know you can take care of yourself. *But…*

He looked down at his glass and then back up at her and held her gaze.

"At some point, Pete and Ana will move in for the kill" he said. "I'm just worried you'll get caught in the crossfire."

They stared at each other for a moment. An ominous cloud had descended on their evening

His words were hugely discomfiting to Marianne. She realised later it was because they had a ring of truth. Pete and Ana had always been concerned with their own agendas, and she only featured in their calculations when it suited them.

When Sam went back to the bar to buy more drinks, Ben texted again. He sent a link to a BBC News story. The headline read "*Ana Novak quits Labour frontbench*."

Ana had resigned as a shadow housing minister after the confidence vote. However, she'd stopped short of calling for Corbyn to resign.

Marianne replied to Ben. *'Such timing. Look forward to writing another statement.'*

Early on Thursday morning, Karen came into her bedroom and shook her awake. She had *the Daily Star* open on her iPad.

"You are not going to fucking believe this!" she said.

Talk about a rude awakening Marianne thought to herself.

She looked at her alarm clock. It had just gone 6.30am. Reluctantly, she sat up in bed and tried to focus on the screen Karen was proffering. After a moment, she was able to make sense of the headline.

*'Corbyn Superfans' Sleazy Sh*gfest'*

Squinting, she read the story. It was about the Global Solidarity house. Ned Critchley-Smith seemed to feature prominently.

'The Global Solidarity Group are a coven of young Corbyn fanatics who share a house in leafy Greenwood in West London. They like lefty party politics. But they also like parties that go with A BANG!!! Their house was the scene of a drugs-fuelled orgy when coked-up couples romped naked on the lawn. A neighbour said: "It was disgusting. They were like animals on the Discovery Channel."

This pack of party animals are led by trainee solicitor Ned Critchley-Smith, 23, from Cheltenham. Naughty boy Ned has links with senior Labour figures, including Jeremy Corbyn and he's close to rising Labour star Ana Novak MP…but not that close.'

"Fucking hell" said Marianne. "What a stitch-up."

The story was accompanied by three pictures. One was a pixelated photo of the partygoers copulating on the lawn. Ned appeared in the background, fully clothed and perfectly decent. His mouth seemed to be agape in some sort of shock or horror. He certainly didn't look like he was participating. There was also a selfie of him with Jeremy Corbyn, and another with Ana.

"Madam is going to go apeshit when she sees this" Karen said. "What did you mean by "stitch-up"?"

"Something Joni said" Marianne replied. "She reckons they were gate-crashed. And I think it's probably true. *There were* people shagging on the lawn. But Global Solidarity weren't actually involved."

"It doesn't actually say they were" said Karen. "But it happened at their house. This story just has bare facts, no pun intended ha ha, and loads of insinuation. It doesn't help that Ned is the pictures."

Marianne said: "They must have done some digging. Somebody must have told them where to look. I just hope Ana doesn't want us to write a frigging statement about it."

Her 'phone vibrated at that moment. It was a text from Ana.

'*Come straight to my office as soon as you get in.*'

'Is that Madam?" Karen asked.

"Yep." Marianne felt her stomach lurch.

She showered and ate breakfast as quickly as she could. There was no rational reason why Ana would blame her. In fact, it probably wasn't why she'd texted. She might be in trouble for some whole other reason.

She took the tube into Westminster and felt sick with dread the entire way. To calm her nerves, she looked at Twitter. This proved a bad idea. The first tweet she saw had been posted by Pete who'd gleefully drawn attention to the *Daily Star* story. This had elicited many retweets, replies and terrible puns. Before long, it seemed like the whole of Twitter was about talking it.

As instructed, she went straight to Ana's office. She braced herself before knocking. Her heart felt like it was beating dangerously fast.

"Come in!" she heard Ana bark from inside.

Never had she been so reluctant to enter a room. The blinds were pulled down when she went in. Ana was sitting behind her desk, rubbing her temples. It was as if she was nursing a hangover.

"You wanted to see me" said Marianne.

Ana just stared at her hard without speaking, her lips pursed.

Marianne wondered if she should try to fill the silence but decided against it. Instead, she tried to look back at Ana without seeming insolent.

There was a paper copy of *the Daily Star* open on the desk. Ana carried on staring at her while she closed it and rolled it up. She then hurled it at Marianne, striking her on the chest.

Marianne gasped in shock

"What. The. Fuck" hissed Ana.

It took Marianne a moment to recover herself.

"I do know about the story" she said trying not to stammer with nerves.

"I bet you fucking know about it" Ana said. "It is a vile, sleazy hatchet job. It is *clearly* intended to damage *my* reputation. In fact, I wouldn't be surprised if *YOU* WROTE IT!"

She was roaring with fury now. Her face had assumed the expression of an enraged predator.

"I really don't understand why you would think that" said Marianne, as evenly as she could.

Ana sat back in her chair

"Now why would I think that?" she said, tapping her fingers on the desk. "Let's look at the evidence, shall we? Firstly, there's your fifteen minutes of fame. You enjoyed that *while it lasted*, didn't you? I bet you're missing the attention."

"That just isn't true" said Marianne.

"I'm not so sure" said Ana. "It would have given you some media contacts. Secondly, I know that you've had cosy little chats with Pete Samuelson about this."

"Did Joni tell you that?"

Ana looked as if she'd been caught off-guard for a moment. She ignored the question. "Now, we both know that Samuelson is behind this" she said. "He knew what to look for. Because you told him."

"I had a conversation with him about it" said Marianne. "I just repeated what Joni told me. I wasn't expecting him to do anything with it."

"Why have that conversation with him at all?" Ana shook her head slightly as if despairing

"Well, I…"

"You're quite pally with him, aren't you?" said Ana, her eyes narrowing.

Marianne tried to calibrate her words carefully. "Well, I'm active in the Greenwood Labour Party and we come across each other. But…"

"And you live with Karen Giannapoulos" Ana interjected. "I find it very curious that you kept that from me for so long."

"It was never meant to be a secret."

Ana leaned forward. "The thing is, Marianne" she said. "You seem to have forgotten something very important. You don't work for Samuelson or for Karen. You work for me. Yet I don't have the slightest confidence in your loyalty or discretion."

"I'm sorry you feel that way" said Marianne, not entirely without indignation.

Ana said: "If you had been loyal, if you had been discreet, none of this would have happened. There would be no hatchet job in *the Daily Star*. Your problem is that you're too susceptible to flattery. You like to gossip too much."

"I don't think that's fair."

"No. No, I'm sure you don't." Ana smiled ruefully. "You must have been working for me for about a year now."

"Yes, I think so."

"Well, I think it's time we did your appraisal" said Ana. "We can talk about your loyalty and discretion. I think we also need to discuss the quality of your work. To be honest, it's not that hot. Perhaps you'd put a date in my diary. Sometime in the next fortnight."

"Yes, but…"

"You can go now" Ana said.

Marianne decided it was pointless to say anything else. She made to leave.

"One more thing, Marianne."

"Yes."

"Greenwood Council is going to have a new leader after tonight." Ana smirked. "Long overdue in my opinion. So you've backed the wrong horse. Always a fatal mistake in politics. You might want to think about that."

Marianne went back to her office. There was only Ben there.

"I need to go out for a bit" she told him. "If Ana should ask where I am, can you cover for me?"

He looked a bit taken aback by the urgency of her manner.

"Sure" he said. "That's fine."

Marianne cantered through St Stephen's Hall on her way out. She was almost at the exit when she ran into Joni. There was no hope of avoiding her.

"Marianne, Marianne!" Joni cried when she saw her. "I need to talk to you!"

Her agitation was bordering on distress. Marianne thought that she looked like she hadn't showered in days or had had much sleep either. Her long hair was all over the place, like a birds' nest.

"I'm sorry, Joni. I really have to run" she said.

Joni grabbed her wrist and stared into her eyes. Her grasp was so tight, it hurt.

"Have you seen those lies and smears in *the Daily Star*?" She was almost weeping. "The neoliberal mainstream media will stop at nothing to destroy Jeremy. Anybody is fair game as collateral damage. They don't care about destroying the reputations of a group of idealistic young people..."

Marianne pulled her wrist away. "I've seen it" she said. "Look, I don't think anyone is going to take much notice of *the Daily Star*. It's tomorrow's fish and chip paper. It will all blow over."

"How can you say that?" said Joni.

"Sorry, Joni. We're going to have to talk about this later." She turned on her heel and ran.

She took the tube from Westminster to Greenwood Town Hall. On the way, she thought about her predicament. She was now in a situation where she could lose her job. It was partly her fault. Perhaps she hadn't been as discreet as she could have been. Then again, she'd been overly trusting in the discretion of others.

"I'm here to see Councillor Samuelson" she told the receptionist when she arrived at the town hall.

"Is the Leader expecting you?"

"No" she said. "But I'd like you to call his office and tell him I'm here."

She waited for a few minutes. Pete's assistant appeared and took her to his office through a labyrinth of tiled, high-ceilinged corridors.

"Marianne, this is an unexpected pleasure" Pete said when she was shown in. He stood up behind his desk. "Welcome to the Leader's office."

She hadn't been in there before. It was a large, light room in the corner of the building with its own conference table. Pete's desk was in the far corner.

Marianne pushed the door closed behind her. She looked at Pete and said: "Pete Samuelson, you are a fucking arsehole."

Pete's mouth dropped open. He looked at her for a moment agog.

"What? Why?" he spluttered. "I don't understand. What have I done?"

"You were responsible for that story in *the Daily Star*, weren't you?"

Realisation dawned on him.

"Oh yes, that." He chuckled Muttley-style. "It was your tip-off that helped."

"I shared that information with you in good faith" said Marianne. "I didn't expect you to go off and use it for some other purpose. Especially one you hadn't told me about."

"Why are you so angry about it?" asked Pete. He looked genuinely baffled. "You have no sympathy for Global Solidarity."

"I'll tell you why!" Marianne snapped. "I am angry because I'm the one who's been compromised. Ana blames me and she's threatening me with the sack."

"I don't get it" he said. "Why does she blame you?"

"Joni must have said something" she told him. "She overheard us talking in the kitchen."

"That's a bummer" he said. "But she can't prove it."

"Doesn't matter. You've put the skids under me."

"I didn't mean for that to happen" Pete said apologetically. "You have to understand that my back is against the wall."

"So you decided to throw me under a bus to save yourself."

"No!" he protested "That wasn't my intention."

"I don't care about your intention!" Marianne growled. "You know something. I *get* the politics of this. There's a battle for the heart and soul of the Labour Party. And you are fighting it any way you can..."

"You understand then?" said Pete, hopefully

"I understand that you're losing this battle, Pete" she said. "And I'm sorry about that because I've always been on your side. But, for future, reference, don't bother asking me for anything else. I am sick and tired of being a pawn in other people's games! I'm not playing anymore."

With that, she left slamming the door behind her.

She made her way back to Westminster. Much to her relief, Joni had gone and there was no sign that Ana had missed her either.

"Was Joni here long?" she asked Ben.

"Nope" he said. "She went up to see Ana and then came back down here for a bit. She was going on and on about that story in *the Daily Star*."

"Did she mention me at all?"

"No" said Ben. "What makes you ask?"

"Oh, just wondered."

This was odd. Joni clearly didn't hold her responsible for the article. If she had, the whole world would have known it. Still, who else could have told Ana about her conversation with Pete? The more she thought about it, the less sense it made.

Nigel Patel's summer drinks party was that evening. Marianne was really not in the mood. She would rather have gone home. Still, Sam and Karen would be there. Sam was excited by the prospect of drinks on the House of Commons terrace. He hadn't been inside Parliament before.

The party started at 7pm. There was absolutely no point in her going home so she worked late. This proved productive as she was able to reply to dozens of dreary e-mails. She went to the ladies' to freshen up before she went.

When she arrived, the terrace was very busy. It was full of suited politicos and their visitors enjoying the early summer evening. Corks popped and the scent of wine pervaded the air. The River Thames glistened and glittered. On the other side of the river, the London Eye slowly revolved.

She found Karen and Sam on the edge of the terrace. They had a glass of wine each. Karen was, unusually, wearing an expensive looking dress and heels and carried a Mulberry bag. Sam wore a navy suit and purple tie. Marianne thought he looked very handsome.

"I almost didn't recognise you" she said to Karen.

"I don't scrub up too badly, do I?"

"Marianne, can I get you a drink?" asked Sam.

"That would be lovely. Thank you."

Sam went to fetch a glass of wine from one of the waiters. Marianne noticed him get side-tracked by Nigel Patel and become immersed in conversation. She hoped he wouldn't be too long as she was dying for a drink.

"Pete told me what happened earlier" said Karen.

"Oh."

"It sounds like you tore him a second arsehole. I'm sure he deserved it."

"He absolutely did" said Marianne

"I'm not defending him" said Karen. "But he didn't know he'd get you in trouble. He things very highly of you."

Marianne sighed. "That's all well and good. The problem is Ana is now on my case. I could be unemployed very soon."

"Have you thought about applying for another job?" suggested Karen. "Nigel over there is looking for a new caseworker and you have all the right experience. Unlike Madam, he's not a total nightmare to work for."

"That's not such a bad idea" said Marianne. "Just need to get a reference from Ana. At the moment, that would be like trying to steal something from the jaws of a crocodile."

"Well she is a bit reptilian" Karen said.

Marianne let out a shriek of laughter.

Karen's 'phone buzzed when received a text from Pete.

"He's won the confidence vote" she told Marianne as she read the message. "By three votes."

"Crikey, that's close. Do you think it had anything to do with that story in *the Daily Star?"*

"Probably" said Karen. "It's funny. Yesterday, all the Labour councillors were shitting their pants over Global Solidarity and their stupid Twitter feed. Today, they're laughing at them. So yeah, it's had an effect. "

Marianne said: "Tell Pete congratulations from me. But make it clear that I'm still pissed off with him and will be for some time."

"I will pass that on" Karen murmured as she typed her response.

Sam reappeared and handed Marianne a glass of white wine.

"I'm really sorry" he said. "But I've got to take a call. One of my young colleagues is trying to deal with a psychiatric emergency."

"That's fine" said Marianne. "You do what you have to."

Karen finished typing. "Right. That's that done. Hopefully Pete will behave himself for the next couple of weeks…oh fucking hell."

She was staring, disbelievingly, over Marianne's shoulder.

"What's up?" said Marianne as she turned around to see what Karen was looking at.

She was confronted by the spectre of a wild-eyed Joni. She seemed possessed by a demonic hatred. Her extraordinary Medusa-like appearance had attracted everyone's attention.

"It was YOU!" she shouted accusingly at Marianne. "Ana told me!"

Karen clearly sensed danger. She stepped between them.

"Now Joni" she said as if speaking to a child. "I don't know what this all about. But you need to calm down. Everyone is staring and you don't want to make an exhibition of yourself, do you?"

Joni didn't seem to hear any of this. She just carried on staring at Marianne's face. She was shaking.

"You are an evil LYING CUNT!" she screeched. "I AM GOING TO KILL YOU!"

She launched herself at Marianne, grabbing her throat with one hand and her hair with another. Marianne screamed. Her glass smashed on the ground as she dropped it. She started to choke as Joni's grip tightened on her throat. There were gasps from the terrace.

Karen yelled "GET THE FUCK OFF HER!" and threw her glass down.

She pulled Joni back by the scruff of her neck. Joni tried to lunge at Marianne again, but Karen restrained her. She tried again. Karen responded by slapping her hard across the face. This momentarily subdued her. She squealed with frustration and begun clawing at Karen.

Karen slapped her a second, a third and fourth time. Blood began to pour out of one of her nostrils. Exhausted and defeated, she gave up. She curled into the foetal position against the wall of the terrace. Rocking herself, she howled and sobbed in anguish. The entire terrace stared on in silent disbelief and horror.

"What the hell is going on?" demanded Sam when he came back.

Marianne didn't know how to answer. She could barely speak.

Joni looked up. "Samir" she moaned. "Samir, is that you? You've got to help me."

"It's alright, Mrs Lessing" said Sam. "We'll get you the help you need."

He pulled his 'phone from the pocket of his jacket and dialled 999. "Ambulance" he said. "It's a mental health emergency."

Joni was admitted to a psychiatric ward that evening.

Chapter Twelve

'*Catfight at the Commons over Corbyn'* proclaimed the *Daily Mail* headline.

"That is *not* what happened" said Marianne.

"They're not going to let the facts get in the way of a good story" said Sam.

They were sat at the table in his flat, drinking coffee. It was Saturday morning. Two days had passed since the incident on the terrace. Marianne was reading from Sam's iPad.

"I probably shouldn't even look at this" she said. "For the sake of my own sanity."

Despite herself, she scrolled down and read aloud.

'*Tensions are boiling over in the Labour leadership crisis. Two political insiders brawled at a boozy bash on the Commons' terrace. The slap-happy socialist sisters are Momentum bigwig Joni Lessing (53) and Remain poster girl Marianne Stuart (32)'*

"Oh, that is just marvellous" she said. "They've basically called us a pair of drunken old slappers. How do they know our ages anyway?"

"Somebody must have told them" said Sam.

Marianne carried on reading.

'*The pair work for Labour MP Ana Novak who last week resigned as shadow housing minister and called for Jeremy Corbyn's resignation. Singleton Marianne Stuart has worked for her since July last year. Mrs Lessing, a married mum of three, was hired in January.*'

"Where the fuck are they getting all this from?" she wondered aloud.

Sam just shook his head.

He said: "They've left out Joni being sectioned because she was acutely psychotic. Then again, maybe that's a good thing."

"Maybe."

She was staying at Sam's for the weekend, on Karen's advice. She'd wanted to avoid being door-stepped by the press. The incident on the terrace had caused a media furore. Karen had told her how to deal with it.

"Switch off all your social media" she'd said. "Don't engage with it. Don't even look at it. Disable your notifications and just lie low for the weekend. Hopefully, this will all have blown over by Monday."

Marianne had followed this advice. Still, she couldn't stop herself reading some of the stories online. She was worried about having to face Ana on Monday. She had started smoking again.

She and Karen had been interviewed by the police the day after the party. They'd wanted the details of the incident. Marianne supposed this wasn't unreasonable. After all, they would have heard many lurid accounts. Joni had ended up bleeding and gibbering on the House of Commons terrace.

Karen had been worried about assault charges but the police accepted she'd used reasonable force in the circumstances. They had seen the CCTV footage. She and Marianne were therefore absolved of blame.

Ana had been out of London on the Friday so Marianne hadn't seen her. Still, she was unnerved by the total radio silence. She'd thought Ana would have been in touch. Surely she'd be worried about the media coverage and would want to know the facts. Perhaps she'd contacted Joni's husband to ask about her welfare.

Marianne hadn't slept well. She'd had a recurring dream: a slow-motion replay of Joni's attack. She could see the expression in Joni's eyes as she lunged towards her. She could feel Joni's hand tightening around her throat. The worst part of it was the mortification, the staring bystanders.

"It just feels so real" she told Sam.

"I know that one" he said.

The next day, Marianne met Bridget for a Sunday pub lunch. They sat outdoors in a walled beer garden which was busy with people soaking up the July sunshine.

"Well, you've certainly been in the wars" Bridget said after they'd ordered.

"Yes" sighed Marianne. "I'm having another fifteen minutes of fame. Like a lot of things, it's not quite so good the second time around."

"I went to see Joni in hospital yesterday" Bridget told her. "I thought you should know."

"Oh? How is she?"

"She's not good. She's very agitated and excitable. She keeps pacing up and down. All she talks about is this *conspiracy* against Saint bloody Jeremy. She thinks that's why she's in there."

"That doesn't sound good. If anything, she sounds worse."

"She's going to be there for quite a while, I think" said Bridget. "She's in this very swanky private hospital."

"Really? How come?"

Marianne had assumed that Joni would have a moral objection to private healthcare.

"Her husband had her moved there on Friday" said Bridget. "I didn't realise but he's high up in Channel Four."

"I've never met him" said Marianne. "She hardly ever talks about him. He doesn't sound like the sort of person I'd imagine Joni being married to. "

"No. No, he doesn't" said Bridget. "Seems nice enough. What I found out from him is that this isn't a first episode. Not by a long chalk."

"I guess we shouldn't really be surprised."

Their food was delivered by a barman to their table with cutlery. They began eating.

"Do you think it would help if I went to see Joni?" Marianne asked.

Bridget looked at her. "My advice would be to leave it for a while" she said. "She's utterly convinced that you and Pete are part of this…what does she call it…*deep state, neoliberal* conspiracy against Saint bloody Jeremy."

"I should probably just stay away then."

"I think so."

Marianne took a sip of her cider. "Well, I think my career is the Labour Party is pretty much over" she said.

"Oh, I don't think that's true" said Bridget. "All of this will soon be forgotten. Especially with Corbyn and the leadership and *who knows* where all *that* is going to end up?"

"We'll see" said Marianne. "Pete and Karen *did* want me to stand for the council next year."

"I'm sure they still do. And you should! You're very highly thought of in the Party, especially after the referendum."

"I'm just wondering if I really want any more politics in my life."

"Well, I can understand *that*. It does take a lot out of you."

"It really does" said Marianne. "But despite everything, I feel I've gained something from it. A sense of... purpose which I've never really had before."

She chewed thoughtfully on her steak for a moment.

"You know, after I got this job, Euan and I went out for dinner to celebrate. We were talking and he called me *aimless*. He wasn't being horrible or anything."

"No, he was just being a man" said Bridget. "Tactless."

Marianne laughed. "Well yes. But it rankled with me because it is sort of true."

"That's all the more reason for you to stick with it then"

"I'm not sure I'll be able to live down the disgrace if Ana sacks me" said Marianne.

"She won't do that" said Bridget. "She'll understand it wasn't your fault. Joni had a nervous breakdown. She'll see that you weren't to blame."

You really don't know what a monster she is thought Marianne.

Later, that evening, she watched a Netflix drama with Karen. She didn't really absorb much of it. She was too distracted. All she could think about was the inevitable summons from Ana the next morning. A sense of dread enveloped her. She felt sick. A night of little sleep followed.

There was no-one in the office when she arrived the next morning. Ben was at the dentist. Marianne checked her 'phone. There were no messages from Ana. She switched on her computer. Ana hadn't e-mailed. She expected her office 'phone to ring but it didn't. Still, she knew it was just a matter of time.

She busied herself with work. There were letters to type and e-mails to reply to. Periodically, she glanced at news websites. The Labour leadership was still the subject of speculation. A challenger was expected to emerge shortly.

The furore over the incident on the terrace had, as predicted, died down. However, there were a couple of e-mails from journalists which she deleted without reading.

A couple of hours passed. She was responding to yet another e-mail about badgers when her office 'phone rang. It was Ana.

"Get up here now" she said in a menacing whisper.

Marianne's trepidation was worse than the week before. Ana was typing an e-mail when she went in. She didn't look up. Marianne stood in silence in front of her desk.

After a few moments, she said "You'll have to excuse me, but I have all this extra work to do. I *don't have* a constituency office manager anymore."

She carried on typing. Marianne just watched. Eventually, she stopped and swivelled round to face her.

"Well, you've really surpassed yourself this time, haven't you?" she said.

Marianne said nothing. She wasn't expected to.

“You know” said Ana “I didn’t think you could embarrass this office any more than you already have. But somehow, you’ve have managed it. And for the second time in a week, no less!”

“It wasn’t my fault” said Marianne. “Joni is seriously unwell”

“That’s just not fucking good enough!”

Marianne stood silently, her cheeks stinging.

There was a short pause before Ana resumed her attack. She looked away briefly and shook her head.

“I have tried to give you a chance. I really have. You’ve *fucked up* at every turn and now…and now, you want to FUCK MY CAREER!”

Marianne opened her mouth to remonstrate before deciding it was pointless. There was another pause. Her attention settled momentarily on the view of Big Ben behind the window.

Ana sighed. She looked down at her desk and then back up at Marianne. Her voice softened. “I have to ask Marianne, what were you thinking? What *were you* thinking? *Who* starts a fight on the House of Commons FUCKING TERRACE?”

“I didn’t start the fight” said Marianne evenly. “I barely even defended myself.”

“I don’t give a shit. All I care about is that the press have dragged *my* name into it. And it is your fault. It really is your fault.”

“All I can say is….” Marianne began.

Ana violently banged the desk cutting her off. The gesture was of such force that Marianne wondered, afterwards, if it had hurt. She sat back in her chair, closed her eyes, and began massaging her temples.

"I really have no choice now. I'm going to have to take advice and make this formal." She opened her eyes. "You know what that means, don't you?"

Marianne nodded sullenly.

"I suggest you go back to work today" said Ana. "We *will* talk more about this."

Dismissed, Marianne returned to her office. On the way, she went into the ladies to compose herself.

How the fuck did I get into this mess? She asked herself, looking at her reflection.

Ben had returned from the dentist. He looked pointedly at her when she walked through the door. He seemed to know, from her demeanour, what had happened.

"I really need to talk to you" he said urgently. "I suggest we go off-site."

They went to St James' Park which was full of lunchtime joggers and American tourists. They sat on a bench opposite a pond.

"This is like being in a John le Carre novel" said Marianne.

She took a packet of cigarettes out of her handbag.

"May I have one?" Ben asked.

Marianne was astonished. "I didn't know you smoked."

"I don't usually."

He took a cigarette from her which she lit it for him, before lighting up herself. They puffed away in silence for a while.

Ben said: "You're going to get an e-mail from Ana today. To ask you to a meeting on Wednesday morning. You'll be able bring a representative."

"She *really* wants to get rid of me, doesn't she?"

"Yes."

"How do you know all this?

"Because I've had to take on all the admin. There's no-one else to do it."

"She must realise that you're going to talk to me" said Marianne

Ben shrugged. "She probably does" he said. "The bottom line is that she wants you and Joni out. She sees you both as liabilities."

"What's happening with Joni?"

"Ana wants to discharge her on health grounds. She's asked for access to her medical records?"

"What! That's outrageous!"

"I don't think she's going to get it" said Ben. "Still, she's had enough letters from her GP."

"Wait!" said Marianne. "Ana's known about Joni's mental health issues all this time?"

"I believe so."

Marianne shook her head disbelievingly. She took a drag on her cigarette and exhaled.

"Joni was useful to her for a while" Ben said. "But she isn't any more."

"So what are my options?" said Marianne. "If I'm going to be sacked, tell me why I should bother going back to work at all."

"You need to try to negotiate" he told her. "So that you can leave on your own terms. If you walk out now, you won't get a reference. It won't look good. "

He stubbed out his cigarette

"Are you a member of the union?" he asked

"Yes" said Marianne

"Take a union rep to the meeting" he said. "You should meet with them beforehand. You might be able to cut a deal with Ana."

"Hmm" said Marianne.

She contemplated the ducks on the pond. Her cigarette was nearly finished. She wanted to light another but decided she shouldn't.

"If you ask me" she said. "Ana caused Joni's breakdown."

"Well" said Ben. "She's not a great person to work for if you're a bit vulnerable."

"It's more than that" said Marianne. "Joni really started unravelling after Ana hit her."

"What!" spluttered Ben. He turned to face her.

"Yep."

"When? Where did it happen?"

"It was a couple of months ago" Marianne told him. "In the constituency office. Ana was supposed to be doing an interview with BBC London. But they didn't show up because Joni had massively fucked up. Ana went *ballistic.* She called Joni a fucking stupid bitch and slapped her across the face. *Twice*."

"Wow" said Ben. "I know full bloody well she has a temper. But that is on another level. Even for her."

"I know!" said Marianne. "I offered to support Joni if she wanted to make a complaint. But she didn't want to."

"Would you really have done that?"

"Totally would" she said. "I wouldn't have hesitated."

She threw her cigarette butt into the grass.

The dreaded e-mail from Ana arrived that afternoon. Marianne contacted the parliamentary branch of her union. She arranged a meeting the next day with her rep, another parliamentary assistant called Imran.

Sam called that night, from A&E, when she was getting ready to go to bed. He was doing a night shift. Marianne told him about her day.

"I found out something very interesting" she said. "It looks like Ana has known all along about Joni's mental health."

"That could be a smoking gun" said Sam. "If that's true, you could argue that she failed in her duty of care to the both of you. I'm no lawyer but you might have a case for unfair dismissal."

"The problem is" said Marianne "is that it's so difficult to *prove* anything. I know she's pretty bloody good at covering her tracks."

"Don't go down without a fight" he said. "That's how these people get away with it. Just remember that whatever happens, I'll be with you every step of the way."

She was glad to have him on her side. It didn't make her any less afraid. However, it made her feel that she could endure anything that followed.

The next day, she met with Imran, the union rep. They'd arranged to meet in the Terrace cafeteria at lunchtime. He was fifteen minutes late. Marianne spotted him as soon as he appeared. He was in his mid-twenties, and distinguishable by his tight shiny suit and Portcullis strut.

"Marianne, hi" he said, shaking her hand. "Sorry I'm late."

He didn't sound especially apologetic. Marianne thought he seemed like a wannabe politician himself. He immediately began talking about himself.

"I have done many of these cases" he told her. "I've worked in the house for quite a few years now."

That's nice Marianne said to herself.

He spoke with an affected received pronunciation accent. His voice had a tinny, inauthentic quality. He sounded like he was mimicking an upper-class English actor from the Golden Age of Hollywood. Marianne was reminded of Stewie Griffin from the *Family Guy* cartoon.

"I have to say your case is particularly special" he said. "*Simply everyone* is talking about it. An actual bitch-slapping on the House of Commons terrace!"

He let out a loud, honking laugh. This attracted glances from other tables.

As long as you're entertained Marianne thought. *That's the important thing.*

"Can you talk me through the process?" she asked.

He didn't manage to tell her anything she didn't already know. She asked about possible outcomes. This was where she'd hoped he might be useful, but he only gave vague answers. He was eager to move the conversation back to himself.

"Ana and I go way back" he told her at one point. "She's been a guest speaker at Young Labour events I've organised."

Oh, for fucks sake thought Marianne.

"I hope that's not going to get in the way" she told him firmly.

"No, no. Absolutely not" he said. His face assumed an odd mock serious expression.

Marianne found him very off-key. She'd meant to discuss Joni and the events leading up to the incident. However, she knew instinctively that he was not to be confided in. In any case, he didn't seem that interested. She wondered if she could ask for another rep but decided it was probably too late.

She was relieved when the meeting ended. It had been like a truly awful date. Imran left grinning and looking pleased with himself. Marianne was not inspired with confidence.

At home, that evening, she and Karen shared a bottle of wine. Karen had suggested it. Marianne was very heartened by this. Over the past few days, she'd felt this intangible distance open up between them. Karen's manner hadn't ostensibly changed, but Marianne just knew things weren't the same. She decided she would test this by talking about Ana.

"Sam thinks I might have a case for unfair dismissal" she told her. "If I had to go down that route."

"*Okay*" said Karen. She sounded dubious.

"Well, what do you think?"

Karen put down her glass. "It's very difficult" she said. "I know Ana's a total fucking bitch and she has no redeeming features. And she's a total nightmare to work for."

"But?" said Marianne.

"I'm just worried that if you pursue this, it's going to embarrass the Party."

"The Party" echoed Marianne.

Fuck the Party she said inwardly

Karen said: "Look, Marianne. I know what you're going through. A long time ago, I worked for a really awful MP, and I ended up having to leave for my own mental health. It's only now that I can go anywhere near Westminster without having an anxiety attack. But you have to think about the bigger picture."

"So what do you think I should do?" asked Marianne.

"Just try to cut some sort of deal with Madam" said Karen. "Like Ben suggested. Leave quietly and don't make a fuss."

"And what do *I* get out of that?"

"It means you can put it behind you" said Karen. "You can still have a career in the Party and stand for the Council. But it would be very awkward if you were suing our local MP for unfair dismissal. Imagine the publicity!"

In that moment, Marianne became acutely aware of the limits to their friendship. Without a doubt, Karen had been very good to her. However, her loyalty to the Party would always take precedence. If it came to it, she wouldn't be on her side. Marianne had this sense of betrayal.

On the other hand, she wondered if Karen was right. What did she really have to gain from fighting Ana? What would really change? One way or another, she was going to have to leave her job. The question was whether she should leave the Party behind her too. It occurred to her, for the first time, that she might be in danger of losing other friends, like Bridget.

Her meeting with Ana was at 10am the next morning in Ana's office. Marianne arrived on the dot. Imran was a few minutes late. She and Ana sat in an uncomfortable silence while they waited.

When Imran did arrive, he exclaimed "Ana, hi. Great to see you!" as he strutted in.

Ana stood up to greet him, smiling. "*You too*, Imran! I don't think I've seen you properly since conference."

Marianne thought, for a moment, that they were going to air-kiss each other but they didn't.

Ana sat back down. "Right, let's make a start" she said. "Marianne, as per my e-mail, this meeting has been called to discuss your disciplinary conduct. In particular, we need to talk about the incident that occurred on the terrace last week. This led to media coverage that embarrassed me, this office and, I think, yourself."

She looked down at a written briefing and read from it.

"Please let me know, if at any time, you would like to take a break."

That's awfully fucking considerate of you thought Marianne.

There was a pause.

"Can I just say something?" she asked.

Ana and Imran looked at each other. Ana nodded, reluctantly.

"The media coverage of the incident is inaccurate" said Marianne. "There was no fight or brawl. I was attacked by a woman who was having a psychotic breakdown. She was restrained and sectioned, as you know."

Ana said: "Well, the publicity was *extremely* embarrassing. And the press reports are all we have to go on."

"That's not quite true" said Marianne. "I can, if necessary, produce a police report verifying my version of events. Would that help?"

"Well, I think that..." Ana seemed flustered.

She didn't finish her sentence.

Marianne interjected. "I have a question. I hope you don't mind."

She looked at Imran for some sort of cue but there none was forthcoming.

"Okay" said Ana.

"I understand that you were aware of Joni's mental health issues" said Marianne. "I would just like to ask what provision you made for her."

Ana stared at her for a moment. "I don't know where you got that from" she said. "But I'm not obliged to discuss confidential information about another member of staff."

Marianne said: "But you have a duty of care to both of us. I was physically attacked at work. But I don't blame Joni because I know she was dangerously unwell."

Imran looked like a startled goldfish. He was clearly out of his depth. Ana stared down at her briefing for a moment.

"I can see you are very emotional, Marianne" she said. "Would you like to take a break at this point?"

"No thanks. Happy to carry on."

"Well, I'm not" Ana said firmly. "I think you've raised some important issues, which I'd like to consider. Perhaps we could arrange another meeting for next week. What do you think, Imran?"

She gave him a meaningful look.

"Erm…yes" said Imran. He was clearly dying to escape.

"Let's do that then" said Ana. She smiled graciously. "Marianne, perhaps we could have a moment."

Imran got up to leave. "Great to see you both. Ana, let's catch up for a drink soon."

"I'd love to" she said.

He sashayed out.

Well you were totally fucking useless thought Marianne.

After he'd gone, Ana sat back in her chair. She regarded Marianne like a boxer sizing up an opponent.

"You know you're not going to win this" she said, her voice very low. "You can play all the games you like. In the end, I will get rid of you."

"Can't we just come to some arrangement?" pleaded Marianne. "I could work my notice and you could agree to write me a reference."

"You've burnt your bridges after that little stunt. Now just get out."

Marianne went back to her office.

"How did it go?" asked Ben, looking up from his screen.

"Not great" she said. "Not great at all. I got the meeting stopped."

"Well that sounds like quite an achievement."

She sat down at her desk. "I suppose it was" she said. "But Ana is now even more hellbent on getting rid of me. That little twat, Imran was fucking useless. She spoke to me after he went. She flat out refused to make a deal."

"Hmm" said Ben, ruminating on this. "That is a problem."

"I think I'm just going to have to wait to be sacked" said Marianne. "Then I could sue for unfair dismissal, I guess."

"Do you really want to do that?"

"No. Not at all." Marianne sighed. "I think I'd somehow end up losing even if I won. Maybe I should just cut my losses and go now."

Ben looked at her thoughtfully. "Something occurred to me last night" he said. "You might have one more bargaining chip."

Marianne was doubtful. "What's that then?"

"You told me yesterday that Ana hit Joni. In the constituency office."

"That's right."

She wondered where he was going with this.

“Do you remember what you told me you saw on her laptop?” he asked. “It was around that time.”

“I’m just trying to think” she said. “Hold on…she has a camera in the other office. She can see what’s going on in there.”

“Exactly.”

“Fucking hell!” said Marianne as realisation dawned. “She might’ve recorded herself hitting Joni.”

“Imagine if you got hold of the footage” said Ben.

“Christ” said Marianne.

They contemplated this for a moment. Marianne broke the silence.

“Are you really suggesting I should *blackmail* Ana?”

Ben shrugged. “I’m not suggesting anything. You’ve got to do what you have to.”

“That would be seriously breaking the rules” she said.

“Nobody plays by the rules around here” said Ben. “Ana certainly doesn’t. The trick is not to get caught.”

He had a point.

“How would we get hold of it?” she asked. “Assuming there is any footage.”

“It’s wouldn’t be hard” said Ben. “I’ll go into her office when she’s not there and get the laptop. I just need you to tell me the date and time so I can find the recording”

Marianne said: “I really can’t ask you to do that. It’s too big a risk for you.”

"It's my risk to take" he said. "And I'm going to do it because you would have done it for Joni. It's quid pro quo."

Marianne didn't know what to say. The implications were almost too big to comprehend. She turned her mind to more practical matters.

"How will you get into her office? What about login details and passwords?"

"I have a key" he told her. "And I know the password she uses for everything."

"When are we going to do this?"

"We don't have time to mess around" he told her. "We have to go in ASAP. Can you check her diary and tell me what she's got on today?"

Marianne looked at her screen. "She's going to Prime Minister's Questions at twelve. And she's staying for the debate afterwards. She should be out of the office for at least an hour."

"We'll do it then" Ben said. "I'll go and get the laptop and bring it back here."

"What if she goes back to her office and catches you? Or comes in here?"

"We'll just have to have some bloody good excuses lined up" he said.

Marianne took a deep breath to calm her nerves. She felt scared. Did they really need to go through with it today?

"Okay" she said. "Let's do this."

Ben left just after 12pm. Marianne watched coverage of Prime Minister's Questions on her computer. She could see Ana in the chamber sat in the middle of the opposition benches. She kept her eyes trained on her.

She hoped Ben would be back quickly but he seemed to be gone an age. She was alarmed when, at one point, she saw Ana leave her seat.

"Fuck, fuck, where's she going!" she shrieked at the screen.

If Ana went back to her office, she might find Ben in there. If he'd already gone, she would certainly notice her laptop missing. Marianne's heartbeat accelerated. She wondered if she should ring upstairs to warn him. There was no point texting him. He'd left his mobile on his desk.

A couple of minutes later, Ben reappeared with the laptop. At that moment, Marianne saw Ana resume her seat on the green benches. She must have stepped out to go to the loo.

Marianne stood behind Ben as he opened up the laptop on his desk. He had no difficulty logging in. Before long, he had found the camera application.

"Okay, I need to know the date and time" he said.

Marianne told him. She'd worked it out while he'd been gone. He typed it in and a new window opened on the screen. She saw a freeze-frame of her standing in the other office with Ana and Joni all those weeks earlier. The camera looked down on them.

Ben played the footage. It had audio. Marianne found that watching it was like having an out-of-body experience.

"You fucking stupid bitch!" screamed Ana from the screen. She struck Joni twice across the face. Ben pressed the pause button.

"Fucking hell" he said.

He played the video again.

"You fucking stupid bitch!" Ana screamed once again. She struck Joni twice across the face, just as she had before.

Marianne and Ben carried on watching. They saw Ana storm out and Marianne go to console Joni. The video clearly showed Joni's nosebleed.

Ben pressed the 'stop' button. He took a breath. "I'm not surprised by much" he said. "But I've never seen anything quite like that."

"It's shocking to watch" said Marianne. "It was even worse to actually be there. Nobody would have believed me if I'd told them."

"No" said Ben. He plugged a USB stick into the laptop. "I'm going to make a file for you."

He spent a few minutes clicking and scrolling. When he'd finished, he handed her the stick.

"Here you go. You know what to do."

"Thank you so much for this" she said. "I can't tell you how much I appreciate it."

"You're very welcome."

He then frowned at the screen.

"She has quite a few videos saved on here" he said

"Can we watch one?" asked Marianne.

"It would be rude not to."

He opened the most recent. It was a recording of Joni in the other office talking to the Idiot-in-the-Beret.

"I know Pete Samuelson is looking for dirt on Global Solidarity" she could be heard telling hime. "I heard him talking to Marianne Stuart."

The video played on.

"So that's how she knew" said Marianne.

Ben looked at her, puzzled. "What do you mean?"

"It's true what Joni said" she told him. "Pete and I did talk about that notorious Global Solidarity house party."

"The one that was in *the Daily Star?"*

"That's the one" she said. "For some reason, Ana knew we'd had the conversation and the only person who *could* have told her was Joni. But I realised she hadn't. It just didn't make any sense."

"What tangled webs" said Ben. He stopped the video and shut down the laptop. "There we have it. Spying, gaslighting and assault by a Member of Parliament."

"You'd better get that laptop back to her office" Marianne said. "She'll be going back soon."

While he was gone, Marianne looked back at her computer. Ana was still sat on the green benches.

When he came back, she said: "Ben, if the worst comes to the worst, please don't admit to anything whatsoever. This all has to be on me."

"It will be fine as long as you hold your nerve" he said.

Ben left at 5pm which was quite a rare occurrence. Marianne knew Ana was in her office. She would be going up to see her very soon. Her hands shaking, she pre-loaded a tweet on her iPhone.

'*Watch this astonishing assault by @AnaNovakMP of her staff member @mrsjonilessing.*'

She attached the video but didn't send the tweet.

Her whole body was convulsed by nervous shivers. She tried to calm herself with breaths. She then went to the ladies' to compose herself. For a few minutes, she just stared at herself in the mirror. She would need every reserve of fortitude she had. What she was about to do could have all sorts of consequences. She steeled herself and went upstairs to Ana's office.

She knocked but went in without waiting for an answer. Ana was surprised to see her.

"Can I help you, Marianne?" she said imperiously.

"Yes, you can".

Marianne sat down without invitation and held up her iPhone. "In a few minutes time, I'm going to tweet this" she told her.

She played the video. Ana watched herself swear at and assault Joni.

Her mouth fell open in disbelief and the colour drained from her face. She was visibly, deeply shocked. Still, she was quick to compose herself.

"You wouldn't dare send that" she said.

"Wouldn't I?"

"Where the fuck did you get it from?"

"Your laptop" said Marianne. "Where else?"

Ana suddenly sprung up. She tried to snatch the 'phone but she wasn't quick enough. Marianne just pulled it back out of her reach.

"I wouldn't bother" she said. "I have several other copies."

Ana sat back down. Her eyes narrowed

"You know you've obtained that video illegally, don't you?" she said. "For the very illegal purpose of blackmail. You could go to prison."

Marianne knew she needed to keep her cool. The threats were inevitable.

"You might be on shaky ground there" she said. "I'm not sure that spying on people is exactly legal either."

"Come on, Marianne" said Ana. "Is it really worth the risk of going to prison?"

"The way I see it" said Marianne "is that the risk is all yours. I don't have much to lose. *You*, on the other hand, have everything to lose. This tweet will go viral in minutes. It will probably be the lead item on the news. In a couple of hours, you'll have been suspended from the Party. By this time next week, you'll have resigned as an MP and there'll be a by-election. Pete Samuelson will love that."

Ana sat back in her chair. She seemed to be weighing up her options. She smirked when something occurred to her.

"Perhaps we should talk about your boyfriend" she said. "You'll remember that I helped him with his immigration status. I could tell the Home Office I was given unreliable information. They'll ship him back to Syria faster than you can say *Sharia law."*

"Right!" snapped Marianne. "That does it. Say goodbye to your career."

She held up her 'phone and went to press the 'Tweet' button.

"Stop!" shrieked Ana, springing up again. "Don't do it. Please! We can negotiate."

Marianne put her 'phone down. "That's better" she said.

Ana sunk back into her chair. She looked at Marianne with a weary resentment. "What is it you want?"

Marianne said: "You told Joni that I was behind that story in *the Daily Star*, didn't you?"

Ana looked irritated by this tangent.

"I told her you had a hand in it" she said. "Which you had."

"You know that's not true" said Marianne. "You just wanted to trigger an incident"

"I could hardly have predicted what was going to happen" protested Ana.

"No, you just chucked the grenade and waited for the explosion"

"Look, there's no point raking over the coals" said Ana impatiently. "Just tell me what you want."

"I'm going to apply for a job in Nigel Patel's office" Marianne told her. "You're going to give me a glowing reference. And I'm going to work my notice."

"Fine" said Ana. "It's a small price to pay to get rid of you. You'll delete the video though?"

"No, I won't."

"Why not?"

"I might need another reference at some point" Marianne said, smiling sweetly.

Ana shook her head. "I don't know what's happened to you, Marianne" she said. "You used to be a decent person."

"It's probably the company I keep" said Marianne. She got up to leave. "Anyway, I must dash. I'm glad we've come to a satisfactory arrangement."

"Fuck you" Ana hissed.

Chapter Thirteen

Friday 21st April 2017

“How does *Marianne Stuart MP* sound?” suggested Pete Samuelson.

“You have got to be fucking kidding me” said Marianne. “Just no. Not ever.”

“Why not?”

“Why not?” she said. “There are endless bloody reasons why not.”

She rummaged around inside her bag.

“I need a cigarette!”

“I thought you’d given up.”

She had, sort of. Still, Pete’s visit to her workplace had been unexpected. She was now in dire need of a soothing nicotine fix. She found her cigarettes and went outside.

She’d got into the office early that morning, just after 8am. She had a busy day ahead of her. She’d borrowed Sam’s mountain bike so she could cycle in. However, she was actually terrified of the roads so she’d ridden mainly on the pavement. It did make her feel less guilty about the packet of Marlborough in her bag.

For the last seven months, Marianne had worked as a caseworker for Nigel Patel. She was based in his constituency office. This was on the ground floor of a Victorian villa on a steep road. There was a veranda at the front where she took her cigarette breaks. From there, she could see the skyscrapers of London shimmering in the distance.

In the end, she hadn’t cycled the whole way in. She’d dismounted at the bottom of the road and pushed the bike uphill. This had made her rather breathless. The office was empty when she arrived. She normally shared it with one other, but they were on holiday. There weren't any volunteers or interns coming in today either. She would be on her own.

She took off her cycle helmet and dropped her bag by her chair. She switched on her computer and waited for it to boot up. Her mobile rang. It was Sam so she answered.

"I don't know what to cook tonight" he said. "What do vegans eat?"

"I don't know. Grass clippings probably."

They had invited Euan and his new girlfriend over for dinner that evening. Marianne and Sam had bumped into them a few weeks earlier. It was at a mutual friend's birthday celebration. Things had been a little awkward to begin with. However, the atmosphere thawed after a couple of drinks. Sam and Euan had got on well which pleased Marianne. She decided the time had come for a rapprochement of sorts. The only problem was that the new girlfriend was vegan.

"I'm really not serving up grass clippings" said Sam.

"Well, it might send the wrong message" Marianne conceded.

The point of the dinner was to normalise friendly relations with Euan. It wouldn't do to insult the new girlfriend's dietary choices.

"Okay, I think you should do the lamb shanks for us" she said. "I'll go online and order some gourmet vegan dish for Sophie. I'll have it delivered before they come. *They* won't know you haven't cooked it."

"That is the most appalling cheating" said Sam. "But needs must."

He rang off.

Marianne had been living with Sam for several months now. She'd left Karen's shortly after starting her new job. Sam's monochrome flat was now more colourful and more cluttered. Marianne had introduced cushions and scented candles. Her clothes were winning the battle for space in their wardrobe. She'd tried to replace the blinds with patterned curtains but Sam had drawn the line at this.

On the day she left Karen's, Sam had helped her move. They had packed her belongings into the back of his jeep. Karen hugged her before they set off.

"I can't believe you're deserting me for Dishy Doctor Sam" she'd said half-jokingly, and half-tearfully.

Marianne sensed that Karen's feelings were conflicted. They were probably a mixture of sadness and relief. She would miss having another woman around to share a bottle of wine with. They'd had an easy companionability. Still, a cloud had hung over them in the last weeks they lived together. They both knew that Karen had picked a side, and it wasn't Marianne's.

They'd stayed friends though. It just wasn't the same as before. Every so often, they'd meet up for a drink and gossip about the Party. Karen was very willing to share her complaints about "Madam". Ana sounded as demanding and capricious as ever. Marianne found it curious that Karen had asked so little about her departure from Ana's office. There were many unexplained details which should have roused her interest.

She hadn't seen Ana since she left. They had avoided each other during her notice period. There had been no leaving card. On Marianne's last day, Ana had arranged to be out of the office. This had saved them both the mortifying awkwardness of a farewell. Still, Marianne's new job had not allowed complete escape. She still had to have dealings with Ana's office. After all, Ana represented a neighbouring seat.

Marianne's replacement was a capable seeming young woman called Beth. She had even met her briefly. They periodically had to liaise by e-mail or by 'phone. Beth was a model of discretion. Still, Marianne intuited that Ana had not ceased to be a monstrous employer. She wondered if she and Beth would one day exchange horror stories.

Ben had left his job with Ana before Christmas. He had gone to work at the National Trust in some policy role. When he handed in his notice, he'd texted Marianne to let her know. She had replied.

'I don't need to ask why. Hope you got a good reference.'

Marianne wondered if Ana had had any suspicions about Ben. She couldn't have *known* that he helped her get hold of the video. There was no proof and he had enough sangfroid not to give anything away. Still, Ana had an instinct for betrayal. She spent enough time practicing it.

Just before Marianne left, Ana had been reappointed to the front bench. She was now a shadow health minister. That summer, Jeremy Corbyn had seen off the challenge to his leadership. As he was much strengthened, many Labour MPs who'd resigned from the front bench meekly returned. On the other side of the House, Theresa May had become the new Prime Minister. Her predecessor, David Cameron was the first casualty of the referendum.

Marianne was busy with e-mails when the office doorbell rang. She was irritated by the interruption. She tried to finish her e-mail but the doorbell was rung again, more insistently this time. She huffily got up to answer.

She opened the door to find Pete Samuelson on the doorstep.

She hadn't been expecting him. They hadn't seen each other for months

"This is a surprise" she said, after a pause.

"I was hoping to catch you" said Pete. "Can I come in?"

"Erm, yes. Sure" she said, standing aside to let him in.

She ushered him in through the hallway. He sat himself down at her colleague's empty chair.

"Can I get you tea or coffee, or something" she asked.

"No, no. I'm good."

She knew this wasn't a social call. He was here because he wanted something. She already had a pretty good idea what.

She sat back down at her desk

"This election is a bit of a nightmare, isn't it" said Pete, as though he were just making conversation.

"Oh God, yes!" said Marianne.

A few days earlier, Theresa May had unexpectedly called a General Election. She wanted a mandate to negotiate Brexit on her own terms. The polls predicted a Tory landslide. Some of the ensuing headlines had made Marianne uneasy. The *Daily Mail* had screeched, from its front page, 'Crush the Saboteurs'. They meant the Remainers who still opposed Brexit.

"It's a bit of a bummer for you" said Pete. "With your job disappearing."

This was true. The day before, Nigel Patel announced he was standing down as the MP for Greenwood North. Marianne had been told about it beforehand. He was part of a small exodus of despairing Labour MPs who saw no future in politics. Nigel himself had been offered a lucrative job with a lobbyist. Unfortunately for her, this meant she would be out of a job.

"It's not ideal" she said to Pete. "But I have learnt over the last couple of years that I am nothing if not resilient. I will find another job."

"Totally" said Pete. "Have you thought about what you're going to do?"

So *that* was why he was here. He'd come to ask her to stand in the local elections. He was in desperate need of more allies on the council. He was still trying to push through the Regeneration Partnership. The controversy and disquiet showed no sign of dying down. Pete was still embattled and there were rumours of another challenge to his leadership. The elections were just over a year away.

He'll be lucky to survive that long Marianne thought.

She had decided she didn't want to go on the Council. It seemed like endless hard work and hassle. Long evening meetings about parking meters didn't appeal to her. Still, she knew *someone* who was interested.

Pete would be horrified she thought. *I'd almost like to tell him.*

He hadn't been her only surprise visitor that week. A few days earlier, she'd answered the door to a woman bearing flowers.

"Can I help you?" she'd asked.

The woman lifted her oversized Chanel sunglasses.

"Joni!" gasped Marianne. "I don't believe it! I didn't recognise you."

This was hardly surprising. Joni's long grey hair had been replaced by a honey coloured pageboy cut. It matched her newly acquired tan. Her aging hippy ensemble had been dispensed with too. Today, she wore a long camel coat over crisp white trousers and a matching blouse. A professional manicurist had clearly seen to her nails. She looked like an expensively maintained corporate wife.

"I've just come to give you these" she said, kissing Marianne on both cheeks.

"Please come in!" said Marianne.

Joni followed her, though the hallway into the office, chatting nineteen-to-the-dozen.

"We've just been in Croatia for the last month" she said. "Have you ever been? You really should go. We rented a villa on the coast. It was the most relaxing holiday I've had in my whole life."

"Well you look amazing" said Marianne. "It must have done you the power of good."

She couldn't believe how well Joni looked. She knew she'd been in hospital for many months. Bridget had been to see her periodically but reported no improvement. Marianne had decided against going herself. She knew from Bridget that she'd been discharged at some point. Marianne felt a peculiar sort of guilt about Joni. She knew, rationally, that there was nothing she could have done. Still, she felt that she'd been too willing to bury Joni in the recesses of her mind.

Joni put the flowers on Marianne's desk and looked around the room.

"Very nice" she said.

"Can I get you a drink" Marianne asked. "Tea or coffee?"

"Do you have any camomile tea? I've given up caffeine *forever.* It made me too wired."

"I'll see what we've got in" said Marianne. "I'll try and find a vase for the flowers too. Please, sit down."

She motioned at her colleague's empty chair. Joni sat down, dropping her shoulder bag to the floor.

Marianne went into the kitchen, along the corridor, and switched the kettle on. After rummaging in the cupboards, she found some herbal tea and a chipped vase.

"I'm not sure what I've done to deserve flowers" she said when she came back.

She carried a mug in one hand, and a vase half-full of water in the other. Joni took the mug from her.

"Oh, it's just to thank you for being such a good friend" she said. "And for looking out for me."

"I really didn't do very much" said Marianne.

She attended to the flowers. She cut the stems off with scissors and put them in the vase.

"Yes, you did" said Joni.

Marianne looked at her handiwork. "They are beautiful" she said. "I can't remember the last time someone gave me flowers. Thank you so much."

"You're very welcome."

Marianne sat back down at her desk. "So, any more long holidays planned? They clearly agree with you."

"Not until the next time I need one" said Joni. "I'm feeling fully recharged now."

"Good!"

"I'm totally raring to go. It's time to take the fight to the Tories. Nothing is more important than Jeremy becoming the next Prime Minister."

Well that's not bloody likely Marianne said inwardly.

She hadn't expected the conversation to take this course.

Joni fixed her eyes on Marianne's. "You know, Marianne" she said in her low monotone. "I have been doing a lot of reading while I've been away and I'm even more convinced than ever that the mainstream media is losing its power. They can no longer perpetuate the narrative of neoliberalism. The rise of the new media has challenged their language, undermined their discourse. You *have got* to start reading *the Canary*. There is a real opportunity for the Labour Party to fulfil its historic mission of liberating labour from capital."

She said all of this at breakneck speed without taking a breath. Marianne tried to think of an appropriate response. However, this wasn't necessary. Joni just carried on, unabated.

"And I want to be at the forefront of this" she said. "On the frontline. Anyhow, I've given it a lot of thought. And I've decided I'm going to stand as a Labour councillor next year. I have a lifetime of experience to bring to Greenwood Council."

Christ on a fucking bike! Marianne thought.

"Don't let your tea get cold" she said to Joni.

When she'd gone, Marianne felt like she'd ridden an emotional rollercoaster. She was relieved, sad and happy at the same time. It had been great to see her. Still, she couldn't help thinking about what they *hadn't* talked about, like the incident on the terrace. Ana hadn't been mentioned once. Joni hadn't asked why she'd left.

And she still can't stay away from politics Marianne thought despairingly.

Back in the present, Marianne said to Pete: "I just want to get this out the way now. I'm not interested in going on the council."

"That's not *exactly* what I wanted to talk to you about" he said.

"Oh?"

"I've come to talk to you about Nigel standing down."

"I don't think I'm going to be able to help with that" said Marianne, firmly. "Nigel has made up his mind and I'm not going to be able to change it."

"No, no. You're not hearing me. They're going to need to select a candidate to replace him. It's a safe Labour seat and whoever gets selected will definitely be the next MP here."

"Yes, I know how it works" said Marianne. She hoped she didn't sound irritated.

"Well, why don't you do it?"

"Do what?"

Pete rolled his eyes. "For fucks sake, Marianne! For a bright woman, you can be incredibly slow on the uptake. Why don't you stand to be selected as Nigel's replacement? Excuse the mansplaining, but it basically means you'd be the next Labour MP for Greenwood North."

"Me?!"

"This is just getting painful now" said Pete. "Yes, you."

Marianne wondered for a moment if he was being serious. The suggestion was ridiculous and absurd not to mention impractical. It hadn't occurred to her, even momentarily, that she could possibly be in the running.

Pete then asked her if she liked the sound of "Marianne Stuart MP". After remonstrating with him, she decided she needed a cigarette break. Giving up could wait. She went out onto the veranda at the front. He followed her out.

""I just wasn't expecting this" she said as she lit up her cigarette.

"So you'll think about then?" Pete said.

"I can't see how I'd even make the shortlist" said Marianne. For a start, I'm not exactly pro-Corbyn."

"That's not such a barrier" he said. "Other non-Corbyn candidates have got through. Look, it wouldn't be easy. Momentum will want one of their own selected."

"No kidding."

"But you have some advantages in your favour" he said.

"Which are?"

"The key thing" said Pete "is that Greenwood North is a heavily Remain seat. It was about 80 per cent in the referendum. Even the Corbynistas here are massive Remainers. And you are like the Remain poster girl."

"Hmm" said Marianne. Something then occurred to her. "Why aren't you going for it?" she asked.

"It's an all-woman shortlist" he told her. "The Party have already decided. It has to be a woman candidate."

"It does sound like a bit of a long shot to me" said Marianne.

"It is! But long-shot candidates get selected, surprisingly often. You stand more than a strong outside chance. I would give you all the help you need. And Karen would help too…behind the scenes of course."

Marianne exhaled smoke and turned to face him. "There are a few problems with this, Pete."

"Like what?"

"Well, I have found life in politics a little…tumultuous. Last year, I had my fifteen minutes of fame as you say, *the Remain poster girl*. Then, *the Daily Mail* practically denounced me as a drunken, brawling slapper. Could be awkward in a selection contest."

"That's all old news" said Pete. "Nobody cares anymore. There's one thing you have to understand about life in politics. Your fortunes can rise and fall. Then they can rise and fall again. You can be flying high one day and on your knees the next. I should know. But you know what? I think you probably understand that better than most."

"I guess I do" said Marianne

Pete said: "The question you have to ask yourself is whether you really want this. I think, deep down, you do. You might be a bit embarrassed to admit it. Still, it's a matter for you."

Marianne wondered if he was right. Perhaps she was afflicted by some inverted false modesty. She began to see a path through the selection process. At the end of it, she would be an MP. She found herself almost frightened to contemplate this. It would be truly life changing for her in a way nothing else ever had been. She might never again, in her life, have such an opportunity.

"It's just such a massive decision" she said.

"So you're not saying no then?"

"No."

She inhaled on her cigarette and they stood in silence for a moment watching the passing traffic.

"There is one thing bugging me though" she said.

"What's that?"

"Ana."

"What about her?"

"Well, if I became the MP here" said Marianne "she'd be my constituency neighbour. I'd have to have to deal with her all the time. I can't say that's exactly an enticing prospect."

"Yeah, might be a bit awkward" said Pete. "Then again, you might not have to deal with her at all."

He let out one of his Muttley-style chuckles.

"What do you mean" asked Marianne.

"Well just look at the polls!" he said. "Labour are going to get smashed in this election. The Tories are targeting marginal Labour seats and hers is as marginal you get. All it takes is a small swing to the Tories and she's *gone*, an ex-MP, a has-been."

He chuckled again, clearly delighted by the idea.

"I know Ana's a total monster" said Marianne. "But I would hate for us to lose the seat back to the Tories. Especially after all the work we all put into winning it last time."

Pete ignored this. "I think you're more than capable of dealing with Ana anyway. You pretty much own her, don't you?"

"I'm sorry?!" exclaimed Marianne, aghast that he would think such a thing.

"I reckon you've got something on her" he said, looking at her pointedly. "A real smoking gun."

Marianne turned back towards the street. "What makes you say that?"

She exhaled a puff of cigarette smoke though her mouth.

"Well, it was very strange what happened last year" said Pete. "She was about to fire you. Then you suddenly land this job. It all happened very quickly. I've often wondered about it."

Marianne wasn't going to tell him. Part of her wanted to. She would like to have seen his reaction. His jaw would hit the floor.

She was certain, however, that she had been right not to tell him at the time. His reaction would have been entirely predictable. He would have tried to have encouraged her, perhaps even pressured her, into tweeting the video. His desire to see his enemy destroyed, vanquished forever would have been all consuming. He wouldn't have thought about the consequences for her.

"Let's just say that Ana and I came to an arrangement" she told him.

"Fair enough" he said.

He knew from her tone that it was pointless to pursue it any further.

Marianne had told only one other person about the video, Sam. After she'd started her new job, they'd gone out for dinner and the subject of Ana had come up. A couple of glasses of Chablis had made her rather garrulous. She felt some inexplicable need to test him. She wanted to see how he'd react. Would it change things between them?

"My God" he said when she told him.

"Are you shocked?"

"Yeah, I guess I am. It was pretty…dirty."

Marianne looked him straight in they eye. "Does it change the way you feel about me?" she asked.

He didn't answer her for a moment. She wondered if she'd done the right thing. Still, she had to know.

After a moment, he took her hand in his. "Not at all" he said. "You're in that world and you do what you have to do to survive. I understand that. And let's face it, I *am not*, and *never will be*, in any position to judge you."

"Thank you" breathed Marianne.

The relief of unburdening herself had made her rather tearful.

"I am just so glad to be able to talk to you about it. The last couple of years have been really interesting but I'm just not sure who I am anymore."

"Time will help with that" said Sam. "At least that's what my New Age hippy counsellor keeps telling me."

Marianne snorted and they dissolved into laughter.

Back in the present, Pete said: "We need to have an awkward conversation about something."

"Oh?" said Marianne

Pete had never been known to find any conversation awkward.

"Erm, yes" he said. "It's about Sam."

Marianne raised her eyebrows. "What about him?"

"Don't get me wrong, Marianne" said Pete.

He paused for a moment as he made a rare attempt to choose his words carefully.

"I really like Sam and I think you and he are great together. And I know that he'd be really supportive..."

"For Christ's sake, Pete, just spit it out!" snapped Marianne, exasperated. "You usually do."

"Okay" he said. It's just that there are rumours..."

He paused again, overcome by an embarrassment that he was unused to.

"What rumours?" she said.

Pete cut to it. "Rumours that he was involved in an ethnic cleansing in Syria."

"That's total bollocks!" said Marianne. "Who the fuck is spouting this crap?"

"I'm sure it's bollocks" said Pete. "It's just a motley crew of pro-Assad Trots. Nobody would believe them. But, with social media, these things can spread like wildfire."

"It wouldn't be Sam running" said Marianne. "It would be me."

"Yeah, I know. But a partner with a dodgy past...okay, *perceived* to have a dodgy past can be a liability. I know it's not fair but it's not a good look for a candidate."

Inwardly, Marianne conceded he was probably right. She knew by now that politics was often far from fair.

"What are you suggesting I do?" she said. "Dump my boyfriend?"

"No" said Pete. "We just need you to get your story straight and be prepared for any awkward questions. It just means we can manage the situation *if we have to*."

Did Ana go through this? Marianne wondered.

She found it hard to imagine. Then again, she really knew so little about Ana. She was strangely unknowable, even after all this time.

Pete's phone buzzed inside his jacket. He took it out to look at it.

"Fucking hell!" he exclaimed, staring at the screen.

"What's up?"

"It's Ana. She's resigned from the front bench again"

"What?" spluttered Marianne. "Why?"

"I'm just trying to find out" he said, scrolling down. "Okay, this is all about the EU Withdrawal bill. She's resigned because…she wants to *abstain* on the next reading."

"She's resigned to *abstain*?" Marianne was incredulous. "Who the fuck does that? It makes no sense."

"I'm just looking at the Twitter speculation" Pete said. "It looks like she's desperate to avoid upsetting her local Remainers. So she's not going to vote *for* it."

"I should think not" said Marianne.

"But, get this. She doesn't want Momentum to think she's anti-Jeremy. So, she's decided she's not going to vote *against* it."

He looked up from his 'phone grinning.

"She's trying to ride two horses as usual" he said. "But I think this time, she'll fall off and end up with a *very* bruised arse."

He guffawed at this.

Marianne stared at the skyscrapers in the distance and took a drag on her cigarette.

"Well, that's just not fucking good enough" she said.

The End

Printed in Great Britain
by Amazon

35465899R00176